# THE LAZARUS PROTOCOL

DAVID BRUNS

CHRIS POURTEAU

SEVERN RIVER
PUBLISHING

THE LAZARUS PROTOCOL

Copyright © 2018 by David Bruns and Chris Pourteau.

All rights reserved.

Severn River Publishing
www.SevernRiverBooks.com

This is a work of fiction. Names, characters, businesses, places, events and incidents are either the products of the author's imagination or used in a fictitious manner. Any resemblance to actual persons, living or dead, or actual events is purely coincidental.

ISBN: 978-1-64875-543-9 (Paperback)

# ALSO BY BRUNS AND POURTEAU

**The SynCorp Saga**

The Lazarus Protocol

Cassandra's War

Hostile Takeover

Valhalla Station

Masada's Gate

Serpent's Fury

Never miss a new release! Sign up to receive exclusive updates from authors Bruns and Pourteau!

severnriverbooks.com/series/the-syncorp-saga

*For our wives*
*Christine and Alison*

# 1

## REMY CADE • VICKSBURG, MISSISSIPPI

The troop carrier lifted out of the landing zone in a spray of muddy mist. Corporal Remy Cade slogged through the soggy meadow with the rest of his squad. Although the rain had stopped for now, the Mississippi humidity made it feel like he was breathing through a wet towel.

From desert to deluge. That's how the reporter on YourVoice poetically described his unit's new assignment. After eighteen months in the Sinai, the rep of Graves's Diggers was solid gold. In the Drought Wars of East Africa, there was no problem too big or too small for Colonel Graves and his Diggers. Their battalion motto was "Consider It Done."

Private Allen James, Jamie to his squad, took a knee beside Remy on the berm of the asphalt road bisecting the water-soaked meadow. "Asshole pilots," he muttered, wiping his face. "They sprayed us on purpose."

"Cheer up, Jamie," said PFC Rita Holmes, the other member of their fire team. "Now you don't have to take a shower this week."

Remy chuckled.

"Knock it off, both of you," Second Lieutenant Raymond Zack interrupted in a harsh voice.

Their squad was saddled with Zack, a brand-new butter bar fresh out of Officer Candidate School. Back in the Sinai, Graves would have taken a newbie officer under his wing and made sure he knew his ass from a hole in the ground before he threw him to the troops. But this was just a pissant little jaunt to the Deep South to prevent looters from trying their hand at a five-finger discount and help storm survivors stay alive. Easy duty compared to Africa. They carried small arms only, and that was just for show. Seeing real soldiers in the streets should keep the peace all by itself.

Now that they were stateside again, things were changing. Promotions were happening, and people were leaving for new assignments. Good people. So many changes that for this last-minute operation, his platoon was operating well below half strength, deploying with only two squads of two fire teams each. The rest of the company was on leave or on loan to another unit. Even Graves himself, newly promoted to colonel, was in Washington for some high-level briefing. Remy knew he shouldn't care, but part of him felt like his family was breaking up.

Just as Jamie opened his mouth to deliver more colorful commentary, Staff Sergeant Hector Akito intervened with a curt, "Lock it up, people."

Remy elbowed Jamie to shut him up. Akito's tone was a low growl, a familiar prelude to a full-blown ass-chewing. Sometimes Remy's best friend failed to pick up on basic social cues.

From what he could see so far, Hurricane Zoey, the second Cat 6 storm from the Gulf this year, had done a number on this place. Other Digger squads were being deployed to Red Cross camps all around Vicksburg to run crowd control and provide what aid they could to storm survivors until the National Guard arrived. As home to the only bridge for a hundred miles that wasn't submerged by the swollen Mississippi River, Vicksburg was a gathering point for thousands of climate change refugees, as the media called them. To hear the news feeds tell it, the good people of Vicksburg opened their community to Louisianans fleeing their swollen bayous with the best of intentions, but things quickly went from *how can we help?* to *keep your hands off.*

The feds made the call to use active duty troops to enforce law and order until the Guardies could get their act together. The public pressure to do *something* was intense with all the news drones, embedded reporters, and heartfelt interviews with little kids clutching soggy stuffed animals. So here the Diggers were, called back from well-deserved leave, to ensure disaster relief went smoothly.

"Glasses on, people," Akito shouted. "Let's move out."

Remy suspected that even Akito thought this was bullshit duty, but he was putting on a show for the newbie platoon commander.

Remy plucked his data glasses from his sleeve and slid them on. The two fire teams of three soldiers each, plus the sarge and the lieutenant, showed up as eight green bubbles in the lower-right of the display.

Sarge's no-nonsense voice whispered in his ear. "Corporal Cade, you have Fire Team One. Team Two, on me."

Remy acknowledged the assignment with no small swell of pride. Here he was, only a corporal and commanding his own fire team. Temporary assignment, of course. Fire teams were led by sergeants, not corporals, but scarcity makes all things possible.

Jamie crowded behind him as they shuffled to their feet. "What are your orders, oh most exalted one?" he whispered in Remy's ear.

"Don't be an ass, Jamie," Holmes muttered. "Remy earned it. He's not a fuckup like you."

"Hey, I resemble that remark," Jamie whispered back with giggle.

"Stow it," Remy said in his best impression of Akito. Jamie laughed harder.

The two fire teams hustled onto the asphalt surface, Remy's team on the right, Akito's on the left, twenty paces between each soldier as they trudged after their platoon commander.

"What're we supposed to do when we find the refugees, Sarge?" Jamie called out as they walked.

"We babysit them there until the Guardies get here, dipshit," Holmes said. "Make sure they stay in their box."

"Cool it, Holmes," Akito said. "These people are all just trying to get through another day. We're here to keep the peace. That's all."

The rain started again, and Remy could feel his wet armor starting to rub at the small of his back. Their gear was made for desert conditions, not this kind of weather. Water ran down Remy's neck, creating a chill despite the muggy weather. He was so lost in his own thoughts, he didn't see Akito call a halt.

The road bent around a copse of dense trees where a pickup truck with

Louisiana plates was stuck deep in a water-filled ditch. It was a beautiful machine, a custom diesel, with chrome everything.

"A gasser," Jamie said, pointing to the exhaust pipes extending over the cab. "They don't make 'em like that anymore."

Remy nodded agreement. Only the uber-rich could afford a vintage gas-powered beauty like this one. It was more a collector's item than something you actually drove, though. For day to day use, they had their aircars. On the other end of the wealth spectrum, the truly poor had no other option besides nursing an ancient gas-powered wreck. Finding gas for them, though, was getting harder all the time.

"Lieutenant." Akito had his head inside the shattered driver's side window. "Blood on the seat."

"So much for keeping the peace," Holmes muttered.

"Recommend we get to the camp before we lose the light, sir," Akito said, looking at the gloomy sky.

The Red Cross tent city was laid out on a neat grid, ten family-sized tents to a side, with the space between them churned to mud. A few dozen solar cars were parked haphazardly along the side of the road.

And not a living soul in sight.

Remy used the muzzle of his AR-21 to lift a flap leading into the nearest tent. The interior had a small rug in the entrance with muddy boot prints. Children's toys littered the floor, and two narrow cots with mussed bedclothes were pushed up against the wall.

Remy squinted into the still-weeping clouds. Maybe the squad could camp here tonight in one of these nice dry tents.

"Sergeant," Zack said, "let's head into town."

"Sir, it's getting late—"

"I'm aware of the time, Sergeant. Our orders are to find the refugees and set a perimeter." He pointed down the road toward Vicksburg. "There's only one way they could have gone."

The gloom deepened as they double-timed it down the highway, crossing into the suburb of Stout. The main street of the small town was lined with two- and three-story buildings, sustainable living structures with shops on the lower floor and apartments above. Despite the encroaching evening, no lights shone in any of the windows.

Concrete planters with flowers and small, decorative trees dotted the pedestrian-only boulevard. After a few blocks, the street opened onto the glassy darkness of the Mississippi River, where a pair of floating casinos abutted concrete piers. In the distance, Remy could see rows of vehicle lights on the I-20 bridge and campfires dotting the opposite shore.

Akito halted the squad at the end of the street.

"What's the holdup, Sergeant?" Zack called.

"Sir, we expected to find thousands of refugees. Where are they? That many people can't just disappear. This place is a ghost town."

The rain was falling harder, forcing Akito to raise his voice. Remy's soaked uniform and battle armor felt like he was carrying an extra fifty pounds. He was tired, hungry, cold, and he felt a blister forming on his right heel.

"There!" Holmes called out, pointing her AR-21 toward the casinos. The outside of the casino came to life with light. If he squinted, Remy could even see movement. That made sense. The refugees had abandoned the camps and moved onto the casinos.

A swoop of movement halfway down the street caught Remy's attention. "Sarge! I'm tracking incoming!"

Jamie had his scope out scanning the street. "It's a news drone," he called, standing up in the pink doorway of a cupcake shop called Sprinkle Dome. As Remy watched, a second, then a third news drone dropped from the sky to hover over the street. Odd to have so many drones clustered in an area where nothing was happening.

Jamie hooked a thumb at the sign above the cupcake shop. "This place reminds me of a strip club I used to go to called the Glitter Dome..." He paused in mid-sentence, the way he always did when winding up for the punch line.

His head snapping sharply sideways, half of Jamie's face evaporated into a red mist. A spatter of something dark splashed against the pale pink door. Remy saw a neat round hole appear in the jamb...

"Take cover!" Remy screamed. His training took over, slamming his body flat against a concrete planter. Behind him, he heard Jamie's body slap against the slick sidewalk. One green dot on the bottom of his field of view turned red.

Remy barely registered the zip of high-powered rounds cracking the asphalt around him. Reflected in the shopfront windows, suppressed fire from the upper floors of the buildings along the street sparked like deadly fireflies.

Jamie was dead. His best friend was *dead*.

Rain mixed with the gore oozing out of Jamie's head wound, creating little rivulets through the mess of clotting blood. He should cover his friend's face with something. Remy started to reach out.

"Don't do it, Remy." Holmes crouched behind her own concrete planter twelve feet of bare sidewalk away. It seemed much farther. "He's gone."

They were US soldiers in an American city. Easy-peasy, that's how this was supposed to go down. He and his best friend were going on leave together in three days ... Vegas. They had it all planned out...

From the other side of the street, Zack shouted into his headset. "Overwatch, this is Digger Squad Bravo! We need immediate evac from this location! One soldier down!"

The answer came back calm and cold. "That's a negative, Bravo. We have multiple firefights in progress. Fall back and secure a defensive position—"

The circuit turned into a hiss filled with static.

Akito roared out a curse. "How are these fuckers jamming us on a military circuit? Remy, have your team lay down cover fire. Team Two, fall back."

Remy rolled to a prone firing position, switching his AR-21 to three-round burst mode. The butt of his rifle thudded satisfying three-beat punches into his shoulder. The enemy fire ceased, but he kept putting rounds into those shattered windows.

Zack's voice broke into the local circuit. "Fire Team One, fall back—"

The explosion was so loud it made the rifle shots sound like puffs from a bee-bee gun. The heavy concrete planter next to Remy rocked with the force of the blast. He pressed his face against the wet sidewalk as chunks of dirt, asphalt, wood, and glass rained down.

The row of green dots on his data glasses blinked and three more turned red. Three greens remained: Akito, Holmes, and some new recruit from the other fire team.

Holmes flashed a thumbs-up to indicate she was okay.

"Sarge! You okay?" Remy yelled into comms.

A streak of light shot over Remy's head and through one of the apartment windows. He pressed his face back into the dirty sidewalk, clamped his hands over his ears. It was too late to run, and he knew what an RPG could do. Another explosion lit up the night sky. More debris rained down on his back.

He could hear Akito's breathing on the circuit. "Sarge?"

"IED, Remy. These assholes set a booby trap for us, and we walked right into it. It's just me and Smithson left, and we are not mobile." The green dots that represented Akito and Smithson shifted to blinking yellow. They both needed medical attention and soon.

Three doors down, the enemy fire resumed. They were ignoring Remy and Holmes. All the fire was directed at the injured Akito and Smithson.

Remy saw his chance.

"Cover me!" he screamed at Holmes. Remy staggered to his feet, lurching across the pedestrian plaza toward the store below the enemy. Behind him, Holmes pumped out continuous rounds at the remaining enemy fire team.

The storefront turned out to be an Italian restaurant. Images of small square tables laid with snow-white linen, silverware, and shimmering wine glasses flashed by as he crashed through the glass front door and rolled against the bar. Outside, Holmes switched to three-round bursts. Inside, the loudest sound was his own breathing.

Headlamp on, Remy edged toward the kitchen, rifle up. He wished with everything he had that Jamie was covering his six.

The cold light from his helmet flashed over a worn range and hanging pans. There were two open doors. One opened to the back alley, the second revealed a set of narrow stairs.

The yellow dot that was PFC Smithson blinked red.

He could hear his breath whistling through his teeth as he climbed the steps to a single door. Jamie's killer was behind that door. Remy closed his eyes.

"Holmes, cease fire," he whispered into the comm circuit.

The incoming gunfire stopped immediately. And Remy listened.

Two weapons in the next room started firing again. A pair of AR-21s, just like the one he carried. These guys, whoever they were, were using military grade hardware on his people. Their own goddamned soldiers.

The ghost of Jamie Allen, fellow survivor of eighteen months in the Sinai, teller of dirty jokes, and the closest thing Remy had to a brother, stood beside him in the dark hallway, lop-sided grin and all.

The grin slid off the spirit's pale face like gravity had pulled it away. The image collapsed into half a bloody face melting into a dirty sidewalk.

Remy kicked in the door. A shape to his left moved and he put it down with two quick pulls of the trigger. Another shift in the shadows, another pair of bullets. He swept the room again.

"Clear!" he said.

In the glare of his headlamp, Remy pieced together the scene. A red-haired boy with freckles wearing black body armor over a yellow t-shirt. A blonde girl wearing an LSU sweatshirt over her chest protector. Both held AR-21s. Neither looked older than Jamie.

Both dead by his hand.

His knees went soft and he found himself sitting amid a litter of glass and expended brass cartridges.

"Why?" Remy said to the corpses. "We came here to help you."

A whirring noise drew his attention to the window. The red eye of a news drone stared back at him.

# 2

## WILLIAM GRAVES • PHOENIX, ARIZONA • SIX YEARS LATER

Three days into the Phoenix Drought deployment, Colonel William Graves reflected on his time as the US military's top disaster relief officer. He knew one thing for sure—he'd take a Category 6 hurricane over a drought any day.

Sure, hurricanes were powerful, devastating events. What the winds didn't rip apart, the storm surge drowned in brackish water and dangerous debris. Bacteria flourished, and diseases so long dormant people didn't even know their names anymore resurrected with a vengeance. But hurricanes were defined disasters. They did their worst and moved on. Waters receded. People rebuilt.

Staring out the window of the Walmart store he'd converted into a command post, Graves watched the baking heat of summertime Phoenix ripple off the pavement in waves. He'd been ordered here to yet another crisis point to manage yet another weather catastrophe. And while the Joint Chiefs rarely denied a request for resources or men, he just as rarely ever felt like he had enough to meet the threat. On days like this, his job seemed like a never-ending problem he couldn't ever solve.

How do you defend against the wrath of Mother Nature? His job had become less a determined dedication to helping his fellow citizens and more a low-grade ache of helplessness. Of feeling, sometimes literally, like he was spitting into a gale-force wind.

No, he decided, hurricanes ended, but droughts just went on and on. He'd take a hurricane any day of the week.

Phoenix was dying. He knew it, his people knew it, and the refugees he'd pulled from the suburbs to the camps knew it too. The only question was how long it would take.

A preventable tragedy. A hundred years of piss-poor water management and stupid, unregulated growth in the middle of the fucking desert had sealed the city's fate.

"Sir?" A young captain appeared at his elbow. Hannah Jansen was a recent West Point grad and one of his most promising recruits. She wore her kinky dark hair cropped close to her scalp, which gave her a tough look. She'd told him her great-great-grandmother had died in Hurricane Katrina in 2005 and her grandmother, a child then, had been saved by the Army; that's why she wanted to serve in the Disaster Mitigation Corps. Graves wished he had a hundred young officers like her. Dedicated, educated, and above all, motivated.

"We've got word from Tucson, sir." She stood at attention, her jaw tight. Jansen didn't rattle easily.

"How bad is it?"

"The mayor ordered a mandatory evacuation over the YourVoice network."

Graves bit back a curse. Second only to the weather enemy were these shortsighted politicians and their social-media habits.

"Get me the Tucson mayor on the line ASAP."

No matter how much he pleaded with them to think their decisions through before making them public, the goddamned politicians always made the expedient choice, whether it was the right one or not. Millions of people displaced by disaster, and all they could think about was losing their job in the next election.

"I have the mayor for you, sir," Jansen said.

A Hispanic man in his mid-thirties appeared on the vidscreen. The mayor's lips were set in a firm line. "Julio—"

"Don't start with me, Colonel," the young man snapped. "We have no water here. *Zero*. The trucks you promised would arrive this morning are still not here." One flick of Graves's eyes, and Jansen darted away to investigate. "These people are scared and they need answers—and *water*. We need *water*."

Jansen was back. She scribbled a note on his blotter: *hijacked*.

"We'll send another convoy, Mr. Mayor," Graves said. "This afternoon, under armed guard. It'll be there by nightfall."

"Too late, Colonel. I've already put out the word on YourVoice and I'm not going to flip-flop on this again. Fool me once."

Graves had talked him into reversing his evac order once before, and Julio Martinez had been crucified for it by the WorldNet trolls.

"At least let me send buses up to move people to Phoenix in an orderly fashion." When Martinez started to protest, Graves cut him off. "If everyone drives their own car, we'll just make the problem worse."

In the sunniest place in the country, where people were literally dying from too much solar energy, there was still a high concentration of gas-powered cars. The very rich and the very poor, operating internal combustion engines for very different reasons.

"You don't get it, Colonel. These people are leaving Tucson. For good. They're loading up cars and trailers with all their stuff because they are *not* coming back. They're taking everything, their boats—"

"Did you say boats?" Graves resisted the urge to laugh out loud. He was fighting a losing war against a mega-drought and these people were towing boats to Phoenix?

"I don't expect you to understand, Colonel, sitting in your cushy office in Phoenix, but these people's lives are being upended—"

"Thank you, Julio. We'll do our best to accommodate these new refugees. If you'll excuse me, I have preparations to make." He ended the call as Tucson's mayor opened his mouth to reply.

Graves closed his eyes. *One one-thousand. Two one-thousand....*

"You okay, sir?" Jansen asked.

"Yeah." Graves surveyed the busy floor of his command center as he counted his frustration away.

The clothing racks and shelving had been cleared, the contents confiscated and stockpiled for distribution to refugees—the Consumer Goods Confiscation and Disaster Relief Act in action. All those refugees needed tents to live in and at least two square meals a day.

The resulting large, open space of the Walmart floor had been sectioned off into grids, giving the impression of order. The Red Cross Section was a beehive of activity. The refugee influx had doubled since he'd ordered all the water for agriculture across the state diverted to Phoenix. The Power Section was calm. The power grid, heavily fed by solar, was the least of their worries. The colonel's eyes landed on the nearly empty Security Section. The Arizona National Guard was heavily supplemented by regular Army. The combined forces had their hands full keeping looters out of the empty suburbs and securing the few ground wells still yielding water.

Graves sighed. Now they had to provide armed escorts for water trucks as well. What kind of douchebag would hijack a water truck in the middle of a thousand-year drought?

Jansen cleared her throat. She was wearing her data glasses, her right eye hidden behind the glare of data streaming across the lens.

"We found the trucks, sir, in west Phoenix, in a warehouse owned by a black market gang. Do you want us to send in a team?"

Graves counted to five before he answered in a measured tone. Black marketeers were everywhere, scoring profit off misery. And they were no doubt well-armed. "Tell Major Okunye I want that water back in our custody ASAP. Full tactical gear, deadly force is authorized."

"Yes, sir." Her lens flashed as she subvocalized a command.

Graves felt the sudden need to move, to burn some energy. "With me, Lieutenant."

He strode across the white linoleum to the Water Section. Captain Margaret Chou looked like she hadn't slept in days. Her uniform was rumpled, her complexion ashen under her light-brown skin. She set aside a cup of coffee and stood when she saw Graves coming.

"Colonel," she said in a voice as fatigued as she looked. "You've heard about the hijacking?"

Graves nodded. "Okunye's got a team on it, but it's only one convoy. Tucson has fallen, so we're anticipating another wave of refugees in the next few hours."

Chou's face contracted. She led Grave and Jansen to the city map. Green dots showed active water wells, red x's dry ones. The red far outweighed the green. The Phoenix suburbs were color-coded as well: red shading for mandatory evacuation zones, yellow for recommended. Graves's eyes scanned the familiar names: Buckeye, Chandler, Mesa, and the rest.

"We're bringing as much water as we can by tanker," Chou was saying, "but we're not even close to keeping up with the pace of usage. The groundwater situation is bad, but at least it's stable. The Red Cross is running distribution at the active wells, with the Guard providing security. Like I said, not good but stable."

She changed screens. "This is what I need you to see, sir."

Graves studied the image. The bright blue line cutting across the map was the Central Arizona Project, Phoenix's lifeline in the desert. The CAP provided nearly three million acre-feet of water a year, straight from the Colorado River to supply the entire region, including agriculture and water for Phoenix proper. The adjoining graph of water availability showed a bump when the Disaster Mitigation Corps had shut down the water supply to agriculture over two months ago. There were smaller bumps as Graves had isolated suburbs around the city, and then a final surge when Tucson went offline two weeks ago.

But the CAP's supply also trended lower. Small, but noticeable over the span of weeks.

"I know there's a drought going on, but why does it keep going down?" Graves asked.

"Exactly, sir." Chou pulled up another graph and laid it over the CAP supply line. "The story we're getting from the engineers up in Lake Havasu is that our supply is being reduced proportionally to reservoir levels, in accordance with the city's water rights. And that's been true—until ten days ago." She pointed to the slope of the line over the past two weeks. The drop-off for the CAP was much steeper than the reservoir supply's decline.

"They're cheating us," Graves said.

"That's what the data's telling me, sir."

"And you've talked to them?"

"They've been giving me the runaround on releasing this data." Chou offered a faint smile. "I pulled a few favors with some whitehat hackers I know to get this. I also conducted a drone flyby for some on-the-ground stats. It checks out, sir." She held her commanding officer's gaze. "They're definitely shorting us."

Graves ran his knuckles across the stubble of his chin. "What about Department of Interior?"

Chou shrugged. "I just got off the phone with them. I showed them the data, and they were pretty pissed I even had it. They said they'll consider launching an investigation. They'll get back to me next week."

Graves chewed his lip as he considered the chart.

"Sir? If I may?" Chou's face was pinched but determined.

"Spit it out, Maggie."

"This investigation line is bullshit," Chou said, her voice heated. "I think someone's on the take, sir. The water in that dam is being shifted to California and once it's gone, it's gone. What we're dealing with now is bad, but it's about to get a whole lot worse if we don't get the CAP back online. I recommend a backup plan if the discussion with Washington doesn't yield immediate results."

Graves regarded her with a wry expression. "You're a cynic, Captain, but I think you're right." His position gave him the authority to commandeer utilities for the public good, but taking over California's main source of water was a step that would rile Washington. Served them right.

Graves turned to Jansen. "Tell Major Okunye to draw up a tactical battle plan to take over operation of the Lake Havasu pumping station. He should be ready to brief the captain and myself by 1800 hours."

"I think that's the right call, sir," Chou said.

"Let's hope it's not needed."

Jansen followed him from the Water Section. "Intel needs to see you, sir. Priority one."

Graves double-timed it to the Intel Section. A second lieutenant who looked barely out of high school greeted him with a salute. His name badge read *Perkins*.

"You new here, Perkins?" Graves asked in a gruff tone.

"Second day, sir."

The kid looked so nervous, Graves thought he might swallow his tongue. The colonel shot a look to Jansen that said: *He's standing in as intel duty officer on his second day?*

"Well?" Graves said instead. "What is it?"

The lieutenant guided them to a massive wall with multiple vidscreens and nodded to an equally young enlisted woman. The image changed to a drone feed showing a line of six people walking abreast through a desiccated suburb.

"What am I looking at?" Graves tried to control his impatience.

"Sorry, sir. One second." Perkins leaned over another console and zoomed in on the figures. Three men, three women, all dressed in dusty jeans and tank tops. The drone's viewpoint changed as it arced overhead to hover behind them. "There." He stepped back as if the answer was obvious.

"What am I looking at, Perkins? I don't see the significance of six people walking down a street as a major intel threat."

"Their necks, sir," Jansen interrupted. "Look at the tattoos."

"Exactly," Perkins said, pleased with himself. "New Earthers. Neos."

A chill swept up Graves from the base of his spine as he squinted at the enlarged image of a man's neck showing a tattooed split image of a woman's face and the planet earth. The New Earth Order, followers of a mysterious WorldNet prophet named Cassandra, who directed her disciples to certain death in climate-related disasters. He'd seen it play out at other extreme weather events—a Corpus Christi hurricane, an Oregon wildfire, a California earthquake.

All those prior events had one thing in common: when the Neos showed up, things were about to get much worse. His mind ripped through the possibilities—

"Sir? I think I know what it is," Jansen said. She pointed at the screen. The drone operator had zoomed out, giving them a wide-angle view of the desert. A wall of clouds blotted out the horizon. It crawled across the desert like a slow, wasting disease.

"Dust storm?" Perkins asked.

A fork of lightning ripped through the inky blackness onscreen.

"Thousands of people," Graves whispered.

Alarms began whooping around him as the storm showed up on radar.

"The refugees from Tucson," Jansen said. "They're on the highway. They'll be buried by the storm."

"That's not a storm." Graves exhaled, feeling helpless again. "It's a mass grave, falling from the sky."

# 3

## MING QINLAO • LUNA CITY, THE MOON

From the Moon, it really did look like a big, blue marble hanging in black space.

Ming Qinlao studied the subtle white swirl of clouds on distant Earth. If she squinted and was patient, she could see them slowly painting their patterns over the oceans. She remembered gazing up with her father at clouds just like these when she was a little girl. They'd made a game of it, each racing to be the first to find the most exotic animal in their soft designs.

She blinked away her childhood memories, the woman asserting herself once more over the girl. That had been a long time ago. Clouds, blue sky, open air ... Ming didn't really miss them.

The view of the planet from this distance was simple, almost heavenly. But on the ground, she knew, it was a different story. She'd read just yesterday how citizens of Arizona were fleeing their homes for lack of drinking water. Floods, fires, droughts. Mother Earth was angry and mankind, like fleas on a dog's back, scrambled for survival while the planet scratched to get rid of them.

By comparison, life on the Moon was simple, tranquil even. She worked, she ate, she slept, she loved. And that was really all Ming needed. A simple life of order and purpose.

"Ma'am," a voice said with quiet insistence, interrupting her daydreams.

Ming's gaze dropped from the stars into the ancient lunar caldera, where the half-finished dome of LUNa City waited. Management didn't like their precious engineers soaking up radiation on the Moon's surface, but she justified her afternoon excursions as work inspections. Tiny, pressure-suited men, the yellow safety lights on their backpacks making them look like honeybees from this distance, crawled across the structural skeleton. Flickers of intense, white light flared across its surface as they welded.

"Just another minute, Ban. Please." She did her best to keep the irritation out of her voice.

"Very well, ma'am."

Ban never looked at Earth, she noticed. He'd made his choice to stay moonbound long ago. Physically, Earth was no longer an option for him. Not, at least, without a long, painful rehabilitation regimen. Living in space made the human body lazy.

*He's probably counting out sixty precious seconds right now*, Ming thought, imagining the clockwork of her escort's mind clicking and calculating as he paced behind her.

Ban was a good man, but his constant presence wore on her. She understood the company just wanted to protect their investment by providing Ban. With all the competition in the job market from Taulke and the other space development companies, engineers willing to take Moon duty were rare. Engineers willing to sign up for Moon duty on a fixed-cost United Nations contract? Rarer still.

Ming sighed and pirouetted in the low-g—she'd never been able to do *that* on Earth—to face her security escort. Gravity—she certainly didn't miss gravity. Ban made a half-bow and held open the door of the crude lunar buggy they'd taken to the top of the cliff.

She slid into the passenger seat without another word. As they rolled down the slope, Ming's eye flicked, unlocking the do-not-disturb setting on her data glasses. She waited for the onslaught of incoming messages.

Only thirty-two. A slow day. Most were routine inspection requests or change orders to schematics. In the world of government contracts, if something so minor as the thread count on a screw changed, the client demanded accountability in the form of a change order. The United Nations was building LUNa City, the first large-scale multinational civilian habitat on the Moon, so the change orders had to be processed into English, then into whatever language and currency were used by the country paying for that portion of the project, then batched for transmission and processing back to Earth.

The bureaucracy was annoying and sorely slow, but that was the nature of the job—and Ming was good at it.

After passing through the airlock, she exchanged her pressure suit for a red engineer's jumpsuit and prepared to slay the paperwork dragon yet again. She had a reputation for being a ruthless task master, and that's exactly how she wanted it. If you had a meeting with Ming Qinlao, you took it standing up. That made sure the meeting was short and uncomfortable, which tended to keep people on task. Construction crews who wanted to make progress sought Ming out for that very reason. Those who wished to suckle at the government teat a little longer found other engineers to work with.

As she walked into her office, the artist's rendering of LUNa City on the wall caught her eye, as always. It inspired her each time she noticed it. The designer had lavished his attention on the massive, arching dome and underlying high-rise structures, a space that covered an area the size of Minneapolis.

The artist understood his audience. It was the dome that had sold the project, but the real treasure lay beneath LUNa's surface in the honeycombs of tunnels and living spaces currently under construction for the three million people that would eventually live here.

Ban took his position at her door as she surveyed the waiting readouts on her desktop. Would the politicians ever really get serious about living off-planet? The Moon had been inhabited for decades by helium-3 and mineral extraction crews, but not yet by ordinary citizens. Meanwhile, on Mars, Taulke Industries was busy building its own Mars Station. The next step, Taulke promised, would be a terraforming miracle. Anthony Taulke was certainly a genius, but more often than not, his public addresses seemed more hype than history in the making.

Ming's personal comm channel pulsed her a new message. She bit her lip at seeing the beautiful face framed in blonde locks and checked her display's chronometer. Had she forgotten dinner with Lily again?

No, she still had another 45 minutes in her shift. She and Lily had agreed that there would be no personal comms during working hours, barring an emergency. That said, Lily sometimes had difficulty with discerning a perceived emergency from an actual one. Ming accepted the call.

"What's up, Lil?" She kept her voice light, happy. They were about to embark on a two-day leave together. The last thing she wanted was a lover's quarrel.

"You have a visitor," Lily whispered, her eyes darting to the side.

"From work? Tell them to come to my office."

"Not from work." Lily's voice was urgent. "I think you'd better come home now, sweetie. She doesn't look like someone who's used to waiting. On anything."

"Who is it? Did she give you a name?"

"Her card says Xi Qinlao," Lily said. "It's an actual *paper* business card."

Ming's mouth went dry. With a wave of her hand, she indicated Ban should close her office door.

"She's a board member from Qinlao Manufacturing," Lily continued. "She says she knows you." Her tone rose hopefully. "Maybe she's here to offer you a job?"

"Listen to me, Lily," Ming said, more harshly than she meant to. She tried to swallow and found it difficult. "This is very important. Don't tell that woman anything about me—about *us*. Just don't say anything at all. I'll be home as fast as I can."

"Do you—"

"Don't say anything!"

Ming swept out of her office, surprising Ban, who bolted after her. Her home was ten levels beneath the surface, a quarter mile to the north. And the corridors would be full of off-shift workers looking for drink and diversion.

Ming had maintained her Earth muscle tone with regular workouts and pharmaceuticals. Taking advantage of the light lunar gravity, she bypassed the elevator, descending the stairs three at a time and hopping the railing to avoid the dense foot traffic. Ban, with his moonsoft muscles, struggled to keep up.

How had her aunt found her? More to the point, why had she bothered? And why come all the way to the Moon personally?

Any answer Ming could find to any of those questions wasn't good. And the thought of family politics reinserting itself into her life—her well-ordered, comfortable, purpose-driven life—frightened as much as angered her.

She paused at the door to her quarters to compose herself and catch her breath. Ban caught up to her, his chest heaving. "Everything okay, ma'am?"

Her own breathing under control now, Ming's heart still raced. "No, Ban. Everything is far from okay."

She opened the door.

Xi Qinlao was a woman of terrible beauty. Tall even by European standards, rake-thin, with high cheekbones and wideset eyes, the woman could have graced the cover of any fashion magazine—in fact, she had in her youth. But there was a hardness about her now, a coldness in her gaze suggesting her beauty simply was skin deep.

She stood when Ming entered, her silken robes making a soft shush in the stillness of the room. Ming took three steps into the apartment and bowed deeply, a reflexive sign of respect she'd been taught long ago.

"Auntie Xi. Welcome."

Ming's voice fought to get the expected words out. Her least-favorite aunt had invaded her home, the refuge she'd made with Lily. Now that she was face to face with her aunt, fear outpaced the anger roiling in her gut.

Her aunt returned the bow but remained silent. She made a show of looking Ming up and down, then casting her glare around the apartment. The place was a mess as usual, with blankets and pillows bunched on the loveseat where she and Lily left them after watching vids last night. The bedroom door was ajar, and their bed was a sea of jumbled blankets and discarded clothes. The old woman's stony gaze lingered longest on Lily before returning to her niece.

Ming's gaze flitted to Ito, her aunt's bodyguard. He stood stiff in his charcoal gray uniform like a knight in ancient armor, the Qinlao logo embroidered on the sleeve. When she was just a girl, Ito had been her father's bodyguard as well as Ming's self-defense trainer. Thanks to him she knew how to kill a person twelve different ways.

One for each sign of the zodiac, he'd once joked. She'd felt closer to him than almost anyone else in her family's circle. The skin around Ito's dark eyes softened, and his chin ticked down in a barely perceptible nod.

"What's going on here, babe?" Lily asked, bringing her back to the present. Dressed in loose clothes, her blouse spotted with drops from last night's dinner, Lily looked nervous but also excited. Ming could see she was braless and her golden hair was pulled up in a messy topknot, speared through with a plastic chopstick. A rushed attempt to make herself presentable to visitors.

"Introduce us, Niece," Xi said. There was challenge in her voice, not a genuine desire to meet Ming's lover.

"Lily, this is my Aunt Xi..." Ming began formally, then trailed off.

She'd never told Lily that her father was the CEO of Qinlao Manufacturing; never told her anything about her past at all, really. Qinlao was a common enough surname in China.

It was a fair trade; she knew very little of Lily's past. They'd been happy in their ignorance of one another, each content with the romance of a new relationship. Even last year, when Ming bought out Lily's construction contract, her girlfriend had never asked where the money came from. Ming's trust fund, of course. Would she have told Lily if she'd asked? Or would Ming continue to pretend that part of her life had never existed?

Auntie Xi's disapproving gaze brought color to Ming's cheeks and sharpened her focus. Ming cleared her dry throat to continue: "Aunt Xi is my father's sister."

"So your father works for Qinlao Manufacturing?" Lily asked.

Ming pleaded with her eyes. *Please, please, Lil, stop talking. I'll explain it all later, I promise.*

"Yes," Ming said quickly, cutting off further questions. "Auntie Xi—"

"Young lady," Xi interrupted with the air of a queen educating a servant, "her father *was* Qinlao Manufacturing."

"I don't understand," Lily said.

"Ming's father was the CEO and founder of Qinlao, the company was named for him." Xi's gaze swiveled to Ming with all the subtlety of a cannon. "Pack whatever you don't want to leave behind, but be quick about it. I'm here to take you home, Niece."

"Wait," Lily said. "You can't just sweep in here and take her away. I don't care how much money you have, lady. Ming and I live here. She has a *job* here. We're going on holiday! We love each other."

Ming held up a hand to silence Lily. Her ears rang. She regarded Ito again and still saw the softness in his eyes for her. Not the softness of nostalgia, she realized. The softness of pity.

Her aunt had spoken of her father in the past tense. Her father *was* the CEO of Qinlao Manufacturing, Auntie Xi had said.

A weight that had nothing to do with gravity settled on Ming's shoulders. There was only one reason her aunt would come all this way.

"What the hell is going on?" Lily asked.

"What happened?" Ming snapped at her aunt, desperate with a pressing need to know.

Xi shook her head. Even the granite façade of the fierce woman's features cracked for a moment.

Ming's legs weakened. She took a quick step to the loveseat and settled, shaking, into its mound of blankets. They still smelled of popcorn and Lily's perfume.

Lily appeared beside her, arms encircling her in a lover's embrace that was warm, alive, comfortable.

It took effort for Ming to drag her eyes up to her aunt's face. Was there really less gravity on the Moon?

The old woman's eyes were flat. "Dead. Your father is dead."

# 4

## REMY CADE • AIRSPACE OVER ALASKA

The UN dropship banked again so the press corps could get aerial footage of the Alaskan wilderness before they landed. Remy Cade fitted his rebreather over his nose and mouth and blinked to life the retinal display in his right eye.

Somewhere below them, in that tangle of underbrush, were the last remaining fragments of the once-great North American caribou herd. As a kid, Remy had seen history vids of caribou herds numbering in the thousands loping across the frozen tundra.

But that memory felt to him now like something from science fiction. Today, the term *herd* when applied to the caribou was almost a sick joke.

The whole situation felt ... wrong. Why would the caribou herd migrate here, this far north? The dropship, ironically named *Abundance*, had had to lift off a US Navy carrier in the Beaufort Sea above the Arctic Circle just to get here.

The UN Biodiversity Section had tracked the herd for days as it made its way across the barren landscape. They seemed drawn to this stinking, swampy little valley, as if this was where they'd chosen to make their last stand as a species. Hopes were high that some instinctive gene was guiding them to a safe place.

And then, this morning, the devastating news: the herd had scanned positive for chronic wasting disease. They had to be destroyed.

In Remy's mind, a small tactical weapon launched from the carrier in the Beaufort Sea would have been the most efficient means of dispatch. But sending a missile that costs tens of thousands of dollars would have been the very definition of overkill. And the optics would have been terrible.

One thing was certain—when politics and science hopped into bed together, things were never that easy. The United Nations resolution 641.D.5 required any extinction event of a land-based species to be personally attended by the UN's Secretary of Biodiversity. It was Elise Kisaan's job to personally sign the death warrant of the caribou, yet another species lost to the cruel whims of Mother Earth.

And it was Remy Cade's job to protect her. As her bodyguard—and lover—wherever Elise went, Remy was by her side.

Always the newshound, Elise decided to make a photo op out of the death of the caribou. It would accomplish two things, she'd said: draw attention to the sad passing of another victim species of the climate war and demonstrate the commitment of the United States to protecting its citizens.

He surveyed the three soldier escorts carefully selected from UN member nations where Elise needed to strengthen her image. The rest of her entourage included a gaggle of media people, camera drones perched on their shoulders, who peppered Elise with questions.

Remy ignored them. Half their questions were inane and the other half sought to trap Elise into saying something to embarrass the United Nations.

Despite her seeming dispassion—a trait Remy had come to accept as necessary in a job where she pronounced the death of a species on a regular basis—he knew Elise Kisaan to be a caring person. It was the juxtaposition of those two things that had so intrigued him about her, that set her apart from the rest of the fish in the sea. He knew from personal experience how passionate she could be in private.

One of the camera drones turned its all-seeing eye his way, and Remy turned away from force of habit. His security filter was set to *private*, so his image should be auto-stripped from any newsfeeds, but one could never be too careful when dealing with the media.

As the *Abundance* made its final approach to the landing zone, the rotten-egg stench of methane releasing from thawing tundra filled the cabin, and with it his sense of unease. Even with his rebreather in place, the air still reeked.

Remy caught the eyes of the three men forming their military escort and tapped his temple.

*"Stay frosty,"* he pulsed to them.

The two grunts nodded. The third, the sergeant with the name tag *Rico*, rolled his eyes. Remy resisted the urge to march across the cargo bay and instill some respect in him. As the man in charge of the squad, he should respect Remy's position as Elise's bodyguard. That would solve nothing except provide the press corps with footage that would no doubt embarrass the secretary.

The *Abundance* settled gracefully, landing struts sinking deep into the mushy permafrost. The putrid smell of vegetation increased tenfold. Some members of the group tightened their rebreathers.

Everyone gathered at the top of the ramp. Elise waited till the press drones were lined up and focused on her.

"We'll proceed into the valley in three teams, find each animal, take a DNA sample to confirm wasting disease, then deliver a fast-acting toxin to put the suffering creatures out of their misery quickly and painlessly."

As the only child of Indian agriculture magnate Aarav Kisaan, she'd been bred for a role in public life. And yet, when she spoke like this, it was easy to believe she had the animals' well-being at heart. That tension of caring and coldness within this remarkable woman stoked his heart, as it always did.

And he knew her to be a woman of unusual personal strength. When he'd first met Elise, she'd been confined to a maglev chair by a nervous system disorder. When it was revealed she could walk again, the official reason given to the public was a never-well-defined surgical intervention. Questions for details were met with requests for privacy.

His eyes moved over her body as she discussed "necessary measures" and the "sacrifice of one species for the greater good." No one in the press corps, would have guessed she stood before them on two bionic legs. In bed, Remy called her the Billion Dollar Woman.

"Can you talk about containment, Ms. Kisaan?" A young woman from the YourVoice network asked, a news drone perched on her shoulder.

"Of course." Elise pulled her dead-straight ebony hair back into a pony-tail and secured it with a silver ring. Remy suspected it was a maneuver meant to buy her time to formulate a politic answer. Or maybe just to make sure her face wasn't blocked for the camera.

"In addition to treating these magnificent animals with the respect they deserve, we also want to be sure there's no chance of this disease jumping species," Elise explained. "After we depart, the entire area will be covered with a foam shield to neutralize any contamination. Then we'll compost all organic matter so it can be reabsorbed by the local environment. Within a few months, this entire area will have regrown."

Elise had a long, thin face with deep, brown eyes and a perpetual frown. She was a serious person, but plain looking—until she smiled. Then her features blossomed from withering to warm.

She was smiling now, capturing the attention of everyone in the loading bay. Everyone except the short, stocky man from the Chinese state media. He seemed unimpressed by the attractive young secretary's poise.

Raising his hand, he said, "But couldn't this entire situation have been avoided if the United States had confined these animals to a secure loca-tion? That was recommended by the United Nations more than a decade ago. By letting them trek hundreds of miles across open country, you've potentially exposed many other species to a dangerous strain of wasting disease."

Elise focused her attention on the man, who glowered back. Remy thought her smile looked forced now.

"The policy of the United States is to let nature take its course." Her words sounded forced, too. She had vented to him in the past and her personal thoughts were not in line with the UN. "Mother Nature has spoken. If it's one thing we've learned in the last century or so, it's that we really shouldn't argue with her."

She pulsed a message to Remy: *"Make sure he's not with me."*

Remy nodded.

The atmosphere outside the ship was borderline toxic. The rebreathers dealt with the methane, but the stench made Remy's eyes water. The valley was the size of a city block, like a shallow bowl in the mostly flat landscape. In the hazy distance, Remy thought he could make out a mountain range. Maybe these caribou were headed to the mountains and couldn't make it.

In his retinal display, Remy noted the soldiers had gridded the search area and had already made team assignments. Because of the thick underbrush and dense trees, each team would maintain an open channel to avoid someone getting lost. Embracing that basic protocol reassured Remy, but the gnawing fear that something was out of place wouldn't go away.

Sergeant Rico handed out a type of wide-webbed shoe, patterned like a snowshoe, that would allow them to walk across the marshy earth without sinking in. Remy said in a low voice, "Keep your eyes open down there."

Rico shrugged. "Hey, man, I just work here."

Remy glared at the sergeant. Soldiers hated private contractors, and they weren't shy about showing it. He wondered if he should pull Elise out of the op right here and now. Technically, his contract with the Kisaan family gave him the authority to do whatever was necessary to ensure her safety, but the news cameras ... Elise would be furious. And the last thing he wanted to deal with was an upset Elise.

Better to work fast, get this op done, and get her back on the ship as soon as possible. Fingering the Glock on his hip, Remy swallowed his pride and followed Elise into the valley.

The fir trees towered a meter over Remy's head, their soft needles raking at the slippery surface of his body armor. Despite their unwieldy footwear, the group made good time through the undergrowth till they reached the first caribou, a female, lying still on the ground.

The secretary kneeled next to the cow. As she examined the creature, Remy eyed the surrounding area. The encroaching trees gave him a claustrophobic feeling.

"Huh."

"What's wrong?" he asked.

She had her handheld out, analyzing a tissue sample. "This animal's perfectly healthy—except that it's dead."

Remy was no expert on large mammals, but it certainly looked healthy to him, with large, well-muscled hindquarters half-hidden by a shaggy coat.

The animal had curled up on its side with its head tucked down by its front legs, as if sleeping. And it had died that way.

"How long has it been dead?" he asked. He was aware of the YourVoice reporter's news drone capturing everything.

Messages streamed in from the other teams on the open channel. They'd found the same thing—otherwise seemingly healthy animals lying dead on the ground. Remy's paranoia from earlier returned in force. He scanned the surrounding trees line again

"All teams, fall back to the ship," he muttered into the microphone. "There's something not right here."

"Agreed," came Rico's crisp reply. "All units fall back."

"Wait! What's going on here?" It was the Chinese reporter on the open channel. "Is there something here you don't want us to see?"

Other reporters began to question the evac order as well. The channel became a cacophony of angry demands.

Remy reached for Elise's arm, but she pulled away, disappearing into the trees. The YourVoice newswoman darted after her, shouting a new question about the sudden change in itinerary.

"Ma'am—Elise!—we need to fall back!" Remy didn't like the sound of near-panic he detected in his own voice. The back of his head was screaming at him to run.

A pulse message from Elise hit his private channel: *There's one still alive. I can hear it.*

*"I don't give a shit if a hundred are still alive,"* he sent back as he struggled after her. Despite the ungainly marshshoes, her bionic legs had easily outpaced his flesh and blood limbs.

A long, strained bellow like a pinched foghorn sounded ahead of them. Remy crashed through the trees to find a small clearing.

In the center of the glade stood an enormous bull caribou. A huge, curving rack of antlers spread over his head like a wicked crown. He snorted at them, then reared back and bellowed a second challenge at the intruders. Remy unholstered his sidearm, but there was no way a handgun would stop an animal of that size.

"Back up slowly," he whispered to the women.

"No need," said the newswoman, pointing to the ground in front of the bull. Remy heard the clink before he saw the heavy links in the mud. The bull had been shackled in place with a heavy chain around his front hooves. Remy's fear and all he'd seen coalesced into one word in his mind.

*Ambush.*

Someone had killed the other caribou and chained this bull up as bait.

The wall of evergreens on the other side of the clearing wavered in his vision.

*Camouflage field*, Remy realized too late. There was the *pop-snap* of a muffled weapon, and the YourVoice reporter collapsed to the ground, a neat, red-black hole in her forehead. The camera drone, having lost direction from its mistress, dropped to the ground beside her.

Remy gripped the back of Elise's suit, jerking her back into the trees, spinning her body to face the direction of the ship. The marshshoes tangled up her feet, and she went down with a grunt.

More muffled shots. A branch from a fir tree by his shoulder dropped to the ground.

Other shots, unsilenced, echoed across the valley. M-24s, standard military issue. The shared comm channel exploded with civilian panic.

Elise struggled to her feet and launched into the trees. Remy fired blindly behind him as he raced after her. She'd lost a marsh shoe in the haste and her bionic legs were having trouble adjusting to the different types of footing. He cursed, then threw Elise over his shoulder in a fireman's carry and plowed into the vegetation. Tree branches whipped his face and he screamed into the open channel.

"It's an ambush!" Tree branches whipped his face. "We're under attack! I need support to protect the secretary!"

The chaos of reporters screaming and chopped orders from Rico drowned him out.

Expecting a bullet in the back at any moment, Remy redoubled his pace, bursting into the landing zone and safety of the *Abundance.*

But something was wrong. The ship's drive should be hot, the pilot ready to take off the second they boarded. That was evac protocol. Remy put Elise down and she backed away, her glare driving daggers into him. She swayed as her legs stabilized.

Rico appeared at the top of the ramp.

"Sergeant!" Remy said. "We have to get the secretary out of here." He looked around. They were the only three in the landing zone. The *Abundance*, at last, was firing up its engine. "We can come back for the others once she's—"

Rico leveled his M-24 rifle. "Drop your weapon, sir. We have the situation under control." His voice was tight. His finger rested on the trigger.

"Sergeant..." Remy took a breath. "Let's get Secretary Kisaan to safety. Then I'll come back and help you."

"I told you to drop your weapon."

The soldier's arm twitched and Remy froze. He pushed Elise away, out of the line of fire. "Okay." He showed his gun to the soldier, then placed it on the ground. "Now, let's get Ms. Kisaan out of here."

The soldier's lip curled. "Bad choice."

He pulled the trigger.

# 5

## ANTHONY TAULKE • TAULKE ATMOSPHERIC EXPERIMENT STATION, MARS

Anthony Taulke was beginning to hate the color red. He stared through the control-room window at the hundred-meter square enclosure of Martian landscape. Red rocks, red dirt, red dust ... red, red, *red*.

And that red was rust. Ferric oxide. Two parts iron, three parts oxygen. He didn't give a damn about the iron, but he wanted those oxygen molecules. No, he *needed* those oxygen molecules.

He regarded his company's logo hanging on the wall. An old-fashioned rocket superimposed on a bold capital letter T. Staring at it helped him focus.

*Two hundred and eighty billion dollars.*

The figure kept repeating in his head, like a tolling bell.

That was how much of his personal wealth he'd invested in Mars—so far. He'd placed the biggest bet of all time that he could make an entire planet habitable, that he could make a new Earth. The magnetic shield generator in orbit between Mars and the Sun was almost operational. It would, theoretically, keep the Martian atmosphere from being stripped away by the solar winds. But first, he had to create a Martian atmosphere. If he could just get the goddamned Red Planet to cooperate. He only needed a few hundred trillion of those tiny, goddamned oxygen molecules ... was that so much to ask?

The lead engineer on the terraforming project occupied the chair at the control panel. Anthony put his large hands on either shoulder of the seated man. When the first inkling of failure had quieted the control room, Anthony had cleared the space of everyone but the two of them.

He drew a deep breath of perfect, habitat air and tried to ignore the low hubbub of conversation in the next room—dignitaries and investors, enjoying the hospitality of Taulke Industries. Here to witness the next technological marvel from its founder. Another pulse came from his son, Tony, in charge of crowd management.

*"Do your job, son. I need more time,"* he sent back, then muted the link.

"Ronnie, explain it to me again." His hands tightened on the young man's shoulders. "Step by step, like I'm a five-year old."

The young man cleared his throat. "Yes, sir, Mr. Taulke—"

"*Anthony*, Ron," his boss chided him. "I told you to call me Anthony. Now, forget those self-important assholes in the next room, forget all the money and the pressure. We're just two engineers talking here, okay? Start from scratch."

Ronald Maher nodded. "We seeded the test area with the bacteria, but we're only at nine percent efficiency for oxygen production. We need to be at greater than twenty to make the—"

"I know the numbers for the business plan, Ron. Stick to the science."

"There must be something wrong with the scaling algorithm, Mr.—Anthony. We seeded the area with the drones in the same dispersal pattern we used in the small-area test. But we're not getting the same uptake on this run. Look" —he pointed out the window— "the rocks should be turning black as the rust breaks down. They're still red."

"Same drones?" Anthony asked.

"Yes."

"Same delivery height? Same dispersal pattern?"

Maher nodded twice.

Anthony caught his lower lip in his teeth. "Double the dosage."

"But, sir, that means the cost goes off the scale for the project—"

"If we don't show progress, Ron, there won't be a project. Double the dosage and reseed the area."

Maher's fingers worked the control panel. Anthony watched the indicators rise as new bacteria filled the seed drones. The young engineer's hand hovered over the launch button. "This will use all our reserve of the bacteria, Anthony. We'll be stopped for weeks while we brew a new batch."

"Understood." In staff meetings, they nicknamed the bacteria *caviar*, a nod to how expensive it was, but that really didn't do it justice cost-wise. He'd put billions into the bacteria research alone. He could practically put a dollar value on each individual bacterium for that price. "Do it."

Maher launched the drones.

"Get your team back in here," Anthony said. "We need to put on a show with a full cast."

Moments later, the rest of the engineering team had scurried into their chairs, avoiding their boss's gaze like schoolchildren late to class. Their voices created a low hum. They were seeing the numbers for themselves and the gamble Anthony Taulke was making.

He smiled at each of them in turn, what the media called the Billion-Byte Smile, named for the fortune he'd made off his ByteCoin becoming the first globally accepted cryptocurrency. "Thanks for your patience, everyone. Ron here found the issue, a simple glitch in the dispersal pattern. Easily fixed."

One of the engineers, the one who'd developed the dispersal algorithm no doubt, started to speak. Anthony held up a broad palm. "No blame. We're all one team, remember? At Taulke Industries, we succeed or fail together, and every day we try to learn something new. Right?"

He waited until he saw nods all around, then leaned over to whisper in Maher's ear. "Lock out the bacteria loading data."

"Already done, sir."

Anthony pulsed his son: *"Make sure everyone has a full glass. Then bring them in."*

If there was one thing the boy was good at, it was working a room. Tony had managed to acquire his father's excellent taste for the finer things in life, but not his intelligence—or his work ethic. It pained Anthony to admit it, but his son seemed more interested in spending money than making it.

In spite of himself, Anthony felt the unfamiliar thrill of nervousness. Odd. Ever since ByteCoin had vaulted Anthony into the realms of the uber-rich at the ripe age of twenty-five, he'd been on a mission to change the world. God or Buddha or Cassandra or any of the other deities he didn't believe in had chosen him, Anthony Taulke, to make the world a better place. It was his destiny.

At first, he'd contributed to environmental causes and climate science, but he'd soon grown tired of spending his money to help someone else save the world. A few decades ago, he would have been one of the investors in a room like this, waiting to write a check for someone else so they could make a difference in the future of mankind.

So Anthony Taulke decided to change the world all on his own.

He'd started with a space elevator. Everyone said it could not be done. So he did it—and then charged them all horrendously exorbitant fees to ferry their goods and people into space.

And he grew richer.

But his attention kept getting drawn back to climate science, the existential crisis facing humanity. And on that topic, Anthony Taulke had had an epiphany.

What better way to achieve immortality than by saving mankind? It was his destiny.

He was an engineer at heart—a rich engineer, but an engineer all the same. He solved problems with technology. Despite the obvious urgency of the ever-worsening climate, there were powerful factions who didn't want to solve the problems: construction companies who benefited by building seawalls, developers who built new cities far from the encroaching oceans, even religious leaders who wanted their competing sects to suffer the wrath of some deity or another.

So after years of effort, Anthony admitted defeat and went in a different direction. If he couldn't make Earth a better place, he'd make his own planet: Mars.

No one gave a shit about Mars. His only limitations here were money and scientific imagination. But mostly money.

With his space elevator in place, Anthony built his own shipyard to manufacture a fleet of spacecraft to ferry his dream of a new Mars into reality. A few billion dollars cornered the market on the Frater Drive, the very latest in propulsion technology that made the Earth to Mars transit time a manageable three days.

And here he was today, breathing life back into a dead planet.

The doors to the control room opened, and the hubbub entered. Anthony spun on his heel to greet his guests, spreading his arms wide.

"Welcome, ladies and gentlemen. Welcome to the new Mars!"

Only a dozen people, a mixture of government reps and investors, had made the three-day trip from Earth. No news people. There would be time enough for them later.

He caught the eye of Adriana Rabh, owner of the Rabh Conglomerate and one of the wealthiest people in the known universe, even richer than he was. She was a severe-looking woman with dark skin and braided hair. If she alone chose to fund him, she could make all his money problems—and his board of directors problem—go away. Adriana gave a terse nod, then turned toward the window.

"Pop?" Tony's voice. His son's hand landed heavily on his arm. "Maybe we can get started?"

Anthony's smile came automatically. He pointed to the test area outside the control room where black spots stood out on the red terrain. "What you are seeing—that blackness—is where the terraforming bacteria are doing their work. The Red Planet should really be named the Rust Planet, because that's basically what it is: oxidation on a planetary scale. Taulke Industries' proprietary technology is freeing that oxygen for us to use, to breathe."

"So the bacteria eat the rust?" The man asking the question represented the African Nations caucus at the United Nations, according to Anthony's retinal display.

"In essence, yes. It's based on a product I developed back on Earth to seed the atmosphere with carbon-consuming bacteria. That one never got off the ground, so to speak." Anthony paused for the pun, and a handful of his guests offered polite, though muted laughter.

"What about efficiency?" Adriana Rabh asked.

Anthony looked at her sharply, searching for any sign she'd been tipped off to their recent problem. Corporate espionage tech was everywhere, and Anthony was not naïve enough to believe he was immune from corporate cyber-espionage.

Rabh's face was placid, open. But then again, it would be—she was that good.

"What's our conversion rate, Ronnie?" Anthony placed one hand on the lead engineer's shoulder. The young man's shirt was damp with sweat.

"Sixteen percent and rising, Mr. Taulke. Looks like we'll settle out in the mid-twenties, right on target."

Anthony chucked him gently on the back of his head. "Now, Ron, I told you to call me Anthony."

The crowd laughed, genuinely this time.

"At twenty-five percent, the project is more than viable, Ms. Rabh," Tony chimed in.

Adriana Rabh stroked her chin with red-lacquered nails. "If you can show me at least twenty-two percent efficiency, I'm in, Anthony." Her shrewd gaze studied him. Despite a nagging suspicion that his initial fear of corporate spying was right after all, his Billion-Byte Smile never faltered.

"Of course, Adriana. I'll bring you the data myself—so I can pick up the check in person."

She smiled thinly as the rest of the room laughed again.

Tony stepped forward. "The actual process takes a full twenty-four hours, and I'm sure you all have better things to do than stare at red rocks turning black. If you'll follow the gentleman by the door, he'll get you outfitted for a rover ride on the Martian surface."

As the crowd began to move away, a young woman hung behind. She was short and wiry, with cropped dark hair and the pointed ears of a body-morpher. A flash of anger passed through Anthony as she sidled up next to his son like an alley cat. Had Tony actually brought a girl along on this trip? And to the investor meeting to boot?

Tony pulled his father toward the back of the room, away from the engineers. The woman followed them, staring openly at Anthony now, an amused look on her face.

"Dad, this is Helena Telemachus. I think you should listen to what she has to say."

Anthony took the woman's hand out of courtesy. She wasn't as young as he'd first thought. Closer to his own fifty years than his son's early twenties. Her ears were indeed altered to look elfin, and she'd also done something to her eyes to make them glow with a greenish tint. A pair of data glasses were nested in the spiky, raven locks of her close-cropped hair.

"You like my mods, Mr. Taulke? I know a guy, if you're interested." Her voice was throaty and suggestive.

"Anthony," he said reflexively. "Call me Anthony."

"My friends call me H."

"Just H?" The anticipation in his own voice surprised him. Why was he flirting with this woman? Besides, he had actual work to do. He didn't need the distraction.

"Just H."

Anthony shot a look at Tony, who was smirking at the exchange. "What can I do for you, H?"

Holding an index finger in the air, she pulsed him a virtual card. Her full name and title appeared in his retinal display.

"Special Advisor to the White House?" Anthony reassessed every assumption he'd made about this woman. "What does that mean exactly?"

H shrugged. "It means whatever my boss wants it to mean on any given day. Right now, it means I'm here to invite you to a meeting."

A meeting. With the President of the United States. Getting away from politicians was one reason he'd come to Mars in the first place.

"I'm sorry, my schedule is pretty full at the moment, Miss—H."

"Oh, I'm sure it is." She shrugged. "I imagine you'll be very busy trying to get your conversion efficiencies up to twenty-five percent legitimately ... using the advertised dosage of bacteria, I mean."

Anthony's eyes narrowed. "Who are you?" He turned on Tony. "How did she get here?"

"I invited myself, Anthony."

His anger crawled up his neck, red as the Martian landscape. "I think I've heard enough. Tony, put her on the next shuttle back to Earth."

"Please, Anthony." H's hand clamped on his arm with surprising strength. "You need a lifeline, I've got a rope. You're a man of big ideas, but maybe some of them were ahead of their time."

H removed her hand from Anthony's arm. "I'll be in touch." Her index finger lingered.

As she walked away, her laughter lingered in the manufactured air.

# 6

## WILLIAM GRAVES • ARIZONA DESERT

With the Arizona sun hammering down from a cloudless sky, Graves could feel the moisture being baked out of his body. All around him, as far as he could see was rolling sand, like golden waves. Less than a day ago, this area had been I-10 from Tucson to Phoenix, a multi-lane highway. Now, nothing but virgin desert.

The soldier in the lead, with the magnetometer, called out a reading and stabbed an orange flag in the sand. He mushed his way through the loose sand until the flags showed the outline of the vehicle. Four soldiers with shovels tramped forward and started digging. Four miles back, they had backhoes and bulldozers to move the sand and drag cars out, but Graves was leading one of the advance teams, searching for survivors. He shook his head in frustration. The Disaster Mitigation Corps had all sorts of technology, but it was useless here. He and his troops were reduced to using metal detectors and shovels like this was some macabre day at the beach.

He directed the soldier with the magnetometer to keep moving and pulled off his dark glasses to wipe the stinging sweat out of his eyes. The unshielded sun was intensely bright, forcing him to squint. He sipped water from the catch-tube on his shoulder then picked up a shovel.

*Stab-pull, stab-pull.* His efforts didn't so much shovel the sand as shift it to one side, but he found the work a monotonous relief, a way to displace poisonous thoughts with physical labor.

If his team had realized the water shortage earlier, the evacuation would not have happened, and none of these cars would be on the road. If he'd been more forceful with the Tucson mayor about the evacuation. If he'd sent an armed escort with the water convoy, the city of Tucson might have held for another day...

*Stab-pull, stab-pull.*

If, if, if, his thoughts whirled in a carousel of blame, all pointing the finger of responsibility back at him. Last night, Graves had found out the Lake Havasu pumping station had indeed been shorting the Central Arizona Project on water supply, as his team had suspected, but his intervention was too little, too late for these poor people.

His shovel struck something in the sand and stuck. "I've got a hit," Graves called out.

"Me, too, sir," said a young soldier next to him. With her face swaddled against the sun and wearing dark glasses, she looked more like an actor in a sci-fi movie than a US soldier.

He dropped to his knees to find the tip of his shovel buried in a spider-webbed windshield. When Graves wrenched the shovel free, grains of golden sand sifted into the hole and disappeared. He put his face close to the small dark area of exposed glass.

"Move back. We're going to break the windshield."

No answer.

Eager hands swept the sand aside, clearing a larger space. The heat and the sand grinding into the soft skin of every body crevice was forgotten now. When the windshield was mostly clean, Graves stepped back and nodded to a beefy soldier. The young man, similarly camouflaged against the sun, lifted a six foot-long shaft they called the harpoon. A retracted four-fingered grappling hook gleamed on the end. He raised the shaft, called "Stand back!" and punched it through the glass. There was a chunking sound as the grappling hook splayed out inside the windshield, white fingers against the black interior.

Two more soldiers stepped forward. The three of them heaved on the shaft in rhythm. Cracks swept across the glass with a crinkling sound, the center bulged outward, and finally with a sigh like the opening of an automatic door, the windshield folded like paper and pulled free.

Graves dropped to his knees and slid into the opening face-first. It was dark inside, forcing him to strip off his sunglasses. Sand sifted into the car all around him, making little piles on the dashboard, the floor, the empty front seats.

It was a minivan, an ancient internal combustion model with sweat-stained seats and scarred dashboard.

He pulled the bandanna from his face and immediately regretted it. The smell in the vehicle was damp, musty with sweat, sharp with urine. Under that, a fetid smell of being far too late. Already Graves could feel the heat outside sucking the valuable moisture from the space.

"Sir, you should let us go—"

"Quiet!" He needed to hear. "Wait outside."

Graves turned on his headlamp.

There were four of them, a mother and three children, all daughters, ages less than one to maybe four. The woman had put down the backseat and laid out blankets to form a makeshift bed. She lay on her side, the infant pressed close to her chest, her free arm reaching out to embrace all three. They appeared a mixed-race family, some kinky hair mixed in with the woman's own straight, black locks. An ashen sheen tinged her mahogany skin, and her lips were blue with hypoxia. Graves forced himself forward and checked each body for a pulse.

They were all dead.

----

Graves felt a tug on his arm. "Colonel." Another tug. "Sir."

"I said, wait outside!"

He started awake, blinking. The fetid smell of death vanished, replaced by the antiseptic comfort of air conditioning.

Jansen's shaved scalp gleamed in the muted light of the aircar interior. "We're here, sir."

Washington. They'd been ordered to Washington, DC.

Graves swallowed. "Right."

His aide gazed at him with what looked like understanding. Graves wondered if she had nightmares about Phoenix too, though he'd never had the courage to ask.

He stepped out of the vehicle into mercifully weak sunshine. The fresh scent of birch trees washed away the stench of the dream. The area around the Pentagon had been bermed years ago to protect against flooding. The new construction subdued the noise of passing traffic and gave the military installation an incongruous, park-like feel.

Jansen appeared at his side, settling her beret in place. Graves squared his shoulders and led her through the building's VIP entrance. The security bots scanned their biometrics as they walked in. They didn't even have to slow down.

The inside of the Pentagon was cool and professional, a rush of uniformed bodies moving in every direction, everyone in a hurry to get to their next meeting. Islands of laughter interrupted scattered conversations as they passed. They descended to the Pentagon's secure deck, a compartmented area of isolated briefing rooms.

The quarterly disaster threat assessment meeting had been advanced two weeks, which had surprised Graves. Since taking the helm of the Disaster Mitigation Corps, he'd come to feel disdain for the tenuous state of public awareness regarding their changing planet. The newsfeeds, addicted to breaking news, had dulled the public into a disaster-of-the-day feeling of overwhelm. Weather catastrophes were the new normal.

Graves had seen seawalls crumble beneath the onslaught of hurricanes, neighborhoods ripped apart by massive tornadoes, whole communities reduced to ash by wildfires. And now the largest sandstorm in US history had buried an interstate full of Americans.

No one seemed to appreciate the enormity of the big picture. That myopia sometimes made these meetings seem like one step forward and two steps back. A glance at his display said they'd be late in two minutes.

Out of necessity, the population had adapted in the last few decades, albeit at great cost. Migration favored moving inward to the Midwestern states. Those who remained along the reshaped coasts had rebuilt cities devastated by flooding to counter rising sea levels. Even venerable old buildings like the Pentagon had set up levees and elaborate drainage systems, complete with dikes. Dutch history books had proven useful at the close of the twenty-first century.

Graves placed his palm over the locked door of the meeting room. Acknowledging his identity, it clicked open.

A lone man sat at the long briefing table. He wore a dark business suit, modern cut. The material changed color subtly as light reflected off it. Dark green, now navy, now gray. The stranger stood and extended a hand. "Colonel, welcome."

Graves entered and shook the man's hand automatically. "I'm here for the disaster threat assessment meeting." He glanced around, wondering where his commanding officer and the rest of the DTA staff were.

"You're in the right place, Colonel." The stranger resumed his seat.

Graves took a seat, his internal radar pinging. "I'm sorry, you are…?"

"I work for the Office of Budgetary Compliance."

"Oh." Graves shot a glance at Jansen, who shrugged. He wished she could do a quick search for whatever the hell Office of Budgetary Compliance was and why his DTA meeting had been coopted by a slick-palmed bureaucrat in a shiny suit. But she'd get nothing on this secure deck of the Pentagon. All external comms and WorldNet links were blocked by security.

"Shall we get started?" The man spoke in a light tone, his accent neutral. He had vaguely Japanese features and smiled in a way that failed to engage his eyes. Graves disliked him already.

"I've read your report on Phoenix, Colonel."

*Ah*, Graves thought. *He's here about the water poaching.*

The man called up an image on his tablet and slid it across the table. "I wonder what you can tell me about these people?"

The photo showed six people walking abreast with the dark wall of the record-breaking sandstorm in front of them on the horizon. Graves recognized them as the New Earthers the Intel group had shown him.

"They're Neos." Graves pushed the tablet back. "The ones we saw in Phoenix, just before the storm."

The man nodded. "Yes, that's exactly correct. Have you seen people like this at other disaster sites?"

"They're pretty common. They seem to be attracted to extreme weather events. Some sort of twisted nature worship, I guess."

"Do you know how they managed to get into this area of Phoenix? The whole region had been evacuated, right?"

Graves shifted. He hated explaining the realities of military occupation to a civilian. They never understood the exigencies of military necessity and never tired of asking inane questions. "Mandatory evacuations are not perfect, Mister..." The silence extended. Graves plowed on. "They might've hidden when we went house to house. To be perfectly frank, if someone is determined to avoid a mandatory evac order, it's not that hard to do."

Jansen cleared her throat, a signal they'd practiced. Graves guessed his tone must have gotten edgy.

The man seemed not to notice or care. He shook his head slowly as he called up another image. Graves accepted the tablet and held it up so Jansen could see. A video streamed, pieced together from various drone and security camera footage. They watched as each of the six made their way to the deserted suburban street where Perkins had spotted them. The final image showed them facing the coming storm as it approached.

"Each of them left secure housing hours before the storm and walked to the meeting point. Someone told them to go there, Colonel."

"I don't understand, Mister Whatever Your Name Is." Graves was tired, and his bullshit meter had begun to tick-tick-tick. "What does this have to do with water poaching?"

"I'm not here about the report you filed, Colonel." The slick man sat back. His suit phased a charcoal gray. "I'm here because someone knew about the storm hours before you did. Well before our weather satellites even predicted this event. Someone told these six people to go to Phoenix and wait."

"And what does that have to do with me? I'm the guy who gets airdropped into a disaster to make things better; or, at least, not worse. Food, water, shelter, rescue—that's what I do. Tracking cults is not in my job description."

"And you don't find it the least bit strange that these Neos show up at disasters, at precisely the right time and place—almost every time?" The man leaned forward again, his eyes unblinking as he regarded Graves.

"That they seem to be able to predict these events with remarkable accuracy?"

Graves shot a look at Jansen. They'd considered the New Earthers to be demonstrators at best, suicidal crackpots at worst. But the man's confirmation of their own hypothesis that they appeared at the scene of nearly every major disaster was disconcerting.

"What are you suggesting?" Graves asked. Then he held up a hand and pushed the tablet away. "Never mind. I don't want or need to know. As long as they don't interfere with my relief efforts, I don't really care what they do."

The man tapped the tablet several more times and pushed it back to Graves. "Do you know these people?"

The woman was young, not quite thirty, with a thin, austere face, long dark hair, and penetrating eyes. She looked vaguely familiar.

"She's the UN Secretary for Biodiversity," Jansen whispered. "Kisaan. I don't know the guy."

Graves did. He studied the five o'clock shadow of the jawline, the crooked nose, the slight squint in his eyes. "The man is Remy Cade. Used to be under my command. He was caught up in Vicksburg. Good kid. Damned shame how they hung him out to dry." He glared at the man. "He deserved better. They all did."

"Have you had any contact with Mr. Cade in the last year?"

Graves shook his head. "I haven't seen Cade since his trial. I was a character witness, for all the good it did him. Why?" His patience was wearing thinner by the minute.

The man tapped his tablet again, then nodded. "Thank you for your honesty, Colonel. We have reason to believe Mr. Cade and Secretary Kisaan have allied themselves with the New Earth movement. Your biometrics indicate you're telling the truth. Which is lucky for you."

Jansen gasped beside him. While the passive monitoring of personnel biometrics wasn't illegal, it was ethically questionable, to say the least. Graves felt Jansen's anger rising. They were decorated military officers, after all, and this was the Pentagon.

Graves cleared his throat to stop Jansen from speaking. "I certainly feel lucky," he said, sarcasm infecting his tone. "If you'll excuse us, Mr. Nobody, we have a disaster zone to manage."

The tablet pushed across the table again. "I've just been given authorization to read you both into a Special Access Project. You're familiar with the process?"

Graves hesitated only a moment, then placed his palm on the proffered tablet. The gloss of text that appeared was brief. He passed the device to Jansen, who read herself in.

"What is Haven and why do you need us?" she asked, her anger at being monitored still evident.

The man smiled thinly. "Haven is the US military's Plan B in the climate war. We need men and women who can deal with the logistics of unpredictable natural situations."

Graves exchanged a look with Jansen.

"Excuse me, sir," she said. "You haven't told us what Haven is."

The man tucked the device under his arm and stood. "Let's just say we're building an ark for the human species and we want you to outfit it. We'll be in touch."

# 7

## MING QINLAO • EARTH ORBIT

Auntie Xi had traveled to the Moon by private shuttle, of course. Ming had hoped against all reason that maybe they'd take a regular transport home. It would have given her a chance to digest the news of her father's death in the comforting company of strangers. Her aunt wouldn't dare to discuss family matters in public.

Instead, Ming huddled next to a window, watching the Earth grow closer while the Moon—and Lily—fell farther away. The shuttle was a Qinlao executive model, outfitted with a dozen captain's chairs wrapped in real leather. Watching the spiral arms of a whirling white cyclone in the South China Sea, Ming traced the family logo embroidered on the headrest with the tip of her finger.

Gone were the controlled environments and recycled atmosphere of lunar caverns. Soon she'd feel the wind on her cheek, the sun on her face, the humidity of unpredictable weather patterns.

And gravity.

Lucky she'd kept up with her daily weight training and muscle mass supplements. Anyone who made the transition back to Earth after long stretches on the Moon spoke of the pain, the fatigue, the careful movements necessary to keep fragile bones from breaking.

Ming rested her head against the cool of the shuttle window. The pain would be more than just physical pain during her trip home.

"May I get you something?" She could barely hear Ito's voice above the hiss of the air-conditioning.

Ming turned to him. She offered a faint smile but shook her head.

"Hydration is key for a successful return trip," Ito said, handing her a glass of water anyway.

She took it, then threw a glance over her shoulder at her aunt. The back of Xi's chair was to her, and the old woman was engaged in a hushed but animated conversation with a holographic figure Ming couldn't see.

She patted the seat next to her. "Sit." Ito hesitated, looking toward Xi at the rear of the craft. "Please. She's busy. And you're my sensei."

Ito smiled, sitting down. "It has been many years since I was that."

Ming had realized long ago how indebted she was to her father's bodyguard. He'd taught her everything about self-defense he knew: hand-to-hand combat, knives, swords, guns. When she remembered growing up, Ming counted her training days with Ito among her happiest memories. They were islands in the sea of angst and pain her childhood had become after her eighth birthday.

She could remember the exact day her mother had taken ill. Ming had just returned home from third grade, flushed with pride over her grade on a new coding experiment. Usually Wenqian Qinlao was waiting for her daughter with a snack and a smile, but on this day the house was silent.

Anxious to impart her good news, Ming had called for her mother again and again until she finally heard a noise in her parents' bedroom. She'd found her mother sprawled on the floor, her body paralyzed. Drool puddled the tile under her slackened cheek and the room smelled of urine. Upon seeing her daughter, Wenqian made a sound like a wounded animal.

The shuttle's engines droned. Out the window, the cyclone turned almost imperceptibly over the ocean. From here, it was beautiful. Ming could only imagine the havoc it would wreak on land. In a way, the storms were like antibodies, Earth's way of ridding herself of the disease of mankind.

Her mother had been stricken by a gene-hopping virus that corrupted her central nervous system. Her father, Jie, had returned within hours, recalled from Germany where he was closing a major deal with the European space agency. He found his wife a shell of the woman he'd left mere days before. Even now, Ming remembered the words that sounded like a foreign language then: gene therapy, stem-cell treatment, bionic enhancement. It was an agonizing year of physical therapy combined with the latest in stem-cell interventions before Wenqian could sit up, speak, and feed herself. But after millions of dollars and one cast aside doctor after another, they at last accepted that she would never walk again. Her muscles required constant external stimulation to maintain the little progress she'd made.

Bionics were out of the question. Looking back, Ming realized, this was the first rift between her parents. If her father had had his way, he would have remade his wife into a bionic woman capable of doing anything she wanted. She'd be better than before, he'd pleaded.

Wenqian would have none of it. Her one compromise was to adopt one of the new maglev chairs for mobility.

At nine years old, Ming knew nothing of boardroom politics or corporate succession plans. She knew her parents had desperately wanted another child—a son—but the reasons were shrouded in unfathomable grown-up logic.

It was when she saw her mother crying, when her father was away, that Ming learned to hate him. He had taken business trips before, but now—with Wenqian crippled and the house so quiet—nine-year-old Ming had decided his place was at home, with them, to care for her mother.

Ming saw her father less and less as time went on. Despite her resentment, she was elated when he showed up unexpectedly in their Shanghai villa one rainy, autumn afternoon. He kissed her in greeting as he always did, but his eyes were cloudy with emotion. When he held her in a close hug much longer than normal, she allowed that too. Part of her even wished it had lasted a little longer.

"You will need to make a choice, Ming-child. Soon." He hugged her again. "I will not force you. Know that." Then he went into Wenqian's bedroom with her Auntie Xi, followed by a woman and a man carrying briefcases. Ito had stayed with Ming.

She and Ito played chess while they waited. He wasn't very good, but she liked the way his brow furrowed as he considered the board.

"Who are those people with Papa?" she asked.

Ito's concentration broke. He looked out the window. It was raining harder, fat drops thumping against the glass. "Lawyers," he said finally, like he had a bad taste in his mouth.

The door to her mother's bedroom opened, and Auntie Xi left with the lawyers. Her aunt had a glowing smile. Ito's cheek twitched as she passed.

Evading Ito's grasp, Ming ran to the bedroom. She found her father kneeling by her mother's chair, his head in her lap. Wenqian's hand, withered and quivering, softly stroked his hair.

Ito cleared his throat to get her attention. Angrily, she swiped at the wetness on her cheeks.

"Are you crying for your father, Little Tiger?" he asked.

Ming smiled at the old endearment. "I was thinking about the day of the divorce."

Ito nodded, his eyes hooded. "It was a difficult day. For your father, most of all."

That surprised her. "How can you say that? It was mother who was left behind. Traded in, like an old automobile."

Lily crowded back into her thoughts. In leaving her, had Ming just committed the same sin she'd damned her father for? They weren't married, there were no children, no contract to uphold. But she'd led Lily to believe they would have a lifetime of loving together.

"I was proud of you," Ito said, interrupting the cascade of guilty thoughts. "You stayed with your mother."

"Someone had to."

Ito nodded. "You did the right thing. I was so proud of you, but I missed you all the same."

Family. That was why she'd left. The seesaw of emotions, the never-ending sense of obligation. In the end, it was just easier to run away.

On impulse, Ming kissed the old man on the cheek. "And I you, Ito." She hesitated to ask but wanted to change the subject. "How is Sying?"

"Sying is coping," Ito said after a moment's hesitation. "Though your father's death was most unexpected."

Her father's second wife had all the necessary qualifications to serve as the wife of the CEO of one of the most powerful manufacturing dynasties on the planet. She was young, barely a decade older than Ming, beautiful, fertile, and the first daughter of the CEO of a large competitor company. Like some ancient, arranged union aligning ruling houses, the two corporations married their fortunes together. There was no messing around with fate this time: on the day of their wedding, Sying Zhu now Qinlao, was implanted with an embryo, a male child engineered from her DNA combined with Jie Qinlao's. Nine months later, Ruben was born.

Her father made attempts to blend the families, but Ming would have none of it. She saw Ruben as another betrayal, a way for her father to disown first her mother through the divorce, and now Ming herself through a rival sibling. Ming had been determined to grow up an only child.

"How did he die?" she asked.

Before Ito could answer, Auntie Xi put her hand on his shoulder. "May I speak with my niece, Ito?" Although her voice dripped with honey, Ming steeled herself for a confrontation. Ito relinquished his seat, making his way to the back of the craft.

The old woman made a great show of adjusting her chair so she could face Ming, fussing with the lumbar controls and the angle of recline. Ming focused on the ever-larger Earth in the window. The storm seemed headed toward Vietnam. Her aunt placed a long hand on Ming's thigh. "How are you holding up, Ming-child?"

Ming stared at the red nails until her aunt pulled them back. "It's just Ming, Auntie."

The skin around the older woman's eyes creased in momentary frustration, then smoothed again with effort. "Of course, dear—I can still call you *dear*, yes?" She laughed at her own request that was not a request.

"It's a free ... shuttle." Ming injected as much laissez-faire into her voice as she could muster.

A long silence ensued as each woman attempted to wait the other out.

"How did it happen?" Ming asked finally. There was no mystery about the subject of her question.

"An accident," Xi said. "Your father insisted on going to a very remote part of Indonesia to inspect a job site. There was a heavy migrant worker force and, well, you know, some countries aren't as exacting in their screening programs as we are. A virus swept through the work camp." Ming watched her aunt dab at her eyes with a silk handkerchief. "Everyone died. They had to firebomb the site to make sure the virus was contained. It was horrible."

Overseeing a remote jobsite certainly sounded like her father. Always the exacting engineer, he would have wanted to inspect the latest installation himself. And international worksites were natural breeding grounds for the latest virulent diseases. Screenings were mandatory, but companies weren't above bribing officials if they thought they'd save money in the long run by hiring cheaper labor.

"Where was Ito?" she asked. Jie Qinlao's bodyguard had been like his shadow. "Why wasn't he..." With Papa? Dead as well? Shame and silence finished her question for her.

"He was with me. I was dealing with an internal company issue." Xi glanced to the back of the shuttle. "He's taken your father's passing very hard, Ming. It's best not to bring it up."

Ming felt suddenly very alone with this woman. "I want to see my mother," she said. "As soon as we land."

Her aunt shook her head. "I'm afraid there's no time for that, dear. The funeral is the day after tomorrow, and there's a fitting for your dress and—"

"Why are you here?" Ming demanded.

Xi ceased counting off the pre-funeral items on her elegant fingers. The red of her nails shone in the shuttle's pale, synthetic lighting. "I came to get you, dear."

"That's not what I meant. Why are *you* here? You could have sent a message or sent Ito, if you thought I needed a personal escort. So—why you?"

"Because I am your family, Ming. Besides, your father made it clear that he wished for you to attend the funeral, if you could be persuaded."

"Why?"

"He wasn't blind to the animosity you held for him since you were a child, Ming. Maybe he felt like your being there would be a sign of your forgiveness."

Guilt flooded through Ming again. With her father dead, she would have no opportunity to explore reconciliation. The guilt became something softer, more permanent: regret.

"Also, there is the reading of the will. Your presence is required for that as well."

The will. Ming hadn't thought of that. A final cementing of the corporate alliance between her father and his new family.

"I will see my mother as soon as I land. I don't care what appointments you've made for me."

Her aunt bowed her carefully coiffed black hair in a curt nod. "As you wish, dear."

"And another thing, Auntie."

Xi's cold eyes waited.

"My mother will attend the funeral with me."

⸺

Auntie Xi had planned a funeral worthy of a head of state and staged it in the auditorium of the massive Qinlao building in downtown Shanghai. The building's facade was draped entirely in gauzy black by some famous artist from Germany who specialized in "transforming death through art." Her father, a lifelong atheist, was to be lionized by representatives of all five major religions, none of whom had known him personally. The catty side of Ming supposed the five-ring circus was a nod to investors, who'd come from all over the world to pay their respects.

Jie Qinlao would have hated all of it, but since he wasn't around to be consulted for his opinion, she hated it for him.

Her father's cremated remains had been sterilized and placed into an antique vase from the Qin dynasty—another touch of extravagance by her aunt.

Two 3D photographs flanked the vase. The one on the right showed her father last year, a posed portrait in a conservative double-breasted dark suit and red tie, the Qinlao logo revolving behind him. His hair was iron-gray but still full, and his eyes were dark and steely. His expression was the epitome of a strong business leader with a vision for the future.

The picture on the left had been taken when Ming was seven. She loved it but hadn't seen it in years. It was taken at a worksite in Japan, where the Qinlao boring machines cut tunnels for a hyperloop bullet train between the island and the Korean peninsula. Her father's hair was dark in the photo, uncombed and blowing lightly in the wind. Safety glasses nested on the top of his head. He held a wrench in one hand and smiled as, behind him, men swarmed over a piece of equipment.

A young Ming was there just behind him. As the image moved through its frames, she stood tall, reaching for a butterfly she would never catch in that 3D moment.

"It's my favorite picture of him," her mother whispered. Ming agreed by placing one hand on Wenqian's withered arm and lightly squeezing.

The choreographed service crawled by, with one overblown speech following another, as Ming watched her young self attempt over and over to catch the butterfly. She suddenly became aware it was her turn to speak.

It had all been said already, she realized. Her father's life's work, his engineering genius, his business acumen, his international savoir faire. Ming realized it was selfish, but she just wanted to be done with this ceremony.

But her participation was expected. It wouldn't be over until Ming had played her part.

She stood and took two lit incense sticks—one for herself and one for her mother—and held them between her palms as she bowed to the older of the two photos. She pushed aside her anger with her father and stared at the happy little girl behind him, rising and reaching for the butterfly. Then she focused on the engineer in the foreground with the wrench in his hand, ready to work alongside his men to see the project completed to success. Strong, curious, happy. That's how she would remember him.

She heard the whir of Wenqian's maglev chair as it maneuvered next to her. As the sharp smoke wafted over both of them, the sense of loss over-whelmed Ming. She bowed again and replaced the joss sticks, slowly turning to face the packed room.

Her father's second wife, Sying, sat directly in front of her, barely six feet away. Sitting beside her was Ruben, a boy of fourteen now. Sying Qinlao raised her eyes to find Ming's. What did she feel on this day? Ming wondered. Her father had married Sying out of convenience, as a business transaction, but had she grown to love him? Did she miss him, or was she glad to be rid him?

Ming's eyes slid past the widow to rest on her aunt. As ever, she was beautiful, imperious, and haughty. Her dark eyes blazed with pride at the ceremony she had orchestrated.

And here was Ming, standing mute in front of hundreds of business associates and friends. For the deceased's eldest child to remain silent...

*Say something*, her aunt's eyes demanded.

Ming moved in front of Sying and bowed formally, then without a word resumed her seat. Whispers rippled through the crowd. Her mother's maglev purred into place beside her. Ming stared forward, ignoring the glaring daggers from her aunt.

Xi waved her hand at someone across the room. Mournful music filled the room.

"Have you decided?" her mother asked in a labored whisper.

"Decided what?" she whispered back.

Belying the slackness of her face, the old woman's eyes danced with life. "Are you in or out?"

# 8

## REMY CADE • LOCATION UNKNOWN

Remy opened his eyes to a darkened room. He took a breath, and pain arced across his chest. Beneath his back he felt the slickness of a fresh bed sheet. Carefully, his fingers explored the rest of his body.

Massive chest contusion, probably a few bruised ribs, but no skin broken. Flash burns on his neck and the underside of his chin. Behind him, a chorus of soft beeps. He craned his head carefully and found a bank of monitors. And he was wearing a loose gown. A hospital.

Remy sniffed the clean, air-conditioned air. Oddly, a smoky aftertaste lingered on his palate, a bitter sweetness.

*First hospital I've ever been in where they burn incense*, he thought. *Where the hell am I?*

With each breath, the sharp twinge in his ribs returned. He closed his eyes and forced himself to think.

The UN mission in Alaska ... the valley with the dead caribou ... the ambush ... Rico shooting him. Elise! Where was Elise?

He blinked on his retinal display to send her a pulse.

Nothing. No signal.

How was that possible? He enjoyed worldwide coverage thanks to the Kisaans. The only thing that should have interrupted that was an outage of the WorldNet satellite network.

Or maybe the Kisaans had canceled his contract.

Remy tried to rise. One of the monitor tabs popped off his chest, and the machine screamed a warning.

"Lights," someone said.

Soft illumination came up in the room like a fast-rising sun. In the doorway, a well-muscled Chinese man with a shaved head stood dressed in yellow robes.

"Mr. Cade, awake at last, I see." His voice was a pleasant baritone with a musical lilt. A voice used to speaking softly because it didn't need to speak any louder.

Remy took stock of his situation in the light. Injured, but receiving medical care, and facing a physically imposing man. Maybe he was a prisoner, maybe he wasn't.

"Where am I?"

The large man smiled broadly. "In a safe place." He closed the door behind him. His robes seemed to shimmer through the spectrum of the sun as he walked. He pulled a chair up next to Remy's bed and sat.

"What are you, a monk?"

"Something like that," said his host. "You can call me Brother Donald. How do you feel?"

"I asked where I was."

"I should think it is obvious," Donald continued, with a gesture toward the wall behind Remy's head. "You are in the Temple of Cassandra, Mother of the New Earth."

Remy twisted on the bed. On the wall was the sign of Cassandra, a half-globe shared with the half-face of a long-haired woman. The symbol of the New Earth movement. Stretching to see it made him flinch.

"Why don't I have a data signal?" he asked.

The monk reached out and replaced the wayward chest monitor tab over Remy's heart. "Only Cassandra may use data in Her house. The rest of us must soldier on in the old way." He winked. "Face to face."

Remy decided not to ask why a god needed wireless access. "So this place is a Faraday cage, then?"

"This place is many things," the monk said with another maddening smile. "Your injuries were significant, forcing us to keep you in a medical coma for a few days. Perhaps you would care for some food?"

Remy was hungry, but he shook his head. "I need to speak to whoever is in charge. Right away."

Donald effected a half-bow in his chair. "Speaking."

The pain meds were starting to wear off. Remy spotted a button near his left hand.

"If you need more medicine, push the button," the monk said. "You cannot overdose."

Remy's index finger twitched. The searing feeling beneath the flash burns was worse, but he wanted a clear head. "There was a woman with me. Is she here?"

Another broad smile. "You mean Elise. Would you like to see her?"

"Yes," Remy answered. He began to lever himself out of bed again, but his chest objected. Louder, now that the drugs in his system had waned.

"I assure you, she is fine," Donald said, placing a hand on Remy's arm. "I am glad to reunite you two, but I have some questions first."

Remy's temper flared. "I have some questions of my own. Like, what the hell happened in Alaska? Where's that sonofabitch Rico? And—"

"Mr. Cade," the monk said in his quiet, commanding baritone. "All in good time. But first, you must answer my questions. This is not a negotiation."

Remy calmed down. "Fine." He was in no position to negotiate, anyway.

Donald adjusted his robes and sat back in his chair. "I know this may be difficult, but I need you to tell me about your actions in Vicksburg, Mississippi."

Remy's face went flat. "That's none of your goddamned business."

The monk's pleasant expression hardened. "I am afraid you will have to make it my business, Mr. Cade. I know what the official reports say. What I don't know is ... what really happened?"

"I appreciate all you've done for me here, really," Remy forced himself to say. "But I'm going to get out of this bed—I don't care how much it hurts —collect Elise, and we'll be going."

Before he could move, the monk put a hand on his shoulder. Straining against it brought more loud protests from Remy's throbbing ribcage.

"Please." Donald's tone reflected his light touch: non-threatening but firm. "My intent is not to invade your privacy. But before I let you see Elise again, I need to hear your side of the story about Vicksburg."

Remy stopped fighting him. Just breathing was starting to hurt like hell. Moving felt crippling. He glanced down at the button that promised relief.

"Then you'll take me to Elise?"

The monk nodded. Remy pushed the button, and within seconds, the weighted pain across his chest began to subside. He lay back and closed his eyes. "We didn't know what we were getting into," he began.

"My platoon was assigned to crowd control for a squatter camp outside of Vicksburg. It was supposed to be easy duty. We were going to be traffic cops for a few days. These were just regular folks—American citizens—displaced from their homes by the storm. Carrying what they could. Hungry. Thirsty. It wasn't their fault, not really. But they just kept coming. And they got desperate." The drugs made it easier to talk.

"The press called it a massacre, and the Pentagon stayed quiet. It was just easier to let the public believe a platoon of trigger-happy grunts wiped out a bunch of civilians than it was to face the truth."

The monk's eyes were soft but curious. "And what's the truth, Mr. Cade?"

"We were set up. Ambushed, except we were the ones being attacked, not the other way around. We were a combat unit, damn it. Fresh from the Sinai, where every day we fought for survival. When you're fighting insurgents abroad, it's easy to see who's the enemy. They look different, they talk different. Then all of a sudden you're in Mississippi. New mission, but the same tools. But now, the face of the enemy was American citizens, not foreign terrorists. They looked like us. They talked like us. They were us."

He sat up, ignoring the dull pain in his chest. Telling the story again made it hard to sit still, hard to breathe even.

"You want to know what happened? It's simple. We did what solders do when they're attacked. We fought back. My best friend died there along with a lot of good soldiers. Graves Diggers killed twenty-six insurgents—sorry, climate war refugees—including nine women and two fifteen-year-old identical twins from Acadia Parish, Louisiana. And the news drones got it all.

"Vicksburg Massacre Kills Dozens of American Citizens—that was the headline on YourVoice. And that was my platoon's epitaph. Dishonorably discharged, every single one of us. Lucky not to have been sentenced to Leavenworth, we were told, or prosecuted for murder under Mississippi law. Colonel Graves did what he could for us, but the brass let the media write the history. It was just easier. For them, anyway."

Remy clicked the button for another dose of pain meds. "There you go. My version of what happened. Don't you feel enlightened?"

Donald regarded him for a moment, then placed his light touch on Remy's forearm. He rose from his chair. "Your clothes are in the cabinet. I can bring a maglev chair—"

"I'm flying high." Remy swung his feet to the floor, stripping the monitor tabs off his chest. "I can make it."

Together, they walked the long, Spartan hallways of the Neo facility. Now that he was up and moving, Remy actually felt a little better. Or maybe it was just the drugs.

Without access to the WorldNet, Remy tried to recall everything he knew about the New Earthers, which wasn't much. In recent years, they'd gone from minor environmental movement to a religion, mostly due to the emergence of Cassandra, their mysterious leader. Notoriously publicity shy, Cassandra spoke through her ordained surrogates, people like Brother Donald. They promised a new relationship between man and his environment, but they'd been peaceful, as far as Remy could remember.

He took note of his surroundings as they walked. This was not a two-bit operation. The medbot in Remy's room had been top of the line, and any place that could afford med-coma treatment was not hurting for money. They'd traversed a series of hallways. The place had the unmarked shine of new construction about it. The few people they passed wore civilian clothes, not robes, and all of them nodded pleasantly to Brother Donald.

"You haven't asked me why I wanted to hear about Vicksburg," Donald said.

Although the pace was no more than a stroll, Remy was winded. "I'll bite. Why did you want to know about something that happened six years ago?"

"I wanted to be sure I could trust you."

Remy snorted. The last thing he needed was someone else demanding his loyalty. Let the monk and the rest of the Cassandra nuts think what they wanted for now. As soon as he was able, he was leaving with Elise.

"Trust me to do what?" he asked anyway, curious.

They neared a set of double doors. Reinforced construction, like bulkheads aboard a military vessel.

"Protect Elise Kisaan. She is very important to us."

"I'm with you there, Donald. She's a special woman."

The double doors opened into a sitting area. Elise perched on an elegant sofa, dressed in loose trousers and a blouse the color of sand. Her face lit up when she saw him.

"Remy!" She rushed forward and hugged him.

"Be cautious, Elise," Donald said, with a chuckle. "He is still healing."

"Of course, I'm sorry," she said, drawing back. "But I'm glad you're okay. I was so worried."

"I'm fine," Remy lied, scowling as he recovered from her enthusiastic embrace. His eyes drank her in. Elise seemed different, more at ease, more willing to smile.

Brother Donald closed the doors behind him as he left.

"You're okay?" Remy said. "They haven't hurt you?"

Elise laughed in a way that made Remy feel foolish.

"Hurt me? Why would they hurt me?"

"They abducted us, Elise. And they shot me ... who knows what they're capable of?"

Elise lowered her voice and leaned close enough that he could detect the faint scent of her perfume. Fleur, it was called. "Remy—I'm a follower of Cassandra. I'm a Neo." She turned and raised her long, raven hair. There on the back of her neck was the feminine Earth tattoo.

Remy grabbed her arm and spun her around to face him. "Are you crazy, Elise? You're the UN Secretary of Biodiversity. How can you be a Neo?"

Her face became stone. "I've been part of the movement for a long time, Remy. And I want you to be with me. We can be together here. And together, we can help mankind build a new relationship with the Earth."

Remy scanned the room. Surely they were being observed, though he saw no obvious monitoring devices. "Listen to me, Elise," he whispered, "I don't have a data signal, but if I can figure out where we are, I can get us out of here."

Elise laughed again. When was the last time he'd heard her laugh this much? She reached out and took his hand, lacing her long, thin fingers into his. Remy's heart skipped a beat at her touch.

"Stop talking like they're the enemy. They're me, Remy. And this is the Temple of Cassandra. There is no cage here. There's just no signal." She leaned down and pressed a button on the table.

The floor-to-ceiling windows went from opaque to clear, revealing to Remy a vista he hadn't seen in years. Not from this vantage point, anyway. Stars dotted the void, and the planet Earth revolved serenely beneath them.

The Temple of Cassandra was a space station.

# 9

## MING QINLAO • SHANGHAI, CHINA

Marcus Sun had been her father's lawyer for as long as Ming could remember. As the man aged, Ming thought, he looked more and more like Confucius. Give him a robe, a long beard and one of those hanfu square hats, and she was sure Marcus could easily pass for the ancient philosopher.

But today, Marcus was dressed in a dark blue, fitted suit with a skinny blue tie and a puff of feathery yellow silk in the front pocket. When he kissed Ming on both cheeks, he smelled of leather and ink. Marcus was so old-fashioned he used a fountain pen to sign actual paper documents that then had to be scanned and made virtual. His fingers were stained with red ink from his ancient chop, the official seal of the law firm of Sun, Riley and Wilcox, another throwback to an earlier legal era.

The elder lawyer murmured condolences to Ming's mother, then ushered the pair into his office, a luxurious carpeted room filled with heavy, dark wooden furniture. Despite his antiquated method for document management, Sun was not above using technology when he wanted to. He'd skinned the walls with a holo-display to effect the look of a library. Rows of virtual books rested on floor-to-ceiling shelves like leather-bound soldiers. A brightly burning fireplace adorned the wall next to his heavy desk made of prized Zitan wood from southern China.

But it was the view that made Marcus' office unique. The east side of the room was cantilevered from the side of the building in a glass box. The entire extension was transparent. From their position on the eighty-third floor, the old city of Puxi stretched out below. The Han River threaded through its buildings like a fat, brown snake on its way to the barely visible Pacific Ocean. Tiny craft navigated the waters, leaving creamy V-trails in their wake. The sun made a worthy attempt to pierce the smog but was only a faint, brown disk beyond the haze.

Ming left her mother's side to walk to the window. She placed her toes on the edge of the glass floor, welcoming the clench of fear in her stomach created by standing over nothingness. It was the first true feeling she'd had in days, and a welcome relief from the dull ache of sadness for her father's passing. She just wanted all this to be over, to return to her life on the Moon —and Lily. She missed the clutter of their shared apartment, the funk of their bed, the way their bodies fit together in the dark.

Marcus stood beside her. "Most people won't come this close to the edge."

Ming nodded, her eyes on the glimmer of the faraway Pacific. Her gut trembled, but she inched farther over the abyss. A lightheadedness tingled up, all the way from her toes.

"I'm afraid of heights, you know," Marcus said.

Ming regarded him with a questioning look.

"Why would I choose this office?" Marcus laughed. "Your father asked me the same question. I told him: *perspective*. Any time I feel like I'm facing an intractable problem, I come and stand over the precipice. The problem always gets smaller." He gave her a wistful look. "Your father told me I was full of shit ... I miss him, Ming."

She closed her eyes, torn between fear of the view and regret about her father. Marcus had made her laugh, a little, but she really just wanted to cry. She could see Jie Qinlao standing in this very spot, saying those exact words to this man who'd been his closest friend. She could see his crooked smile and the easy laughter they would have shared.

Resentment roiled inside her, lava in a volcano. Marcus Sun had probably seen her father more often than she had since he'd formed his marital alliance with Sying. And he'd done that for what? Money? Power?

"He loved you, Ming," Marcus said softly. "Know that."

Ming set her jaw, biting back the words she wanted to say. They would only embarrass everyone, her mother most of all. The door to the office swung open to admit her step-mother, half-brother, and Auntie Xi, with Ito in tow. As the bodyguard stationed himself by the door, Marcus played host, arranging the group around the large table near the faux-fireplace, far away from the windows. A pair of matching attendants served tea in tiny, eggshell-ceramic cups, before closing the door gently as they exited.

Marcus busied himself arranging a sheaf of papers on the table and positioned his fountain pen precisely across the top of a yellow legal pad. Ming noticed Ruben, her half-brother, staring at the pen with bright eyes.

He was a quiet, thin teenager with sallow skin and a dimpled chin. His dark hair was parted on the right and plastered down with water. He sat very close to his mother.

Ming had never spent more than a few minutes with Sying. Boycotting the attempts at familiarity by her father's second wife seemed the right thing to do by her mother. Whereas Wenqian Qinlao had come from the same hardscrabble background of the inner provinces as her father, Sying was a lifelong member of the coastal business aristocracy. She presented a slight figure who looked as if a good laugh might break her. Her wrists appeared fragile as a bird's wings, with tracks of blue veins barely visible beneath the pale skin. Sying was corporate royalty, bred for one purpose only: to consolidate through marriage.

In other words, Sying was a whore. A well-bred, immaculately mannered whore—but still a whore. The living bride-price for the consolidation of two corporations. And always appropriately dressed to the needs of the social occasion. For this meeting, she wore a black, sheath dress and a dark veil obscuring her eyes. She clutched her son's hand as if Ming might try to take him away.

"Shall we proceed, Marcus?" Auntie Xi seemed impatient and imperious, as usual. She focused her attention on Ming even as she spoke to the lawyer. Ming averted her eyes.

*The Moon. Lily. Vids curled up on the couch*, she thought, a mantra to get through the meeting. *Maybe Mama will want to move there and I can look after her. The lower gravity would be good for her, I think.*

Marcus rifled through his papers, looking for one in particular. "The downside of a paper fetish," he joked. The corners of Xi's mouth turned down in disapproval. "Ah, here we are."

He pulled a folded document from the pile. The paper was yellowed with age and sealed with wax, which piqued Ming's interest. Ruben, so enamored of the pen earlier, leaned forward. Sun showed the document to the group before breaking the seal with a soft crack.

"If you've read the will for Jie Qinlao, he did not address the issue of company ownership. That information is contained in this separate codicil, which exists in paper form only." He smiled wryly with a quick look to Ming. "As you can tell from the age of the paper, he made this plan quite some time ago."

Sun read the document silently, making a few notes on the legal pad with his fountain pen. Ruben watched closely, fascinated as the pen left ink on the pad. Finally, the lawyer looked up. "This document will be subject to your legal review, of course, but here's the summary.

"Two-thirds of my holdings are the property of my firstborn daughter, Ming. One-third to any children with my second wife, Sying. To the latter —the assets will be held in Sying's care until those children reach the age of majority." He placed the paper flat on the table, the pen on top of it, and looked up.

"That's it?" Xi demanded, her voice rising. "That's all it says?" She was dressed in a flowing jade-green robe that made a whispery sound as she moved her arms. Spots of color showed in her cheeks.

"There is no mention of shares in your name, Xi," Marcus said in a measured tone. "Besides, I believe you hold substantial shares and a board position already."

"That's unacceptable," Xi snapped. "My brother must have been out of his—"

"There is one other item," Marcus continued.

Ming's head was spinning. Two-thirds of her father's share of the company had to be worth millions—no, *billions*—of dollars. What Marcus had read meant a lifetime free of financial worry. It also meant a lifetime full of obligation. The Moon and her happiness there seemed to draw farther away with each passing moment.

"What now?" Xi demanded, her lips souring into a pout.

Marcus took a breath. "Jie wishes to nominate his daughter, Ming, as the next chief executive officer of Qinlao Manufacturing."

"Me?" Ming said.

Xi's disbelief filled the room with mocking laughter. "Her? She's just a construction engineer. What does she know about running a company?"

"As was Jie, if you recall," Marcus said calmly. "He always believed character was more important than experience when it came to leadership."

The old woman snorted as she pressed flat the emerald folds of her robe. "I will not allow the inexperience of a child to destroy this family's fortunes. Ming didn't even care enough about her father to come live with him after his divorce."

Ming flicked a glance at Sying, who'd stiffened at Xi's words. She bristled when Xi put a protective arm around her.

"I will be the next CEO of Qinlao," Xi proclaimed. "I will hold the leadership of this company in trust for my nephew, Ruben."

"That would go against Jie's wishes," Marcus pointed out.

"My brother is dead," Xi said flatly. "I am sure the board will support my bid for the leadership. In fact, I've already suggested several ways to expand our investment portfolio that will make the company even stronger."

"I've heard about your investments." The digitally amplified voice of Wenqian Qinlao sounded out of place in the Victorian décor of Marcus' office. "Financial derivatives, transportation companies." She made a sound like a fart with her mouth. "My husband was an engineer. He was a builder. He would be outraged by your plans."

"Well, thankfully, Jie's not here now, is he?" Xi said, any pretense of mourning pushed aside.

Behind them, Ito sucked in a breath at the flagrant disrespect.

"Yes, but I am," Ming heard herself say. "And I accept my father's wishes."

No one spoke. She noticed Marcus fighting a smile. Behind her, Ito cleared his throat the way he used to when she'd impressed him in their sparring so long ago. Xi, for once, was silent.

Feelings that had been brewing in her ever since Auntie Xi had invaded her life on the Moon coalesced inside Ming. A sense of family honor. A new appreciation for her father, who'd seemed so cold since setting his first wife aside to ensure his dynasty survived. Or maybe, Ming thought, it had been she who'd grown cold.

Ming gripped her mother's hand and received a spasm of reassurance in return.

"That's not how these things work, Ming-child," Xi said. Her words swam in acid. "The board needs to vote for any executive appointment and you, my dear, do not have the votes."

"Are you sure about that?" Wenqian Qinlao's mechanical tones seemed all the more potent for their lifelessness.

Xi's lip curled as she surveyed her ex-sister in law. "Quite sure."

"I think we can settle the matter right now, actually," Marcus said. "More than two-thirds of the voting shares for the company are held by the people in this room. Even if the board wanted a different candidate, they would not be able to overrule the will of the family."

"Fine, Marcus," Xi said. "If Ming and her mother vote together, their combined votes do not outweigh those of Sying and myself—"

"I vote my shares for Ming," Sying said.

Silence spread into the four corners of the office.

Xi gasped. "What? Sying, we discussed this—"

"On one condition," Sying interrupted.

Marcus sat back in his chair, watching Ming. Jie Qinlao's firstborn child felt her face grow hot. If it made her uncomfortable being stared at by her father's oldest friend, how could she possibly have what it took to be a chief executive?

From his position next to the door, Ito cleared his throat. "I would like to vote my shares for Ming also."

Marcus smiled. "Thank you, Ito, but you don't own voting shares."

Ito nodded. "I still support Ming."

Despite the anger blanketing the room, Marcus chuckled softly. That short space of time away from the center of attention was enough for Ming to gather her wits. She calmed her pulse with the force of willpower.

People believed in her. This was her father's wish. Ming reached across the table and picked up the codicil to her father's will.

It was dated the day of her parent's divorce.

"It was always you, Ming-child," her mother whispered at her side. "Always. Now I ask you again: are you in or are you out?"

Ming turned to Sying. "What is your condition?"

Her step-mother raised her veil and locked her dark eyes on Ming. Xi started to speak, but Sying stilled her by holding up a milk-white palm.

"You will teach my son to be more like his father," she said. Her voice was soft but firm.

Ming's insides churned, a tornado of emotion. The loss of her father. The realization that her idyllic life with Lily was over. The heartfelt support of those around her. The firm resolve to thwart her aunt's lust for power. And the weight of responsibility that came with taking up the standard of Jie Qinlao's legacy as it settled on her shoulders.

All those years she had blamed him, hated him, and now…

"I accept," Ming said.

Auntie Xi stood in a whoosh of green silk and strode to the door. "The board will not stand for this," she said. Ito snapped the door open for her. She paused in front of him. "You're fired."

The bodyguard's face remained impassive.

Ming stood, releasing her mother's limp hand. "Ito, you work for me now."

# 10

## ANTHONY TAULKE • SAN FRANCISCO, CALIFORNIA

Anthony was not a morning person. Never had been. Standing at the kitchen counter, he sipped his morning coffee and watched the sunlight stream through the spans of the Golden Gate Bridge.

Far below, downtown San Francisco buzzed with ant-people. He watched them scurrying about their business from his penthouse perch atop the Taulke building. He missed his house overlooking the Malibu seawall in L.A., where Louisa, his third-partner-almost-wife lived with their two young children. But the daily commute to San Fran had proven too distracting. It was the twins. They caused too much chaos to make a daily trip home worthwhile. When he was focused on business, Anthony had little patience for life's disruptions.

How had he let Louisa talk him into having kids, anyway? Except for Tony, he'd avoided the parent trap in his previous relationships, though Louisa had somehow won him over. When Anthony was honest with himself, it was his disappointment with his eldest that had deterred him from having more children. Until the twins came along, anyway. Maybe they were his last-ditch attempts at getting it right.

Tony ... what could he say? Not a chip off the old block. Like his mother in the sense that she'd been a people person, but so unlike her also. Marian was a reserved and caring individual who'd died far too early. Tony's interests were all directed inward.

*Maybe that was my fault.*

He exhaled a breath, trying to recapture his inner calm. The real truth was that he didn't like his own son very much. Tony was the kid who always took the path of least resistance. If there was a shortcut, Tony found it. Maybe he felt like if the world had taken his mother, it owed him everything else in balance. Or maybe he was just a spoiled rich kid.

No, it was more than that. His son used people. Other people were simply a means to Tony's ends, whatever the consequences. Anthony had made his own share of enemies on his way to the top, but he did it the old-fashioned way: he beat them fair and square through superior intellect and skill. And now he was using his "winnings" to make the world a better place for mankind —okay, Mars a better place for Taulke Industries—but was there really a difference? With the fortunes of Taulke rose the prospects for humanity.

A calendar notice from his virtual assistant flashed on his retinal display.

*"Eight a.m. meeting in the boardroom."*

He glanced at the time. 7:42.

Must be a mistake. Anthony queried the notice for more details.

*"Adriana Rabh. Discuss financial investment."*

He set his coffee cup down so quickly it sloshed hot and steaming onto his hand. His virtual must have scheduled the meeting and forgotten to tell him. He rarely saw anyone before ten.

But for Adriana, he'd fly to the Moon at midnight if that's what it took. And she was coming to him—that could only be good news.

Anthony trotted into his bedroom, where he selected a conservative blue blazer, a pair of khaki trousers paired with a lightly starched white shirt, and his favorite loafers sans socks. He surveyed his reflection, assessing the eclectic-entrepreneur-turned-innovator look, and added a red pocket square for flair. He patted the slight, loose waddle under his jaw with disdain, then swept his fingers through his curly salt-and-pepper hair.

Might be time for a cosmetic touch-up.

Another time check: 7:58.

He jogged down the curving steps from the penthouse to the board-room level, sweeping past the stunning western vista of the Pacific Ocean. A line of thunderclouds limned with morning sun crept up from the south, trailing hazy rain behind it. He'd designed this entire floor to impress even the most hardened investor with the immense wealth of Taulke Industries.

On the south side of the building Anthony spied a single, docked aircar, a Cadillac. The luxury craft was jet-black with tinted windows, no insignia, and no security people. If Adriana wanted to keep their meeting secret, it might mean she wanted a very large share in the Mars venture. Anthony smiled. The familiar buzz of a deal in the making was more intoxicating than any stimulant in the world.

He paused outside the boardroom and shot his cuffs so they extended exactly a half-inch from the blazer's sleeves, then pushed through the heavy wooden door.

Helena Telemachus sat slumped in a plush leather seat, a leg draped casually over one arm of the chair. Her eyes appeared vacant as she studied the display on her data glasses. She looked up when he strode in.

"Surprise!" she said, waving jazz hands. "Remember me?"

Anthony kept his face still as he took in her short, dark hair and elfin ears. His virtual reminded him Helena preferred to be called H. He extended his hand, doing his best to project that her presence wasn't at all a surprise. "H, of course."

"You're a minute and a half late," she said playfully. "Ms. Rabh would not have been pleased. She's a stickler for promptness."

H took his proffered hand and pulled herself to her feet. She was lighter than he expected. Her loose blue jeans and hoodie looked out of place in the boardroom with its walls of oak luminous in the San Francisco sunshine. She flipped the data glasses up into her hair. "I'm afraid Adriana won't be joining us, though. Three's a crowd, right?"

H laughed like the tinkling of a wind chime.

Anthony jerked his hand away. "What are you doing here?"

"Mars? We agreed you'd take a meeting, remember?"

Anthony adjusted his jacket. He regretted the red pocket square now. He felt like an idiot. "I'm afraid I have other appointments today. Perhaps we can reschedule," he said, with no intention of doing so.

H grinned but didn't move. "Let's see, I bet your schedule has you booked to see Ulysses Corp, Sanchex, and Amerigrow this morning?" She waited as he checked his display.

"How do you know—"

"Yeah, those are all me. Like how I spelled out U-S-A?" She put her hands on her hips, appearing very pleased with herself.

"You hacked my personal schedule?" Anthony felt a chill in spite of his rising anger. She'd hacked his virtual assistant without setting off any of the security tripwires he'd personally implemented. That took real resources. And balls.

"Don't sweat it, Tony. I'll have you back before tea." She pointed to the docked Cadillac. "I'll drive."

"My name is Anthony, by the way. Tony is my son."

H smirked. "Yeah, I know. Notice I didn't invite junior to this meeting?"

---

"You can take it off now, Anthony," H said as the aircar touched down. He heard her fingers tapping a control panel.

Anthony slipped the hood off his head and raked his hair back. The faux leather hood was more than a blindfold; it was a dampening field that blocked all external connections. His retinal display flashed its offline indicator. The last location it registered was the Taulke building and it wasn't picking up his present position. How was that even possible? He paid premium rates for worldwide coverage.

"Ready?" Not waiting for an answer, H opened her door and got out.

Anthony squinted in the bright sunlight. They were at elevation. His lungs had to work harder but seemed to gain less air for the effort. Rugged mountains surrounded them, and a fenced installation grew out of the far landscape. His internal clock told him they'd flown for maybe thirty minutes, so that could be Washington State, or Arizona, maybe Mexico— was there a mountain range in Mexico? He tried once more to engage his virtual.

*Offline* flashed again.

"Don't bother trying to connect to the 'net. We've got the whole area dampened. National security, you know." H donned a pair of dark glasses as she walked. "Figured out where we are yet? Don't let me down, Anthony. I've got a bet riding on you."

A drone buzzed overhead as they approached a log cabin overlooking a broad valley. The valley floor was spotted with scrub brush. Beautiful scenery, but nothing cluing him in to their location. Anthony spied a nest of lightning rods and boxes on the cabin's roof.

"Arizona?" Why was he trading banalities with this ridiculous girl? *The ridiculous girl that hacked your virtual,* he reminded himself.

H heaved a theatrical sigh. "Thanks for playing, Anthony, but no, we're not in Arizona." She leaned in. "Hopefully you'll do better with the boss." She held the cabin door open for him.

Anthony blinked in the sudden dimness, afterimages from outside blotting his vision. Slowly, he made out the profile of a dark-skinned man dressed in a flannel shirt and jeans and seated at a rough, wooden table. Without broadcast makeup and a suit, he almost didn't recognize Howard Teller III, the President of the United States.

Teller rose, extending his hand. "Welcome, Mr. Taulke. I've been looking forward to meeting you." There was no mistaking that voice. Deep, smooth as cream, but with a timbre of understood power.

"Mr. President." The handshake was textbook firm and reassuring.

"Coffee?" Teller indicated a thermos on the table and an empty mug. Anthony nodded.

The president studied Anthony's face, then stared out the window for an uncomfortably long time. Anthony sipped his black coffee and tried his virtual again for the hell of it.

"You know what the problem is with politics today, Anthony?"

"No, sir."

When Teller leaned in, Anthony could see the famous gold flecks in the man's soft brown eyes. "Money."

"Money?"

Teller nodded as he fiddled with his coffee cup. "Money—there's not enough of it. In politics, I mean. Used to be, you and I would have met long before now. I would have come crawling to you on my hands and knees begging for cash to get elected. We would have a preexisting relationship, one built on trust. But today?" He sat back in his chair, a disgusted look on his face. "It's all polls and public opinion—and no one has to put their money where their mouth is. There's no accountability."

"I see," Anthony said, not really seeing at all. He'd always been taught that making all elections publicly funded had been one of the greatest achievements of the mid-twenty first century. And here was the President of the United States calling bullshit on the whole system.

"Oh, don't get me wrong, the old way of doing things was imperfect, to be sure. And there were people who abused the system, but it had its good points." Teller smiled. "So, have you figured out where we are yet?" He glanced at H, who'd sequestered herself across the room, once again draped over a comfortable chair. "H and I have a friendly wager going."

Anthony shook his head. "I'm afraid not, Mr. President."

"Los Alamos, New Mexico. Home of the Manhattan Project."

"The Manhattan Project? As in atomic bombs?"

Teller leaned in. "In the mid-twentieth century, the men and women who worked here created a great weapon in order to save lives, to save the planet from continuing war. And they did it in total secrecy. Millions of dollars—would've been billions today—and hundreds, thousands of people all working together for the greater good of mankind."

"Really," Anthony said, his tone skeptical. "You have a funny way of seeing the beginning of the Nuclear Age, Mr. President." It was only after he said it that Anthony wondered if he'd just offended the most powerful man on the planet.

"I see it like my predecessor, Harry Truman, saw it," Teller said, rising and walking to the window. "The Manhattan Project saved American lives by making moot the need to invade the Japanese mainland. But semantics aside, Anthony, the war we're facing today is worse—much, much worse. Total destruction by our own hand. We've turned the planet against us— and we as a world can't seem to get our shit together to fix it. Floods, storms, gene-hopping viruses—they're spiraling out of control. Whole populations are picking up and moving. Humanity is running around like Chicken Little, only this time, the sky really *is* falling.

"What happened in Mississippi, the deaths of all those people in Arizona, the wildfires in the Northwest. These are just the beginning of the end. People are desperate, scared. And frightened people do stupid things. All over the planet, we're in a war for our own survival as a species and we don't even know it."

Teller returned to the table and sat down. When he looked at Anthony, his gaze was fierce, determined. He placed his hands flat on the table.

"In the old days, the money people would have wised up by now. We all have to breathe the same air, right? But now politics is all driven by the public's self-interest. Mob rule via the ballot box. 'Don't build that dam, don't spoil my view, don't bring those refugees into my neighborhood and lower my property values. I'm afraid of fusion power.' It goes on and on."

Toying with his coffee cup, Anthony felt vaguely like a kid called to the principal's office.

"Somebody has to do something, Mr. Taulke," Teller said. "And that someone is you."

Anthony blinked, his poker face sliding off. "Me, sir?" He laughed to fill the empty air. "I already tried, remember? I wanted to use bio-seeding to reduce the carbon compounds in the atmosphere." The hot memory of bitter defeat filled him anew. In a lifetime of business successes, the bio-seeding initiative had failed in spectacular fashion. Public ridicule had been deep and widespread. "I failed, and you know why, sir? Those politicians you were just talking about, they turned public opinion against me."

Teller nodded. "You're right, Anthony. You're absolutely right. And you had the right idea back then, too. But poor execution."

Anthony flushed, his anger getting the better of him. "Poor execution?"

Teller waved his hands. "Calm down. Not what I meant. There's profit in suffering, Anthony. You tried to convince the public to take their medicine but never had enough money or smarts to beat the private interests set against you. The climate change industry manipulated public opinion through the media, and the public ate you alive. That's all the media seems good for these days: filling people's heads with nonsense until they believe anything because everything sounds like bullshit."

Anthony took a moment to rein in the old frustrations. He tried to bleed the sarcasm from his tone and failed. "What's *your* solution, Mr. President?"

Teller took a moment, poured himself another cup of coffee. He offered Anthony another cup, but he demurred.

"Secrecy," the president said finally. "How long would the Manhattan Project have lasted if the public knew we were building the greatest weapon in the history of the world out here?" He swept his arm toward the window. "They would have protested, and Congress would have wanted hearings. Even the Allies might have protested, looking beyond the war to the world after and the US having too much power in it. The whole thing would have died the death of a thousand cuts and we'd all be speaking Japanese today. The secret to success was secrecy."

Anthony processed what Teller was saying. "So you want me to restart my atmospheric seeding program?"

"In secret."

"What about the UN? I mean, climate is a worldwide problem. We can't just seed the United States."

"Do you not understand the meaning of *secret*, Anthony? I'll handle the UN when the time comes."

Anthony took a moment, but only a moment, to consider Teller's offer. "I'll need money, Mr. President, and lots of it."

"H told me about the shortfall in your cash flow. She'll get you whatever you need."

A passing cloud shadowed the sunlight streaming in through the window.

"How did you know I'd say yes?" Anthony asked.

Teller's lips bent upward. The changing light gave his expression a feral quality. "I just offered you a chance to literally save the world, Anthony. No one says no to that."

Anthony couldn't stop the grin creeping across his face.

Maybe someone would say no. Certainly not Anthony Taulke.

# 11

## MING QINLAO • SHANGHAI, CHINA

"You got your hair cut!" Lily's face was puffy with sleep and she had the creases of crumpled bed sheets imprinted on her cheek. She was still blinking the sleep from her eyes.

Ming's heart skipped a beat at the sight of Lily's naked skin. Her gut ached, and not from Earth's greater gravity. Lily looked adorable in her morning messiness.

"Yes," she said. "Do you like it?"

"Guess I'll have to." Lily rubbed her eyes and moved closer to the lens. Her handheld's field of view panned wildly across the rumpled bed and the clothes on the floor, then gave a teasing peek at their loveseat against the outer wall. "Are you wearing makeup?"

Another pang of homesickness. Ming drank in the morning sounds of Lily shuffling in the bedcovers. The two-hundred forty thousand-odd miles separating them seemed suddenly small.

"Yeah," Ming answered. Her voice felt lifeless. "Part of the job." The increased gravity made her face feel like it was slagging off, but the makeup artist had done a phenomenal job making Ming appear young, confident, and in charge. If only she felt that way.

Faced with Lily in all her waking beauty, Ming's resolve in accepting the reins of Qinlao Manufacturing seemed to evaporate. She was giving up her quiet life of predictability on the Moon for … what? A seat at the table of the rich and powerful? A chance to carry on her father's legacy? Or was it sticking it to Auntie Xi that appealed most? She'd had another sleepless night, wrestling with the choice she'd already made.

Lily's face fell from joyful to concerned to resigned. She drew back from the lens. "You're not coming back are you?"

The aching, empty space beneath her breastbone collapsed. She hadn't known how to say it, how to break it to Lily … to herself. And now, Lily had gone and done it for her. The two-second time delay in Earth-Moon communications made things worse. The hurt and anger on Lily's face hung there, accusing.

"No, I'm not." What else was there to say? A bunch of words that amounted to those three. Ming opened her eyes to the air to keep them dry, to avoid crying and ruining her mascara. "I'm sorry."

"We could've avoided this, you know." Lily's face hardened in anger. "Why didn't you tell me who you were right at the beginning?"

Why, indeed? Not telling Lily about her family when she'd met her was understandable, but that didn't explain why she'd kept up the pretense even after they'd moved in together.

Pretense, a fancy word for lie. A lie of omission, but a lie just the same.

"I—I wanted you to love me for me, not my family's money."

Two seconds passed.

"Bullshit," Lily spat.

Ming blinked in surprise at the sudden hatred in her ex's voice. Her ex. The finality of that realization hurt more than she expected.

"Don't quote me some rom-com line about what true love is supposed to be," Lily said. She pulled the bed covers up. Ming saw the gesture for what it was: you're not entitled to this intimacy anymore, Lily was saying. I've revoked your privileges.

Lily's features hardened like wet stone. "Did you think I was stupid? No one has the cash to just buy out a work contract on the Moon. I knew you came from money, but I thought—I hoped—you loved me enough to tell me the truth."

"I'm sorry, Lily," Ming said again, feeling smaller by the second. "I never meant to hurt you. But I need to stay here."

"And what am I supposed to do?"

The two second delay felt like an eternity.

Ming started to speak: "I'll pay for your—"

But the screen was already dead.

Ming dabbed at her eyes and checked her reflection. She'd managed to save her makeup, at least. She drew a deep breath and pulsed a message to Marcus in the next room to bring her mother and the stylist team in.

Even with the pain meds her joints ached from dealing with Earth's heavier gravity, and she had a persistent, low-grade headache from the operation to implant her retinal display. The constant influx of information still felt weird in her head. One more thing Ming would have to get used to in her new world. She stood, drawing her silk dressing robe more tightly around her shoulders.

"That's done," she said when they had arrived. "What's next on the agenda?" Her voice sounded cold even to her.

A young man wheeled in a rolling rack of business clothes for her to choose from, while an older woman fussed with Ming's hair. Her mother indicated outfits the young man should pull from the rack for a closer look.

"We meet with the board in an hour," Marcus said. "It's a formality. They know no one has the votes to overrule the appointment, so they'll go along with it—for now. I expect Xi to start lobbying for her diversification plans as soon as she finds her footing, so we need to be ready to counter her." He made a sour face. "Also, Xi got herself appointed as the board representative for the investor meetings this afternoon."

Ming waved away the hairdresser. "Will that be a problem?"

Marcus hesitated, but Wenqian said in her amplified voice: "Xi will lay low for now. She's making a new battle plan. Be careful what you say in front of her."

"You'll be there, Mother. You can tell—"

"Your mother will not be there," Marcus interrupted. "You need to present an image of independence and strength. Any notion that Jie's daughter is any less capable than the man she's replacing will just play into your aunt's hands."

Ming nodded. She'd relied on her mother in the past few days—had it been only a few days?—but Marcus's advice felt sound. "I understand. You'll be there, Marcus?"

He inclined his head. "If you wish."

"I wish." She turned to the clothing rack, considering her choices. Jie Qinlao had been famously informal in his dress, often showing up to meetings in coveralls from his visits to the shop floor. It worked for him; it was authentic. But she needed her own space, her own image.

Wenqian had chosen three outfits: a yellow sleeveless dress, close-cut and slim; a conservative, dark-blue business suit with a cream-colored, scoop-necked blouse; and a neo-modern gray morning coat, complete with a silk cravat and dark trousers for contrast.

The last combination struck Ming as contemporary yet traditional. Unexpected, playful, with a hint of masculinity. And all that together implied mystery, the unknown.

She chose the morning coat. Marcus frowned, but her mother nodded in agreement.

The boardroom of Qinlao Manufacturing was a window on the world of the old and the new. The transparent eastern wall overlooked the bustle of Shanghai on a mostly clear day. Construction cranes expanded the ever-growing city skyward. Outside, aircars and drones darted between plumes of smoke from car exhaust and factories below. On the opposite wall hung a mosaic of Qinlao's past, from the very first ion drive manufactured half a century earlier to the latest micro-implant, like the one Ming now wore in her own eye. In each invention—from large to small, from complex to simple—Ming saw a bit of her father.

Her stomach, still fluttering from dumping Lily, grew lighter still at the thought of formally stepping into her father's shoes. Outwardly, she smiled serenely.

The unusual outfit had done its job. She'd noticed the curious glances when she'd entered, flanked by Ito and Marcus. The grayhairs on the board were trying to reconcile the unknown variable Ming represented with the sparse details their spies had reported. It was good to have them off balance for now, second-guessing their first impressions of her until she had a chance to solidify the desired image.

Marcus took his time introducing the board members. Dong Huan was one of her father's earliest investors, an ancient man with a hunched back and a gap-toothed smile. He owned a fraction of a percent of shares, but he'd been on the board from the beginning, one of the first venture capitalists to show faith in Jie Qinlao's potential. Ming took the old man's hand and bowed low in a sign of respect.

She granted similar deference to two other minor shareholders, also old friends of her father's, one an economist and one a professor at Tsinghua University.

There were two Westerners, young white men in expensive suits who represented a hedge fund and a pension plan for California. They nodded at her and shook her hand with neutral, sweaty grips. She knew they cared only about profits and were allies of Auntie Xi's diversification plans—as long as they made money.

Then there were the major shareholders. Auntie Xi, of course, whose smile appeared painted on. She hung in the background of every introduction, quick with a word or a sidelong glance to her allies. Finally, Ming was introduced to the representatives from two major family manufacturing conglomerates, strategic partners of Qinlao Manufacturing: the Hans and the Xiaos.

Ming approached JC Han before Marcus had a chance to formally introduce them. Jong Chul Han was a contemporary of her father's, and the two men were cut from the same blue-collar cloth. Weathered, sunburnt features showed under a carefully combed, silver-gray pompadour. The Hans led the Korean peninsula in manufacturing prowess.

He took Ming's outstretched hand in both of his own. His grip was dry and strong as he bowed to kiss her hand. She allowed the ancient affectation out of courtesy.

"We've met before," Ming said.

"Indeed we have, young lady. In Japan, on a job site. You were seven years old and the apple of Jie's eye. He was a good man, Ming. I am sorry for your loss." His voice was low and warm, grandfatherly. Despite his familiar manner, Ming liked him immediately. She vaguely remembered the meeting he'd mentioned, and the memory carried mixed emotions for her father. Tears threatened.

"You are very kind, Mr. Han. That was a long time ago. I am honored you remember me."

The old man chuckled. "Forgetting you would be difficult. Your father spoke of you often."

She studied his face, trying to discern if this was flattery meant to garner favor with her as the new CEO.

"He told me just last month you were the most productive construction engineer on the Moon," Han continued. "Reminded him of himself, he said. Efficient, without patience for waste."

He leaned in close enough for Ming to feel his warm breath on her cheek. "Don't look so shocked," Han whispered. "I am glad you are taking his place, Ming. He would be so proud right now." When Xi leaned in to listen, he backed away.

That left the Xiao family; or rather, their virtual representative. In place of an actual attendee, the Xiaos had sent the hologram of a lawyer. Even on her first day, Ming recognized the obvious sign of disrespect that had, prior to the meeting, sent mild-mannered Marcus into a fit of rage. As the largest shareholder in Qinlao and the largest manufacturing conglomerate in China, the Xiaos had expected to be consulted in the choice of Qinlao's new CEO. Marcus suspected they'd even been promised it by Xi.

Ming had deliberately saved them for last. She approached the holo-station where the life-sized image of the lawyer stood waiting. The holo was quite good, with only a tiny bit of transparency in the image. He appraised her with cool eyes, then bowed. "It is an honor to meet you, ma'am."

Ming did not return the bow. "But not enough of an honor to travel here in person?" she asked, careful to keep the rancor from her voice. This was more than the chance to make a first impression on the Xiaos. It was also an opportunity to demonstrate to the board just who Ming Qinlao was.

The man's professional mask faltered a bit. Clearly, he hadn't expected to be challenged by a twenty-something engineer from LUNa City. "Scheduling issues prevented Mr. Xiao from attending, I'm afraid."

"I was talking about you."

"Oh ... I was only notified at the last minute." The man's image shuffled its feet. "No personal insult was intended, I assure you."

"Who said anything about a personal insult?" Ming asked. "I would never expect such a petty gesture from such an esteemed family." She waited, watching the lawyer weigh his options for response. Just as he was about to speak, Ming said, "No matter. Please convey my best wishes to the family and thank them for their support."

Ming sent a signal from her new retinal implant to break the connection. The lawyer's image evaporated.

"What are you doing?" Xi was at her side, hissing in Ming's ear. "The Xiaos could crush us if they wanted to."

"Setting a tone, Auntie," Ming said, turning away from the old woman to survey, face by face, the rest of the board. Some wore shocked expressions, mirroring Xi. Others were smarter, their faces impassive. Marcus was smiling. "I am Qinlao Manufacturing now, and I will not be disrespected."

Her gaze settled on Xi. "By anyone."

--------

The rest of the day was a blur. The board vote to confirm her as CEO had been uneventful and unanimous. While surprising to Ming, Marcus explained that no board members, not even Xi, wanted to be seen as publicly unsupportive toward their new chief executive officer. "Consider it a last gesture of respect for your father," he said. "But make no mistake, Ming—you have enemies there."

Marcus had also organized a brief press event. Ming's speech was short and sweet, with an emphasis on maintaining the course set by her father. She was sure to mention the board's unanimous approval of her instatement, an ad-lib of which Marcus approved. "It will help stabilize the value of QM stock," he said.

Her outfit looked stunning on the newsfeeds and she even picked up a few fashionista commentaries. Everything had gone just right on the first day.

It was well past ten when Ito opened the door to her father's apartments adjacent to the Qinlao headquarters. Ming dismissed him for the night and wandered alone from room to room.

An office; a workshop with half a dozen incomplete prototypes on the benches; a kitchen stocked with noodles and tea, her father's two dietary staples; and a slew of spare bedrooms. One was stately and spare, clearly her father's. In another, the décor and video gaming chamber suggested it was where Ruben stayed when he and Sying visited. Ito's quarters were just off her father's office.

Ming inhaled deeply as she walked. The whole apartment smelled of him, a combination of oil, cleaning solvent, and pipe smoke. The elements that had defined her father's life.

She picked up the image of the two of them at a job site, the one from the memorial service. Its 3D motion made her smile. Unlike at the service, there were no eyes but her father's in the photo watching her now. Ming looked around for a picture of Sying and Ruben but found none.

She dropped into a deep leather chair, still holding the image-in-motion. Crinkles formed at the corners of Jie Qinlao's eyes as he smiled. Her father had been a man who smiled with his whole face like the happiness was radiating out of him. In the background, little Ming grasped after the butterfly. The picture reset and little Ming was kneeling again, her father's expression once more becoming serious.

Over and over, the photo reset and replayed its captured moment from her life.

Had she misjudged him? Ming and her mother had never wanted for anything when she was growing up. Papa visited Mama regularly until Ming herself put a stop to it. In fact, all the tension between her father's old family and the new had been a result of Ming's petulance. A hurt, little girl's black-and-white interpretation of her father's actions.

She argued with herself. He'd left her mother when she'd needed him most. He'd found a younger wife and had a son, all for the sake of the company.

But today, JC Han had told her how often her father had mentioned her. He'd known about her posting on the Moon. He'd even complimented her engineering prowess.

The picture cycled again. Her father, wrench in hand, smiled at her. Who was this man she thought she'd known well enough to hate?

The doorbell rang. Ming sat up in her chair, wiping her cheeks. She hoped the makeup proved waterproof after all. The time on her retinal display said it was after midnight.

Ito met her at the door to the office, dressed in a robe. He showed her a personal access data device with an image of their visitor.

Ming stared at the PADD. The young man waiting in the foyer was long and lean, his dark hair cut in a stylish rake, his eyelids painted with shadow. He wore the latest in tight-legged trousers and a bespoke, plaid jacket. In the crook of his arm, he held a huge bouquet of real flowers.

Xiao Deng-bo, Danny Xiao, the eldest son of the Xiao manufacturing empire. Ming vaguely remembered him from company social events in her youth. The memories did little to entice her to receive him, but she had new responsibilities now. This was not really a social call.

Ming retied her cravat and slipped on her gray coat. She nodded to Ito. "Let him in."

Ito keyed the entry and returned to his room. She noticed he left the door cracked.

Danny Xiao's tall, thin frame cast a long shadow. He bowed deeply to Ming and presented the flowers to her.

"Congratulations, Ming."

She accepted the bouquet with a gracious smile. The heaviness of its scent filled her nose. They were beautiful. "Thank you, Danny."

"Your auntie said I might find you here."

Ming kept her expression fixed, hospitable. "Oh, did she? Well, in that case, please do come in."

# 12

## ANTHONY TAULKE • SAN FRANCISCO, CALIFORNIA

Anthony never would have dreamed his biggest opposition to saving the world would be his own son.

"I don't see the profit in it, Pop," Tony said, sitting across from him. "What's in it for us?"

Anthony stared at him. Tony may have inherited his father's cosmetically enhanced square jaw, rich wavy locks, and dark eyes, but that kind of comment just reinforced what Anthony had feared for a long time now: there was something disconnected inside this kid. A wire pulled loose. Something.

"We're talking about saving the world, Tony. You know, our *species*." As if speaking the obvious might elicit compassion in Tony for his fellow man.

His son sniffed. "And I'm trying to save you—and our company—from your own humanitarian instincts."

Anthony bristled at *our company*, but let it pass.

Tony raked a hand through his hair. "What happened to Mars as the new Eden? You'll take resources to work on this little save-the-world sideshow—the one that failed before, remember? If you want to save humanity, develop Mars. It's cheaper!"

Convincing Tony to help him was supposed to be the easy part. Anthony needed him to work behind the scenes within the company. Set up sub-projects, move money, reassign people. Run things off-book. As CEO, every move Anthony made would be studied and dissected by Taulke Industries' board of directors. He needed an inside man, someone he could trust.

Instead, he had to settle for Tony. Anthony tamped down the spark of anger that threatened to fire his words.

"That was then, Tony. This time is different." Anthony winced. Even he thought his argument sounded lame. Were things really so different now? He had the clandestine approval of the President of the United States, but climate change was a global problem requiring a global solution, and that meant buy-in from the United Nations. Did President Teller really have the juice to pull off a global initiative?

"Is this about the money?" Tony asked. "I never should have introduced you to H. She said the White House wanted to invest in Taulke Industries. I thought she meant the Mars Project, not some crazy-ass, save-the-earth bullshit. What about Adriana Rabh? And the other investors?"

"Teller's a bird in the hand, Tony."

Anthony launched himself from his leather chair and strode to the window overlooking the ocean. He needed a moment to regroup. He'd established his office in the penthouse atop the Taulke building as his war room for the new project.

A brand to sell the venture, that's what he needed. A quick, impactful way to win over the court of public opinion. He'd spent half the night considering names. Something that would sound good for the history books. Simple, recognizable, and laden with historical significance.

He'd settled on the Vatican Project. Recognizable in any language, symbolic, but also a poke in the eye to all the religions that had failed to pray their way out of a global catastrophe. One day they'd have to acknowledge it was Anthony Taulke, not God, who'd saved the planet. His son had laughed out loud at the name.

"Did you at least get the money?" Tony asked. The boy's tone was infuriatingly condescending.

Nodding at the serene Pacific vista, he said, "It came in this morning, but I need—"

"—to run this project off the books," Tony finished for him. "I get it, Pop. You need my help."

Anthony stayed silent, considering his son's reflection in the window. Surprised at himself, he'd been hurt by Tony's rejection of the name Vatican for his venture. Now, it sounded like he might be coming around.

Tony pushed himself out his own chair in a way that mirrored his father's movements. "Fine. I'll open a couple of skunkworks projects and funnel the money back to you in ByteCoin, so it's untraceable."

"Thank you, Tony."

"Don't thank me yet, Pop." Tony rested his hands on the back of the chair, his powerful shoulders set. "You haven't heard what I want in return."

Anthony felt his upper back muscles clench. "In return?"

"We're businessmen, Pop." Tony chuckled. "You get something, I get something. One hand washes the other. You know, all that crap you taught me growing up."

A half-dozen responses sprang to Anthony's lips. *You miserable sono-fabitch, I put you on the board. You greedy...* He bit them all back. There was no time for that argument now. He needed the boy, and Tony had his old man right where he wanted him. Now was the time to make the deal—when the other guy needed it most.

Just like Anthony had taught him.

"Well?" he said through gritted teeth. "What's the ask?"

Tony turned the screws. "Ask implies you have a choice, Pop. You don't."

Anthony glared at his son. He may have taught this kid the art of the deal, but he never taught him to gloat like a prick. That was a skill his son had developed all on his own.

"Get on with it, Tony."

"Mars."

Anthony's eyes narrowed. "What about it?"

"It's mine now." Tony smiled. "You save this world. I get Mars. We'll see who corners the market on salvation. Deal?" He walked up to his father and thrust out his hand.

Almost without thinking, Anthony took it. He didn't need a family squabble now. He had a job to do, and he needed all hands on deck. He could feel his heart beat a little faster at the thought of a new project. The early stages were the best, when the outline was still murky and anything was possible. Tony could have Mars. It was a world-sized money pit.

Screw Mars. He was going to save his world first.

"Deal," Anthony said. He deliberately turned away from Tony's self-satisfied smile to face the infinite expanse of the Pacific. A stiff breeze was pushing fog inland, uncovering the bones of the city below him. Disappointment, rage, excitement—they all swirled inside Anthony, stirred by lack of sleep. It created in him a sense of disconnection.

"I'll get started setting up Vatican right away," Tony said, heading out the door.

"You do that."

*That kid will be the death of me.*

---

He'd just poured himself a second bourbon when his virtual announced his second visitor of the day. This one, at least, he was looking forward to.

Viktor Erkennen liked to cultivate the persona of a mad inventor. Short and stout with a shrewd gaze, Anthony's oldest friend eschewed cosmetic enhancements, preferring to sport ragged gray stubble on his sagging double chin and allow his thinning gray hair to frizz around his head like a halo. He walked in wearing an ill-fitting, rumpled gray suit with a too-long coat. Anthony couldn't help but smile as he embraced Viktor. Despite his ratty appearance, Viktor was a germaphobe, and he smelled of fresh soap. He carefully dabbed at his cheeks with an antibacterial handkerchief where Anthony had kissed him.

"Still think I'm going to infect you, Viktor?"

"Just a precaution." Viktor had a soft, feminine quality to his voice, but the tone was playful. "I'm never sure where those lips have been."

Anthony laughed, a genuine sound of comfort and relief. Viktor was such a breath of fresh air after dealing with Tony.

"I saw Junior downstairs. He looked very full of himself."

Anthony growled, pouring his friend a drink. He added a single ice cube to Viktor's.

Erkennen pursed his lips. "Ow, touchy topic, I see. Well, the apple doesn't fall far from the tree, you know." He jerked a thick thumb at the closed door. "You made that."

"Don't remind me." Anthony sat down again. Hearing the obvious from an old friend like Viktor was painful.

"I'm sorry," Viktor said, dropping into an open chair. "That was cruel."

Cruel, but true. Anthony clapped his hands. "Yes, well, I have good news for both of us."

Viktor's eyes brightened under his thick, black eyebrows. "Do tell." He steepled his fingertips.

"I'm launching a new venture and I want you to join me." Anthony paused, then chuckled lightly. "Actually, that's not true. I'm re-launching an old venture and I want you in on it."

Viktor's eyes widened. "The atmospheric seeding project."

"Exactly."

Viktor rose from the chair. His short legs propelled him around the room. "A UN charter? Are the Chinese in this time? We can't do it without the Chinese. We learned that lesson last time." He stabbed at the air as he spoke.

"Not quite," Anthony replied. "It's a US project. A secret project, commissioned by the president. A Manhattan Project kind of thing."

"President Teller?" Viktor stopped pacing, his steady gaze focused on Anthony. "What's in it for him?"

*Why is that the first thing everyone asked?* Anthony wondered.

"It's the world, Viktor. He wants to save the planet."

"He wants to save his own political skin, you mean." Erkennen began pacing again. "Politicians have been paying lip-service to this problem for a hundred years. It's a little late, isn't it? Wait, let me guess," he said, finger in the air. "He wants a working prototype he can take to the UN before the election in November? Save Earth, save his political hide."

"Are those two goals mutually exclusive?" Anthony shot back.

Viktor studied Anthony's face for a long time. "Not necessarily, I suppose. The seeding idea we had before was a good one, but bacteria have serious limitations. Fortunately, I've had some real breakthroughs in the last few years on nanites."

"Nanites. Really?" Anthony rested his elbows on his desk. Moments like this were what he missed. They were few and far between on the Mars Project, where he'd spent more time worrying about budgets and manpower than how to innovate technology.

"By combining nanites with an engineered bacteria, we get the best of both worlds. The efficiency and the growth factors of a biologic but the precision of mechanics. There's even a possibility we could tune the biologics." Viktor's eyes sparkled as he spoke. "It's just a concept now, but it's feasible. The team I've got on this will blow you away, my friend."

In the back of his mind, Anthony considered the problems he was having with control of the oxygen-producing bacteria on Mars. If he could apply the Erkennen nanites to his own venture ...

He pulled himself back to the problem at hand. Maybe he was just like all the rest of them, looking for his slice of the pie from the bigger picture. Maybe he really had taught Tony everything he knew.

"What about dispersal?"

Viktor rubbed his eyes. "We can use aircraft for the first test, but that's not practically scalable. To cover the entire planet evenly, we'll have to build a network of low-earth orbital satellites. But we'd need every nation in on that. It'll cost a fortune." He ambled to the window and gazed at the ocean. There was a long silence as Anthony mixed two fresh drinks, then joined him. Viktor Erkennen barely came up to his shoulder.

"You need my nanites," the scientist said as he took his glass. "Maybe on Mars too, eh?" Viktor smiled at Anthony's self-conscious blush. "Listen, my friend, together we can save the whole fucking solar system. Not just this old backwater garden we're standing on."

"Two men, two planets," Anthony said with more bravado than he felt.

Viktor slapped him on the back. "That's the spirit!"

When the door closed a few minutes later behind his old friend, Anthony stayed at the window. Gray-green thunderclouds massed on the horizon, lightning cascading across their swollen underbellies. When he caught his own reflection in the window, Anthony Taulke raised his glass in a toast to himself.

Not a bad first day on the job.

# 13

## MING QINLAO • SHANGHAI, CHINA

Ming switched off her retinal display and kneaded her temples with the heels of her hands. The UN commission was stonewalling her, she was sure of it now. She'd given two years of her life to those bastards in charge of LUNa City's construction, and now, when she needed them to come through, they were screwing her over. She cursed, pounding her frustration into the desk.

Ito appeared in the doorway, one eyebrow raised. His gaze swept the room, security conscious as ever.

Ming managed a weak grin. "It's just me, Ito. I'm ... frustrated."

"Your father used to do the same thing," he said. "He swore a lot, too."

Her expression bloomed into a smile. "Did he?"

Ito nodded. "He said you should always let the other party know where you stand." Ito bowed and left, closing the heavy carved door softly behind him.

Ming felt the grin evaporate from her face. It was an odd feeling, occupying her father's space in the Qinlao corporate offices, like she was a voyeur in his old life. She'd done her best to make the office her own. The artist's rendering of LUNa City from her office on the Moon hung on the wall directly opposite her desk. Despite the current challenges with the UN contracts office, the image still inspired her.

Sying and Ruben shared a posed picture in a heavy silver frame on one corner of the dark wooden desk. Mahogany, Ito had said, a valuable wood from the tropics. On the opposite corner sat an image of her mother, healthy in her youth, in an ebony frame.

Next to it, framed as a paperweight, a smaller version of the photo of Ming and her father at the Korean job site when she was seven. She'd switched off the 3D animation to freeze it when her father's smile, and her own attempt to catch the butterfly, had reached their fullest expressions. Unlike the others, this photo was not for decoration but for everyday use, a reminder of the pragmatic approach to business she shared with Jie Qinlao.

Ming pushed away from the desk and strode to the eastern window. The chair, a highly-engineered auto-stow model, slid under the antique desk. Just like Jie Qinlao to mix the old and the new. The ocean was invisible, hidden by low-hanging clouds, but the sunset turned their tops a beautiful red-orange. People on the street, tiny from this height, wore air-filter masks, making them appear as faceless drones crowding the sidewalks.

She worked her shoulders to loosen them. The pressure made her want to give up corporate leadership and retreat to her safe haven on the Moon with Lily and her old life of comfortable predictability.

The forces arrayed against her were closing in. There was no pity in the world of high-stakes business, no second chances, no do-overs. If Auntie Xi was orchestrating everything that was happening—and Ming was certain she was—the older woman was winning handily.

First, Danny Xiao. A bold move on her aunt's part, inserting Danny into her life. Ming was in no position to snub the eldest son of a board member and the largest manufacturing conglomerate in China. So she had gone along with the charade to buy herself time to find a way to distinguish herself to the board.

Ming had seized on her contacts with the UN lunar project. Closing a deal on Phase III of LUNa City's development would be a prize for any company. She knew the LUNa project inside and out. There was no way anyone could beat her proposal.

But an anonymous complainant had questioned the safety of the technical specifications, and now the entire letting process was on indefinite hold. Even Ming doubted Auntie Xi had the influence to derail the LUNa City contract. Maybe she'd gotten some help from the Xiao family.

Or maybe Ming was just being obstinate.

She frowned at the beautiful clouds. After all, a Xiao-Qinlao union made perfect sense. Together, they would form the largest manufacturing conglomerate in the world. But how would such a merger impact her father's company? Jie Qinlao could have merged with Xiao years ago, yet had chosen to remain independent.

She turned from the window. More importantly, what would it mean for her? There was no chance the new board created from the merger would allow an untested young woman to remain as CEO. Based on her impotent performance so far, Ming wasn't convinced they'd even let her remain on the board at all.

For now, she had the voting bloc to stave off a takeover, but she needed a win, and she needed it soon. Her step-mother's support of Ming to become CEO had been welcome, if unexpected. When she was honest with herself, Ming wasn't sure she could fulfill her part of Sying's bargain. To teach Ruben how to be more like their father? How was she to do that? She hardly knew the man herself.

Ito pulsed her on her private channel. *"Your mother is here."*

Wenqian Qinlao's maglev purred into the office. She sagged against the side of her chair but offered an engaging smile. Her bright eyes searched her daughter's face. "How are you, Ming-child?"

Her first instinct was to chide her mother for using her childhood pet name, but in that moment, she took comfort in the personal connection. "I don't know how father did it, Mama."

"Your father used to say the only way to eat an elephant is one bite at a time—and to start with the tail."

Ming resisted the frustration she felt. She didn't need patronizing proverbs now, she needed a business deal to save her job. Doing her best to keep her tone neutral, she said, "That only works if you have an unlimited amount of time, Mama."

The old woman shrugged the shoulder that wasn't paralyzed. "You need a break. I have a surprise for you. Something to take your mind off your work."

"I'm meeting Danny tonight."

"Cancel it."

"Mother." Ming tried to wring the impatience out of her voice. "I need to keep up appearances."

"Nonsense," Wenqian whispered. "Tell him you need a night off. Blame it on me."

A night off sounded wonderful. She'd seen Danny nearly every night since he'd shown up at her door after the memorial service. Night clubs, restaurant openings, art gallery parties. Wherever there was a gathering of paparazzi, Danny was sure to be there. She wasn't sure he actually worked at his family's company. He just seemed to party his way through life.

Ming had even allowed him into her bed when she felt she couldn't hold him off any longer and still keep him interested. The sex had been transactional, a way for her to maintain control of their relationship, and as infrequent as she could make it. The encounters had been in the dark—something Ming insisted upon—and only served to accentuate the loneliness she felt after breaking up with Lily.

And she'd had the gall to call Sying a whore.

But each interaction cemented their relationship even further in the eye of the public and would make it harder for her to break away when the time came. The weight of expectations was a constant, concrete albatross around Ming's neck.

To hell with it. She pulsed a message to Danny to cancel their date.

"Come now, Ming-child. My car is waiting on the roof."

---

The aircar rose swiftly in the darkening sky to the highest traffic lanes, the ones normally reserved for cross-country travel. Traffic was light as usual, since only the richest citizens in Shanghai could afford personal air vehicles.

"Where are we going?" Ming asked. Her mother smiled but said nothing.

Stonewalled again.

Ming peered down through the rips in the cloud cover, where the frenetic density of Shanghai's city lights gave way to the more sparsely lit countryside. They were headed west into the growing twilight. Ming turned to Ito. "Do you know where we're going?"

He shrugged, but a grin played around his lips.

Half an hour later, the aircar coasted down into the clouds. Gray mush whipped past the windows until they broke into the clear. Below, a lake shone like glass.

She knew this place. Jie Qinlao had grown up in a tiny hamlet in the Sichuan province, a mountain gathering of homes barely deserving the title *village*. This was a region of dying mining towns, where automation engineers and maintenance techs, people who rarely went below ground, held the few remaining jobs.

On Ming's fifth birthday, her father had brought her here. He'd built a mountain retreat, and staffed it with locals, including groundskeepers, gardeners, farmers, and all the men and machinery needed for a completely self-sustaining estate. He'd even taught her how to fish on the lake. Ming had not been here since that one visit.

The aircar flared and landed gently on the rooftop pad. Wenqian drove her maglev past a line of retainers who bowed as they passed. "Follow me," she said. Her augmented mechanical voice sounded odd among the night sounds of nature.

The tiled hallways were stylish, illuminated with hidden lights. The whispering whir of her mother's chair and the steady tread of Ito's boots escorted them deeper into the structure. Ming's annoyance had turned to curiosity, then emerging memories of having been here before. In spite of herself, Ming enjoyed the intrigue of the moment.

A short elevator ride took them to the ground floor of the house. Ming smelled salt water when she exited. A pool? They turned a corner, entering a room with a high ceiling. It might have been a gymnasium at one time, but now it was outfitted with a lab and a room-sized glass box filled with water. A man and a woman in white lab coats sat behind a monitoring console.

In the water, wearing a breathing mask, was Lily.

Ming stopped short, stunned.

She closed the distance to the tank slowly, then extended her fingers to touch the glass. Lily mirrored her from the other side.

"Surprise!" she said, waving her hands. Her voice, amplified through the mask, projected from speakers mounted above.

Ming opened her mouth to speak, then closed it again as her heart caught up with her eyes. Lily was dressed in a two-piece bathing suit. Ming devoured her curves, the contours of her white flesh. It was all she could do to keep from crying.

"What are you doing here?"

"It was my doing," her mother whispered behind her. "I've hired the best bone doctors in the world, the best gravity rehabilitation specialists. We'll find a way for you two to be together. You need someone, Ming-child. Not that Danny Xiao." Wenqian's voice, even synthesized, was laced with distaste. "Someone you can love."

"Get out," Ming said softly.

Wenqian gasped. "I'm only thinking of—"

"Get out!" Ming screamed. "All of you! Now!"

She whirled on the room, her eyes blazing. Ito guided Wenqian's away from the tank. Everyone, family and medical staff alike, hurried from the room.

Ming strode to the console. She found the controls for the cameras and recording devices and shut them all off.

"Are you angry with me, Ming?" Lily's voice sounded plaintive through the speakers. Instead of answering her, Ming shut them off, too.

She turned back to the glass box. Lily, unable to be heard, pressed her hands against the glass, a stricken look on her face. Ming stood, staring at her former lover through the glass.

Lily was as beautiful as she remembered. Her hair floating like a halo of spun gold. Her breasts firm in the water, her nipples teasing against the bikini top. Ming's mind cascaded with hungry memories. She felt the renewed ache of loss at the sight of her lover behind glass.

She pointed to the top of the tank and climbed the ladder. Lily's head popped up. She removed the mask and slicked her hair back. "You're angry with me," she said. Her voice was hoarse, and Ming noticed dark circles under her bloodshot eyes. How much pain must she be in, suffering Earth's gravity for the sake of a lover who'd rejected her?

Ming shook her head slowly, holding back tears. She stripped off her clothes and stepped into the water.

The tank was warm, body temperature, and tasted of salt. Ming sank to the bottom, then pushed back to the surface where Lily floated, waiting. She'd removed her bathing suit, and the two were both naked now, together. Ming reached out and pulled Lily in to a tight embrace, kissing her deeply. Lily's fingers roamed over Ming's body.

"How much does it hurt?" Up close, Ming could see most of the small blood vessels in Lily's eyes had ruptured.

"I've been here two weeks. It's getting better ... a little." Lily's hands traced Ming's hip. "They say after maybe six months of regular osteo-drugs and exercise I should be able to stay outside the tank overnight." She kissed Ming again, then pulled away, flinching. "Do you mind if we put on masks and stay submerged? Being out of the water gives me a headache."

Ming said nothing, but slipped on the extra mask and joined Lily below the surface.

"Are you angry with me?" Lily asked again. The masks had a built-in diaphragm which let them talk. Her voice underwater sounded hollow and muffled.

Ming shook her head. "Not you."

"I want us to be together, Ming. We belong together."

Ming sighed. "My life is complicated now."

Lily laughed, a harsh gurgle. "Danny Xiao, you mean."

Ming's eyes flashed. "That's business. You don't know what you're talking about." She regretted her harsh words as soon as she said them.

Lily traced Ming's arm with her fingers, her touch feather light in the water. "Let me stay. I'll live here in this house, in this tank, for now. I'll get stronger. You can visit on weekends. I love you, Ming. I need you."

Ming stripped off her mask in a burst of bubbles and Lily did the same. When their lips touched, Ming could not taste where her lover began and the water ended.

Ming's hair was still damp when she took her seat in the aircar for the trip home. She let the silence build in the cabin as they rose into the midnight sky. The clouds had cleared, revealing Shanghai as a yellow glow on the horizon, infecting the otherwise dark, peaceful countryside.

"Thank you, Mama," she said finally.

"I only did it to please you," came the whispered reply.

"Now, send her back. Immediately."

"Why?" Wenqian switched to her amplified voice and her tone was harsh, judgmental.

Because you're hurting her, was what Ming wanted to say. That sounded humane, but it wasn't the truth.

"She's a liability," Ming said. She watched the lights of a small town pass beneath them. Ahead, Shanghai and her life there loomed like a gilded prison cell. "She's a weakness that my enemies will use against me."

"I'll see to it." Wenqian's whisper-voice again. "I only wanted you to be happy. I'm sorry, Ming-child."

"And don't call me that anymore," Ming snapped. Her mother retreated farther into her chair.

She felt Ito watching her. Ming met his heavy gaze and set her jaw. He could chastise her if he wanted, but this was her life and she would live it by her rules.

Ito delivered a barely perceptible nod, then turned his eyes forward again.

# 14

## WILLIAM GRAVES • MIAMI, FLORIDA

Miami was lost.

Graves stared at the big screen. Jansen stood by his side as always. Together they watched the Atlantic Ocean easily top the seawalls built less than five years earlier.

Billions of taxpayer dollars spent with the assurances of the Army Corps of Engineers, now unable to hold back the fury of Hurricane Victoria, the second major storm to hit southern Florida in as many months. A wall of oceanfront condos succumbed to the raging sea, swaying, leaning, then finally toppling into the pounding surf.

The remote camera died.

Graves felt hollow, empty inside. The scale of the devastation pressed him down like a heavy weight. Miami had been mostly evacuated, but many obstinate Floridians had stayed in their homes, afraid of looters.

"Shall I have the evac troops fall back here to Tampa, sir?" Jansen asked. The eye of the massive storm was projected to cross the bottom half of the Florida peninsula. Their job here was done until the storm had cleared the area. Then he could start the recovery and rebuilding process—again. Assuming there was to be any rebuilding this time.

All along the US coastlines, the rising oceans had eaten into cities. The larger population centers, including Miami, had spent money on seawalls, elaborate pumping systems, and levees. All a waste once Mother Nature upped the ante. Now, monster hurricanes were judged on a scale of 1 to 10, not 1 to 5.

New Orleans had been the first major city to go, which surprised no one with its history of routine flooding. Then Houston flooded for the third time in a hundred years, another gimme to the prediction crowd. One by one, coastal cities submerged, becoming modern Atlantises: Myrtle Beach, Annapolis, Fort Lauderdale. The list got longer every year.

And now, Miami was slowly being eaten away by the sea. Maybe not this year. Maybe not in ten years. But in his lifetime, it would become a sunken city as well. Graves was sure of it.

"I need some air," he growled. He spun on his heel and exited the mobile command center trailer.

Outside, the atmosphere was heavy with moisture. A ragged wind whipped cloud fragments across the pewter sky. To the south, a wall of bulging blackness hugged the horizon. They were set up in the deserted parking lot of a big-box store. Graves paced the cracked pavement, trying to purge his dark mood.

He was so weary of the disaster treadmill. Destroy, rebuild, repeat. All those lives lost, property destroyed. This was his third trip to Miami in as many years, and the outcome was always the same. In a few days, with heartbreaking optimism, millions of people would return to the city and attempt to rebuild their lives. A year from now, another storm—maybe bigger than this one—would destroy their lives again.

Graves set his jaw. Not this time. He had the power to declare a city uninhabitable, and this time he'd exercise it. Damn the politicians. He was tired of attempting the same mission over and over and never accomplishing anything.

The whir of an approaching aircar drew his attention to the leaden sky. A four-seater corporate model slowed, then descended rapidly to the ground. A lean man dressed in a dark suit and tie emerged. When Graves locked eyes with him, he detected the flash of an implant in the man's right eye.

"Colonel Graves?" he shouted over the wind. "I need you to come with me, sir."

"And you are?"

"Adamms. Secret Service." The man flashed his ID.

Graves gestured toward the mobile command post. "I'll need to—"

"Already been taken care of, sir," Jansen called from the steps. "The situation's in good hands, sir."

Graves returned her salute and slid into the aircar. Beige leather, real wood trim. Definitely not a military model. Adamms sat across from him and looked out the window as they lifted off.

The command post grew smaller behind them. At this height, the pregnant darkness of the far horizon loomed even larger. A fat raindrop splatted on the clear roof of the car.

"Where to, Mr. Adamms?"

The man did not answer him.

The car flew straight north for a while. Graves assumed they were headed back to DC. Somewhere over the Carolinas, the pilot made a sweeping turn to the west and ascended into a high-altitude, cross-country transit lane.

Graves watched the countryside blur by. Interstate highways crossed the land below like gray synapses connecting clumps of city-nerves. He spotted a good-sized town approaching as they passed over Tennessee, wondering how many of Miami's refugees would move into that state to start a new life.

Tennessee became Arkansas. Looking down, he saw no evidence of state lines, but Graves knew there were state governments talking about setting up border controls to manage the flow of refugees. The worse the weather, the more nervous people got. He dreaded what he knew to be inevitable. It was only a matter of time before another Vicksburg happened.

"We're headed to Kansas, sir." When Adamms wasn't shouting across a windy parking lot, he had a pleasant speaking voice.

"What's in Kansas?"

Adamms pulsed him a data packet. "The Joint Chiefs have selected you as their representative for this test."

Graves settled his data glasses on his nose and leaned back into the soft cushions. *Atmospheric Alteration Through Enhanced Bio-Seeding*. He skimmed through the report. High altitude dispersal ... nanite-enhanced bacteria ... carbon-reduction projections. He blinked the report closed and stowed the glasses in his breast pocket.

"Well, that's ambitious," he muttered.

Carbon reduction in the atmosphere through environmental engineering. The Holy Grail of climate control. A worthy goal, but about seventy-five years too late. Better to invest in figuring out how to levitate cities now.

He resumed his watch of the countryside. There had been a scheme like this one, what twenty years ago? By the multi-billionaire inventor ... Taulke was his name. Graves had never seen actual scientific results from Taulke's experiments, but he did recall how the newsfeeds had taken turns lampooning him, then shitting on his science.

The guy went off to Mars after that, he remembered. Smart man. *Might as well find a new planet*, Graves thought, his frustration in his present never-ending mission front and center in his mind. *This one's toast.*

The aircar descended into flat green country—exactly what Graves imagined Kansas would look like. He saw a pair of military drones flash by the window. They were armed.

He raised an eyebrow at his companion.

"Test area's been cordoned off," Adamms said. "We're the last to arrive. Twenty square miles of zero human intervention. Total news blackout, too."

The aircar shed speed, then landed in front of a military mobile command post not unlike the one Graves had just left in Florida. When the car door slid open, humid warmth washed over his face. He smelled earth and green things and fertilizer mixed with the sharp, plastic odor of temporary buildings. In a way, it made him feel at home.

Stepping inside the trailer was like passing into another dimension. In the far corner of the building, a technician sat behind a workstation, a vast screen with multiple data sources crowding the space. His right hand, encased in a data-manipulator glove, stabbed and curved through the air.

"Colonel Graves?" A tall man with dark, curly hair and square shoulders approached. His lips parted to reveal a star-quality smile of perfect teeth. "Anthony Taulke. May I get you a drink, sir?" He guided Graves to a makeshift wet bar. "Wine, maybe?"

"What? No. Thank you." If Taulke himself was involved in this effort, Graves hated it already. He had no desire to encourage a rich-man's Jesus complex about saving the Earth.

The food smelled wonderful, though, some kind of meat—real meat—simmering in a rich broth. His eyes swept the table. No MREs here. Caviar with toast points, cheese, fresh fruit, and a full bar on the side.

With a touch on the elbow, Taulke kept Graves moving forward. "May I introduce you to EPA Director Freddy Pinchot and Laura Ellis, Secretary of the Interior?" Graves recognized them both from newsfeeds. He shook hands automatically, before being pivoted by Taulke to a rotund, graying man.

"Viktor Erkennen, my partner in the Vatican Project."

Graves recognized both names from the briefing he'd received in transit. Taulke seemed to be warming up to launch a sales pitch.

Graves put up his hands. "Mr. Taulke, I'm here on orders. The only thing I know about this project is what I've read on the way here. I barely understand the basics. But I know one thing this idea has failed before." He had Floridians to save and a city to condemn. No time for pussyfooting around.

Taulke's expression faltered. Erkennen elbowed his taller partner in the ribs.

"Fair enough, Colonel," Taulke said, a cheaper version of his failed smile back in place. He motioned for the two people from DC to join them. Both held glasses of wine, and gravy spotted the EPA director's shirt front. Graves tried not to judge, though he didn't try too hard.

Taulke clinked his wine glass with a spoon. "Ladies and gentlemen, over a hundred and fifty years ago, the United States embarked on a top-secret effort to end World War Two. The Manhattan Project created a weapon of immense power that was ultimately used to sue for peace with the opposing Japanese forces."

Graves blew out a breath. Looked like he was getting the sales pitch after all.

"Today, we're fighting a different war: a war for the planet. A war for our very existence on Earth. And that war requires a new weapon, a weapon that can counter the carbon poisoning our atmosphere. Together with the best minds at Erkennen Labs, Taulke Industries has taken the concept of bio-seeding to a whole new level. Today, we'll show you a proof of concept demonstration that reduces carbon levels in a localized area."

"Then what?" the EPA director asked, eyeing the bar. "You don't have the best track record when it comes to saving the world, Anthony."

Taulke snatched the open wine bottle from the bar. He continued speaking as he refilled Pinchot's empty wine glass.

"That's about to change, Freddy. After today's success, the president intends to ask the United Nations for international support to implement the Vatican Project on a global scale." Taulke monitored the room as his words sunk in. "That's a massive effort, with every country contributing resources to launch a fleet of satellites needed to provide planetary dispersal of the agent. Today, we'll be using a single, high-altitude aircraft to show a localized test."

"What about side effects?" Graves asked.

"Apart from lowering carbon levels? None." Taulke laughed at this own joke. "In all seriousness, Colonel, you raise a good point. The nuclear weapons developed by the Manhattan Project set off an arms race that consumed our world for well over a century. Those weapons still exist today, in fact, which is why we've taken the added precaution of adding a nanite kill switch to the bacteria's DNA. We can shut down the reaction at will. Total control at the touch of a button."

Taulke spread his arms like the ringmaster in a circus. "I'm getting the high-sign from our technician that the deployment of the agent has already begun." He lit up a wall of the trailer to mirror the technician's screen. In one corner, there was a vid-feed from a drone showing distant aircraft making a lazy figure eight in the sky. The rest of the screen showed a dynamic graph of atmospheric elements. The carbon line, highlighted in bright red, jittered around the 500 parts-per-million mark.

Taulke touched the screen. "This shows the carbon-based concentrations, compounds like carbon dioxide and methane, that contribute to our global temperature rise." As they watched, the line wavered, then began a slow decline.

Pinchot's eyes got bigger. "Carbon sequestration in the air?" The EPA director got a distant, thoughtful look on his face. "If this works, Anthony ...

my God, the economic advantage the United States would have! We could put anything we want in the air and just filter it out later. No restrictions on manufacturing due to environmental concerns. That's brilliant!"

Taulke turned sharply. "The point of this demonstration is to show that we can reduce atmospheric carbon so we can mitigate the problem of climate change. Humans get a second chance, if you will. I didn't create this to encourage polluting, Freddy."

Pinchot smiled widely. "You just deliver the technology, Anthony. We'll worry about the policy implications."

Taulke shifted on his feet. The look on his face told Graves this was not the reaction he wanted to his demonstration. "Mr. Director, I want to make it clear that we developed this tech to—"

"You said you had a kill switch?" interrupted Interior Secretary Ellis. "Can you control the reaction any other way?"

Erkennen stepped forward. "In theory, we can adjust the effectiveness of the nanites to allow for localized control. We will maintain a dedicated, quantum-keyed frequency to stop the reaction at any time. I can demonstrate."

Erkennen pulled a slim, silver case from under the table of food. He flipped up the lid to reveal a computer screen and a slim ring of matte-black metal. He slid the ring over his pudgy wrist.

"The quantum encryption combines with the wearer's DNA to establish a control link to the nanites. The combination of the two effects results in an unbreakable cryptography. Absolute security. Once the link is established, it cannot be overridden." He held up his hand to show them the black bracelet. With a flourish he touched the screen. "The nanites are dead."

Graves turned to the wall screen. After a moment or two, the carbon line on the graph began to rise again.

"Very impressive, Dr. Erkennen." As Secretary Ellis swept her hair behind her ear, Graves did a double take when he glimpsed a Neo tattoo on the fair skin of her neck. He moved closer, but her collar slid over the spot. "But a security question—is that the only key?"

Erkennen inclined his head and winked. "Madam Secretary, I can assure you, this is the one and only key on the planet."

# 15

## MING QINLAO • SHANGHAI, CHINA

It was after midnight when Ming returned to her apartments adjacent to Qinlao HQ. Although she'd barely left her office the entire day, her muscles ached like she'd run a marathon. No, a marathon would at least have provided the benefit of some post-exercise endorphins. With this ache, there was no runner's high—just the promise of more pain tomorrow.

With all the effort of maneuvering around Auntie Xi's corporate intrigue, Ming had neglected her daily regimen of re-building muscle mass. Her lunar routine kept her from suffering as Lily had during her visit, but Ming's own rehabilitation required constant attention to reacclimatize her to Earth.

Leaving the lights dim, she collapsed onto a barstool in the kitchen and let the chill of the stone counter seep into her sore forearms.

*Lily.*

Ming had received no word from her since ordering her returned to the Moon. For Lily to be angry with her—or worse, disappointed in her—hurt Ming's heart. She'd wanted to reach out a hundred times, but she stayed silent. Lily deserved to be left in peace. She turned her arms over, letting the cool stone soothe their other side.

For all her efforts to secure the contract for the Moon project and prove herself as the leader of Qinlao Manufacturing, Ming still felt like an impostor in her father's stead, a little girl playing at Papa's work.

She'd found refuge in Ito's teachings—translated them from personal combat to business, encased herself in emotional armor. She approached her outings with Danny Xiao as perfunctory tactics to achieve a larger goal. She endured his fumblings in the bedroom by splitting her emotional self from the physical. Sometimes she imagined herself still on the Moon with Lily, not selling herself to the highest bidder for the sake of the company. If Danny's reaction was any indication, her acting had gotten better with practice.

Ming had adopted a similar routine in her daily work life. She didn't allow herself to feel but simply absorbed knowledge in hope of gaining an edge as CEO. She parried arguments of *we can't do that* with facts supporting *how it can be done*. More facts, better facts.

And yet she couldn't escape the feeling that, each day, she drew further away from her goal. Her aunt was winning. It was just a matter of time.

Ming attempted to exhale the stress from her shoulders. The only answer she knew was to work harder. She had two more briefs to review tonight to prepare for the next board meeting. Popping a stim tablet, she relished the bitter taste on her tongue. She needed to review the briefs before she fell asleep on the sweet, cool surface of the counter.

Through the open doorway to the office, she spotted the LUNa City rendering on the wall. Her life here on Earth had become a lonely one. Ito was the closest thing Ming had to a friend, and there was always the necessary distance of servant from mistress. Her playacting with Danny served only to accentuate how empty she truly felt. The night with Lily in the water tank had been a bright oasis of intimate sharing. It had also been a stark reminder of what she did not, and could not, have for herself now.

She often wondered if she'd made the right choice in sending Lily home. Her lover might offer comfort, but not the empathy she craved. Lily had always been a soft, safe place for her to fall after the rigorous routine of directing lunar engineers. Lily was fun. But she was no equal. What Ming desired, truly, was someone who would stand beside her and offer her strength when she needed it. Someone who could match her intellect as well as her passion. When she thought of Danny Xiao permanently in that role—even merely for show to the outside world—her sadness threatened to leap the cliff into depression.

Ito appeared in the doorway. "You have a visitor," he said.

Ming blinked slowly.

"Who?" If it was Danny Xiao, she'd scream.

But her bodyguard was already retreating.

"Ito!" she called, exasperated, then jumped up to follow him to her father's study. He waited at the door for her to enter, then closed it softly behind her.

Sying Qinlao, her back to the door, occupied one side of the leather couch in front of the fireplace. She turned from the flames of the faux-fire to greet Ming with a smile.

"Ah, finally. I was beginning to wonder if you were ever coming home tonight."

Ming frowned. "Sying. A ... pleasant surprise. Not to be inhospitable, but I have work to do—"

"Sit." Sying patted the couch next to her. The gesture seemed friendly, genuine. Ming circled to the front of the couch and sat on the edge of the cushion.

Sying was dressed casually in an embroidered silk robe with matching slippers. Her dark hair was loose around her shoulders, and her makeup softer, less severe than when Ming had last seen her. She'd always regarded Sying as a trophy wife, a China doll in the game of business politics whose job was to demonstrate her husband's wealth and power. But the Sying sitting beside her was relaxed and radiated an air of strength Ming hadn't sensed before among the perfect fashion and deferential customs.

"I like your shoes," she blurted out. I like your shoes? God, she was tired.

Sying inclined her head but did not laugh, as Ming expected her to. She slipped them off and tucked her feet under her. Her toenails were painted jade green.

"They match the robe," Sying said, "but they're not very comfortable."

Ming laughed, an actual laugh, and the ache in her shoulders diminished. Sying stretched a thin white wrist toward the end table where a bottle waited next to two tumblers. Jameson's Irish Whiskey: Jie Qinlao's favorite.

"Drink?"

Ming nodded, watching her pour. It was like she was meeting Sying for the first time. Every movement was elegant, controlled, purposeful. Almost a ballet in banality. She wished she hadn't taken the stim now. Her knee jiggled with pent up energy. Sying seemed unaware of it when she handed Ming the crystal glass.

"Why are you here?" Ming asked. It seemed too abrupt and loud for the reskinned space with its flickering fireplace. *Must be the stim talking.*

Sying tasted the whiskey. She rolled the liquid around in her mouth before swallowing. The woman even made drinking alcohol look refined. "I'm protecting my investment."

Ming sipped and swallowed too soon. She coughed at the burning in her throat, self-conscious at her clumsiness. "I don't understand," she said when she could talk.

Another nip of the Jameson's. More long moments as Sying savored the smoky taste. "Your performance—or lack of performance, I should say—has exposed my position." Sying's voice was matter-of-fact, not accusatory.

"Is this about Ruben? I promise you, I'll work with him when I have a spare moment."

"It's not about Ruben." Sying's eyes were large and dark, thoughtful and beautiful. To Ming they seemed full of secret knowledge. "Do you play chess?"

Ming nodded.

"What is the most powerful piece on the board?"

"The queen, of course."

"Exactly, the queen." Sying's eyes flashed. "She can move in any direction, as many spaces as she wants, take any piece she wants." Another savoring sip. "So tell me: what chess piece do I represent in this game we are playing with my husband's legacy?"

Ming sipped her drink again, trying to imitate Sying's action of rolling the whiskey over her tongue. The alcohol was taking the edge off the stim.

"A pawn."

Sying turned her gaze on the fire. "Chess is a game of strategy, Ming. I was a pawn ... once. My family contracted marriage to your father to ensure their company survived. I was sold, in a way. My mother told me I would live out my life like a rare bird in a golden cage. Prized for the joy I brought to others when they looked upon me." She refreshed her glass and poured another measure into Ming's. Ming didn't stop her. This was the most she'd ever talked with this woman who'd displaced her mother. And she was growing more fascinated by the moment with her.

"Then a strange thing happened. Your father taught me to play chess. He taught me to choose my role in the game, not let it be assigned to me. I choose to be a queen, Ming, not a pawn. Unfortunately, my dear, your amateur moves are fucking up my game."

Ming sat back in her chair, stunned by the sudden rebuke from this elegant woman. Sying appraised her with hard, unflinching eyes. Her voice became husky with passion. "You think you can outwork these people, be the smartest person in the room, know every detail of every project so that no one can get the drop on you. But this game we are playing is not business, Ming, it's politics. You have to outmaneuver your opposition."

"But that's what I'm doing," Ming said. "I'm pretending to have a relationship with Danny Xiao to buy time. I need to land a deal that will get the board off my back. If only the goddamned UN oversight committee—"

"And how is that going for you? I assume you know it was Xi who sparked that UN investigation. They knew you'd go for the low-hanging fruit and you walked right into their trap. You're acting like a pawn."

Ming turned away, staring into the faux-flames instead of Sying's harsh eyes.

"Think, Ming." Sying's feet touched the floor, and she leaned across the couch. Her face was only a few inches from her step-daughter's. "As long as you're associated with the Xiaos, why would anyone do a deal with you? If Qinlao merges with the Xiaos, they will have the upper hand. Even if you manage to hold on to power, it will only be after months of negotiation. What company wants to do business with the weaker party in a merger?" Her breath painted Ming's cheek. "You are acting like a pawn."

Ming gulped the last of her whiskey. The liquid burned all the way to her empty stomach. Her head felt light, her thoughts unconnected to her body. Everything Sying said made perfect sense.

"I have a plan." Sying's expression was still and composed. "But I need your help."

Ming placed her glass on the floor. "Tell me."

Sying set her own glass aside. "The damage with the Xiaos is done. Your aunt has what she wanted: a weakened CEO. Now, she can push her own agenda with the board. She doesn't have the votes to remove you, but she can limit your power and bleed your influence away slowly. Eventually, you'll be voted out. That's bad for the company and worse for you. For us." Sying gripped Ming's hand in both of hers. Her delicate fingers were warm and surprisingly strong. "You need a bold move. One that upends your aunt's plans, puts her back on her heels. A move worthy of a queen."

"What is it?" Ming asked, returning Sying's tight grip.

"You need to get married."

Ming pushed Sying away. "What?"

The older woman drew close again, her eyes intense. "Anything less will give the Xiaos an opening that leaves you in a position of weakness. You brought this on yourself. The moment you let Danny Xiao into your bed, you sealed your fate."

"I don't see how marriage helps me." Marry Danny Xiao? The thought of a lifetime with that vacuous clothes model...

Sying's laugh was hollow. "That's because you think of marriage as two people in love coming together. This is a business transaction, a contract between companies that also happen to be families. You can beat your aunt at her own game. You need Qinlao to become the largest manufacturing conglomerate in China—in the world. Bigger than the Xiaos, bigger than anyone."

Ming's thoughts whirled. "I'll never marry Danny Xiao," she said.

The doorbell rang.

"Who said anything about marrying Danny Xiao?"

Ming stared at her, confused again. "I don't understand."

Sying took her hand again. "Do you trust me, Ming?"

Ming found herself nodding. She did trust this woman, but why?

Sying was a queen. She chose her destiny and made it happen. This was true power, Ming realized. And she wanted it for herself.

Slipping on her shoes, Sying stood and straightened her robe. Ming could see the mask of social propriety slip back into place.

"That is JC Han at the door. The Han family is in financial trouble. They've overextended themselves, and some of their creditors are demanding they settle up. He would be open to a contract negotiation that would pair his son, Ken, with you."

The doorbell rang a second time.

Sying fluffed her hair about her shoulders. "I'm confident I can strike a bargain with the elder Han to allow us to keep control of the company following the merger. The Hans will run the Korean subsidiary, of course, for appearances' sake, but all the rest is ours."

She bowed to Ming. Not a mocking bow, but a respectful, kind gesture. "With your permission, Ming, I will negotiate that deal."

Jie Qinlao's firstborn child and heir apparent stood. The ache of obligation had lifted from her like a cloud. She'd watched this woman shed her emotional skin three times in the last hour. Which Sying was real?

"What is the son like?" Ming asked. "Ken."

Sying tilted her head. "What are they all like, Ming? Danny Xiao is typical. A rich playboy who wouldn't know work unless he was sleeping with her. These are not men like your father. Jie was a founder, he earned his way in the world. These next-gens ... they're lazy and self-indulgent."

"Like me?" Ming's cheeks burned. "I'm a next-gen."

Sying paused. She reached out to stroke Ming's cheek, her touch as gentle as a feather. Ming shivered. The stim and the whiskey together, she supposed.

"I know about your lover. Lily? She was willing to stay, willing to bear the pain of rehabilitation. You sent her back. Why? Because you don't love her anymore?"

Ming shook her head.

"Why, then?" Sying persisted.

The doorbell rang a third and fourth time in rapid succession.

Ming's eyes sought the fire, then the wall, the floor, until finally she was able to look at Sying. "She would have been used against me ... somehow, some way. I didn't want that."

"You didn't want her to suffer you mean?" Her eyes held Ming's, demanding truth.

Ming started to confirm that, then shook her head. "She made me weak."

Sying smiled then, and Ming's heart felt light.

"Exactly, Ming. That was the moment you chose to be a queen. That's why I'm helping you. Now, if you'll excuse me. I have a meeting—"

"Did you love my father?" Ming blurted out.

Sying paused, her eyes locking with Ming's. "It was never about love, Ming. It was business. Always business."

Ito appeared in the doorway. Sying nodded. "Show Mr. Han into my quarters, Ito. And make sure we have his brand of whiskey in the room."

"All right," Ming said. "Make the deal."

Her step-mother leaned in and kissed her on the lips.

"Then let me be the first to say *mazel tov*."

# 16

## ANTHONY TAULKE • SAN FRANCISCO, CALIFORNIA

Anthony flinched as the cosmeticist dug the needle deeper into his jaw muscle.

"Damn it, Alix, that hurts!"

Alarmed, the young man stepped back. "I'm sorry, Mr. Taulke. I must have touched a nerve. There should be no pain with the procedure." He was completely bald with pale, androgynous features, reminding Anthony of the sculpted flesh of a peeled potato. Firm, white, and glistening with the sheen of the damp-look makeup all the kids wore these days.

*God, I'm getting old*, Anthony thought. *Now I'm complaining about what the kids are wearing.*

Anthony leaned back in his chair, trying to relax. Clenching up only increased the likelihood of pain. "Just be careful."

Alix smiled with his perfectly shaped white teeth. He lifted a fresh, hair-thin needle from the tray. "Beauty has a cost, sir."

"Oh, I know exactly how much it costs, Alix. And part of what I'm paying for is a pain-free procedure. Let's see that I get my money's worth, okay?"

Alix's expression appeared painted on now. "Of course, Mr. Taulke." He slid another micro-needle into the meat of Anthony's jaw. Was that a spot of liquid warmth as the needle delivered its payload? Anthony couldn't tell.

After his forty-eighth birthday, he'd shifted to monthly micro-cosmetic touch-ups, avoiding the need for more drastic surgery later. That was the theory, anyway.

"That'll do it, Mr. Taulke," Alix said, his manner crisp. "Now, you know the drill. You need to stay in this position for at least forty-five minutes. Gravity is your friend, for once." The bald sculptor of skin tittered at his own joke, trailing his finger along Anthony's chin. "I worked on squaring your jawline today—it's getting a little saggy." He slipped his fingers into Anthony's curls. "The volume of your hair is still excellent, but I am seeing more gray. A touch at the temples looks distinguished, but too much up top and it fades you out, so I did some dermal toning on your scalp. A short nap would do you good as well, sir." His touch was light and a tad too sensual.

Now that his skin was no longer being invaded by needles, it was a lot easier for Anthony to relax. He should have scheduled a massage, but it was too late now if he needed to stay face up for most of the next hour.

He closed his eyes.

The young man's fingers withdrew, and Anthony heard the door close.

Sleep. If only. True sleep was rare these days. Most of the time Anthony needed pharmaceuticals to make it happen. He'd forgotten the stress that embarking on a new venture created, and the secrecy of the Vatican Project robbed him of his usual trick of basking in the public's adoration of his genius.

Viktor Erkennen was taxing his nerves as well. True, his smart bugs, as Anthony thought of them, had made the atmospheric seeding project viable, but his ability to scale the manufacturing process for the bio-nanites was well behind schedule. President Teller was demanding a planetwide rollout plan from Anthony, something he could present to the United Nations, and soon. But whenever Anthony pressed him, Viktor just laughed it off and promised him everything was fine.

And then there was H, still hacking his virtual and scheduling herself appointments whenever she wanted. Even more annoying, she'd made a game of it. She'd scheduled her last appointment for eleven at night under the name Mickey Mouse. Anthony hadn't shared his reservations about Viktor with H yet, but he was sure she'd show up and demand an update for Teller at the least convenient time possible.

Anthony's pulse rate was climbing, probably not helpful to his cosmetic treatment. His thoughts were running together, so a nap was completely out of the question. But he was trapped here, paralyzed for the sake of vanity, for at least another half an hour. He blinked on his retinal display and scanned the news.

He ignored the disaster porn. Another Cat 6 hurricane, a dust storm in Nevada, the daily status of Antarctica's sheering ice sheets... It all reminded him of work, and that's the last thing he wanted to think about right now. The political news wasn't much better. President Teller had won another flash poll, giving him the momentum to push his latest gun control proposal through Congress, which was sure to bury it in committee. No one was in the mood to give up their guns these days. Too many people moving in too many places.

Anthony settled on the tabloids, where a headline from *The Public Eye* caught his attention: *Qinlao Heir on Track to Wed Xiao Heir*. The story had all the trappings of a pure, paparazzi hit piece. The accompanying vid showed a slight young woman on the arm of a tall young man with a stylish, jutting haircut and wearing the latest in Asian fashion. Anthony recognized the man as Danny Xiao, heir to the Xiao manufacturing fortune, and a close confidant of Anthony's son, Tony.

The young woman struck him as different, somehow. She was the daughter of Jie Qinlao, whom he'd met once at an economic summit in Reykjavík. The Chinese manufacturing magnate had struck him as extremely capable, extraordinarily intelligent, and someone unafraid of hard work. Anthony vaguely remembered Qinlao's passing a few months earlier and an invite to the memorial service. If he recalled the situation correctly, the CEO of Qinlao Manufacturing had been killed by a rogue virus on a remote job site. QM's stock, of which Taulke Industries owned a couple hundred thousand shares, had taken a nosedive immediately following the death of its founder. Alert to any potential threat to his liquidity, Anthony had taken notice. He'd been relieved when the stock bounced back in short order, largely on the strength of the news that the young woman who'd caught his eye in the gossip column had taken the company's helm. Lately, the stock had begun to fluctuate again amid rumors of infighting among QM's board of directors.

Like everyone else, he'd expected Xi Qinlao would be named CEO following her brother's untimely death, a rumor Anthony suspected Xi herself had leaked. But Qinlao had named his eldest child his successor, and so far, she was holding her own in that position. Perhaps he should have gone to the memorial service after all. He might have gotten to know the daughter better. Despite her questionable taste in men, she struck Anthony as someone to watch closely.

He ran a quick search on Ming Qinlao in the company database and was surprised to see she'd gone to undergrad with Tony. But whereas his son had bailed after a bachelor's degree, Ming had continued on to a doctorate in electro-mechanical engineering. Earning that kind of advanced degree took some doing. Estranged from her father ... served for two years as a construction engineer on the UN lunar project ... solid credentials. Rumors of a long-term relationship left behind on the Moon when she returned to head Qinlao Manufacturing.

Staring at her beautiful, intense young face, Anthony judged her an impressive young woman, indeed. He read the headline again: *Qinlao Heir on Track to Wed Xiao Heir*. Surely she knew that if she merged with the Xiaos, she would lose control over her father's creation. QM would be absorbed by the larger manufacturing company and lose all control over its own future.

Stepping into the role of CEO after Jie Qinlao would be a daunting challenge for even an experienced business executive. But as a newcomer with no track record of business success, Ming would be under tremendous pressure to distinguish herself before the board. And knowing her aunt's frustrated expectations for power, Anthony knew there would be little leeway for trial and error.

He found himself nodding. Young Ms. Qinlao needed a win to stay in power...

The Vatican Project needed a manufacturing partner; one who was hungry and willing to work hard for success. Viktor was already having difficulties producing the nanites in quantity and they hadn't even started designing the delivery satellites yet. Maybe there was a play here for Anthony. President Teller would balk at bringing in another partner, but if he could advance the project's deployment schedule...

Excited now, he closed down his external feeds and called Tony. When he answered, Tony's hair was mashed against his head, his eyes bleary with sleep. Clearly, his son didn't suffer the same insomnia as Anthony. He heard bedclothes rustle and a woman giggling.

"Pop? What is it? I'm, uh, in the middle of something here." Another giggle.

Anthony did his best to hide his disgust as he compared his son to Ming Qinlao. It was eleven in the morning on a Tuesday, for God's sake.

Tony rolled his eyes. "Pop, what's the emergency?"

Anthony held back a sharp retort and tried to center his emotions. Stretching his face at the moment was probably a bad idea. "How well do you know Ming Qinlao?"

Tony screwed up his face. "Ming? We were at Stanford together in undergrad. Tight ass with a tight ass ... always studying ... goody-goody. Why?"

"I'll be in Hong Kong on Friday. I want you to set up a meeting for me."

"A meeting? Is this about your thing—"

"Just set up the meeting, Tony. Friday. Hong Kong. Peninsula Hotel for lunch."

"Oh-kay. Sure thing, Pop. I'll get on it just as soon as I take care of something here." There was a titter in the background as Tony winked at the screen.

Anthony cut the connection.

# 17

## MING QINLAO • SHANGHAI, CHINA

Ming stood in Marcus's office overlooking the yawning precipice. Outside, a crystal clear day etched every detail of the city in sunlight. A line of aircars crawled through the sky like shiny beetles, creating corresponding shadow bubbles that crept across the cityscape below.

She edged her toes out into open space, welcoming the familiar clench of vertigo in the pit of her stomach. Drawing a deep breath, Ming willed the feeling away. She was in control.

"Having second thoughts?"

Marcus approached, careful to keep his distance from the edge.

"Just getting some perspective." Ming replied, handing Marcus's words from their previous meeting back to him. The old man laughed. She offered him a smile while seeking out Sying and Ruben, who waited on the leather couch. Marcus had reskinned his office to show a forest, and Ruben watched a squirrel race up and down the gray-furrowed bark of an ancient English oak tree. Ming thought Marcus's Anglophilia oddly endearing in a Chinese man so traditional he preferred to write with an ink pen.

Sying sat with her legs crossed at the ankles, knees together and angled just so. Her dress was a royal blue skirt with matching jacket and silver buttons. She offered Ming and Marcus a demure expression appropriate for public consumption.

Sying's coaching had been no less profound than Ito's tutoring of Ming's martial skills when she was a little girl. As he had taught Ming the art of self-defense, Sying had become her new sensei in teaching her the subtleties of shadow maneuvers in business.

Her gaze swiveled to her own mother, and her positivity waned. Wenqian wore a sour look as green as her dress chosen for the occasion. Her demeanor had nothing to do with her disease. Since the scene with Lily at the woodland estate, Ming held Wenqian at arm's length, despite the guilt she felt. Wenqian wanted what was best for her daughter, this Ming knew. But what a mother wanted for her child and what Ming needed to succeed as CEO of Qinlao Manufacturing seemed two entirely different things. Today's pending ceremony and the polar opposite expressions on Sying's and Wenqian's faces proved that.

"It's a good match, Ming," Marcus said. "Brilliant, actually. It gives you the space you need from Xi to reset the business." He lowered his voice. "I won't ask how you found out about the Hans' financials."

Ming felt a frisson of delight shoot up her spine. From the way Sying slipped effortlessly from model wife to master plotter to how she navigated through the thicket of corporate-family relations, the woman was a wonder to Ming. She had so much to learn from Sying.

Turning back to the transparent box cantilevered from the building, Ming took another step over nothingness. She wasn't a fool or a child. She recognized the signs in herself.

Ming Qinlao was in love.

Marcus's head ticked as he received a pulsed message. "They're here."

JC Han led his wife Maya, son Ken, and their family lawyer into the room. Jong Chul was a solidly built man. The ruler-straight part in his oiled, iron-gray hair gleamed, and he wore a broad smile on his weathered features. He greeted Sying and Wenqian with formal bows, shook hands with Ruben, and kissed Ming on both cheeks. She embraced him, remembering his kindness to her at that first board meeting, when he'd made sure to tell her of her father's regard for her accomplishments. And he'd done so out of Xi's earshot. Her trust in Jong Chul's honorable character had convinced her of the wisdom of Sying's strategy.

Dressed in a severe pantsuit that looked more appropriate for a funeral than a wedding, Maya Han merely nodded stiffly at her. The woman's eyes were dark and full, with a flame flickering behind the black coal. Maybe her mother and Maya could find solidarity in their shared opposition to the marriage.

Ming crossed to Ken. He was a chubby kid, only a year older than Ruben, but was doing his best to mimic his father's formality. She took both his hands in hers. "I'm Ming. It's wonderful to meet you, Ken." His hands were clammy and trembled in her grip.

"You're so pretty," he whispered. Then, cheeks flushing with a schoolboy's embarrassment, Ken said the obviously rehearsed, "It is an honor to meet you, my future wife."

She smiled at the boy's earnest effort to impress in his role of corporate princeling. How this arrangement would be for Ken over the long term wasn't something she'd considered before. He was a few centimeters shorter than her, so she leaned down to whisper in his ear. "Don't worry, Ken. We'll be great friends." She deposited a gentle kiss on his cheek.

Maya Han's fiery gaze attempted to cook Ming where she stood.

"This way, please," Marcus said. He led them to the long table where contract screens lay side by side. Marcus manned one station, the Hans' lawyer the other. The details had been hammered out in advance. All that was left was this signing ceremony.

Ming and Ken took their places in front of each contract station. They even looked like a pair, she thought. Somehow Sying had found out what Ken Han would be wearing to the wedding and had designed Ming's complementary dress: a sleeveless sheath of pure creamy silk with a matching short jacket and pearls as accessories. Ken was outfitted in a dove-gray suit that made her dress glow beside it. When released to the newsfeeds, their wedding picture would be stunning.

*Just the thing to drive Auntie Xi crazy*, Ming thought with a secret smile to Sying. Her step-mother's eyes flashed in response. Ming's shoulders shivered under her gaze.

She took Ken's hand tenderly as they presented their biometrics to the screens and sealed the contract. Marcus nodded to the other lawyer as the funds transferred to the Han account.

"I now pronounce you man and wife," Marcus said.

Ming leaned down and kissed her new husband. His lips were soft, quivering, and he didn't close his eyes. His whole body seemed to shake.

"I have a present for you, Ken."

"For me?" His voice went up, delighted. He was an adorable child. A way to ensure Qinlao Manufacturing survived. They were nothing more to each other than guarantors of their respective company's fidelity to their deal. Ming wondered if that had been explained to Ken.

"For you." She passed him a square box tied with a white bow. He tugged the bow apart and lifted the lid. Inside was a badminton shuttlecock.

"You got me a shuttlecock? Thanks ... I guess."

Ming laughed. "No, silly, I got you a badminton team. You now own the Seoul Scorchers."

His eyes went round. "I *own* the Scorchers? Me?" He looked at his parents. Jong Chul smiled proudly. Maya's dubious expression tried to seem happy for her son.

"Yes, you," Ming said.

Ken's reaction was priceless and perfect. Another triumph for Sying, who'd chosen the gift. "A team of your very own. I know how much you like watching them play."

Ruben watched them, eyes shining with envy.

Jong Chul prodded his son. "Oh, yes, I have a gift for you too, Ming," the boy said, his rehearsed voice returning. He pulled a rectangular box from his jacket pocket. Ming opened it to find a wide bracelet made with hundreds of tiny diamonds and fitted with a platinum clasp.

"It's beautiful." Ming held out her wrist. "Would you put it on for me, Ken?"

The boy struggled with the clasp. Ming felt the flop sweat of his nervousness slide along her skin. At last he'd secured it, and she held it out for all to see.

Sying took her hand to inspect the bracelet. Ming's pulse raced at her feathery touch. "It's beautiful," her step-mother said.

The clock was ticking. Ming took a deep breath. "I'm sorry, everyone, but I have another meeting I cannot miss."

Maya Han gasped. "What do you mean another meeting? We have only just—"

But her husband placed his hand on her arm, and his wife went silent. "We understand, Daughter," he said, his new name for her carrying both humor and affection.

Ming kissed Ken on the cheek. "I'll see you soon, Ken. Enjoy the team." Her last image of the room was Sying's secret smile.

---

Ito waited for her at the aircar dock.

"Congratulations," he said with the exact inflection of a servant. His face was as unreadable as a slab of granite. Ming ignored his tone. Her old master simply didn't understand the rules of the new game she was playing.

"Thank you, Ito," she replied, playing her part in the necessary script. She settled into her seat and held out her wrist with the diamond bracelet. "My wedding present."

Ito nodded, then steered the car into the skylanes above the Qinlao building. The trip to their destination, the Dim Sum Delight restaurant, took only a few minutes.

"I may need you for this next meeting, Ito," Ming said as she stepped onto the restaurant's landing. She pulsed a message to Danny that she had arrived and received an immediate reply.

The Delight, Shanghai's most famous dim sum establishment, occupied a clear, rotating bubble ninety floors above the streets of the old city. The view was even better than the view from her own office. Ming climbed the stairs to the restaurant slowly, rehearsing the next few minutes.

Danny met her at the entrance, his smile wide, white, perfect. Dark shaggy hair hung playfully across one eye in the latest style, and he sported three new diamond studs in his left ear. He wore a short black silk jacket over a T-shirt with three diagonal slashes that revealed a peek at his perfect abs when he spread his arms. Tight black leggings completed the avant-garde ensemble. Danny could have graced the cover of any fashion magazine in the world—and frequently did.

And Ming was here to dump him. Publicly. Painfully.

He did an elaborate elevator eyes routine on her own outfit. "Whoa, were you at a wedding or something?" He laughed at his own joke. Ming smiled.

Danny had reserved a too-large table next to the convex window overlooking the city. The appetizer arrived as soon as they sat down. Ming sat quietly as he rattled on about something inane, as usual. She laid the linen napkin across her thighs and lifted a steaming shrimp roll into her mouth with ebony chopsticks. As the delicacy melted on her tongue, she realized she was famished. Ming took another and touched the corners of her lips with the napkin.

"Sake?" Danny held the ceramic bottle with both hands, the traditional way. She nodded and he filled her small cup, then his. He lifted the cup, staring at her across the rim. "A toast."

Ming raised her cup.

"To us," Danny said.

Ming returned his salute, then pulsed a message to Marcus.

*"Send the press release."*

The sake burned all the way down to her empty stomach.

It took one minute and forty-eight seconds for the news of her marriage to Ken Han to reach Danny Xiao. His dissection of the latest Paris fashion trend ceased at why wide belts were coming back, and the sake he'd been pouring slopped onto the lacquered table. Danny's eyes sought Ming's, then dropped to her white dress. He defocused to read his retinal display again.

"What have you done?" he demanded, harsh and low. Danny assessed the other diners in the restaurant with the fearful countenance of a trapped animal. He gazed around to see if anyone else had yet seen the news.

"You're married?" His voice was hoarse with heat, his face rigid. "To the Han boy!" Heads turned their way from a nearby table. Controlling himself again, he said, "He's what, sixteen?"

"Fifteen," Ming replied. "But his family is rich, and I get to keep my company." She explained her decision as if reporting on the weather. Part of her was enjoying this. That part of her that would never again have to endure his groping hands in her bed. Behind her, she heard a buzz ripple through the room like wind before a coming storm. Probing eyes sought out Danny. He twitched under the scrutiny, focusing on Ming.

"You fucking *bitch*."

Danny stood, flipping his hair out of his eyes. His perfect abs winked at her from the slashes in his t-shirt.

"I'll fucking ruin you and that shit company of yours. For this? I'll ruin your whole goddamned *family!*"

He'd clearly stopped caring who heard. Danny threw his napkin on the table and stalked away. The spilled sake seeped into the linen.

Conscious but careless of the other diners around her, Ming took another shrimp roll. She really was famished. Might as well grab a bite while waiting for the rest of the fallout.

Auntie Xi's first call came one minute and twenty seven seconds later. Ming rejected it. The other diners had returned to their own life dramas, though with occasional, furtive gazes thrown her way as she ate.

"More sake, ma'am?" asked a nervous waiter, a new ceramic decanter in hand.

Ming held up her cup. "Yes, please."

After calling three more times, her aunt pulsed, *"Answer my call, Ming. We can still salvage this, if we take action now."*

Ming finished the shrimp, ate a steamed bun with bean paste filling, and told the waiter to send the bill to Danny Xiao. And to be sure and give himself a healthy tip. When she walked back downstairs, she found an impassive Ito waiting by the aircar. As they ascended, Ming pulsed a message to Xi.

*"I'm in a meeting, Auntie. We'll talk tomorrow."*

"Where to, ma'am?" Ito asked with cold efficiency.

Ming studied the city. It really was a beautiful day. And only getting better by the minute.

"We're headed for a new opportunity, Ito."

Her bodyguard waited a moment. Then, when no clarification was forthcoming: "Could you be more specific?"

She laughed. Maybe Ito was beginning to thaw toward her again. Or maybe he was just being impertinent.

"Peninsula Hotel. Hong Kong."

The aircar arced skyward. Ming stared out the window at Shanghai, growing ever smaller below.

*Let's see what Anthony Taulke can do for me.*

# 18

## ANTHONY TAULKE • HONG KONG

Anthony loved how the Peninsula Hotel in Hong Kong reeked of history. The white-washed stone walls and broad French doors spoke of an earlier time, a colonial era of pith-helmeted British soldiers marching around in khaki shorts while elegant ladies sipped tea with their pinkie fingers raised to the heavens.

Once, in the late twenty-first century, the hotel management tried to erase their colonial past and make the Peninsula just another Hong Kong high-rise. Someone with a nose for branding had put a stop to that nonsense.

He sat at a table for two by the window overlooking the street. The churn of humanity flowed by on the sidewalk, appropriately separated from the hotel by a narrow strip of green grass and a wrought-iron fence. Soft violin music played in the background, and the white noise of nearby conversations soothed his senses. Tea appeared on the table alongside cucumber sandwiches, sans crusts of course. He nibbled one. Bland on bland. Maybe some things were best lost to history after all.

Anthony considered ordering himself a drink, then decided that would be rude before his guest arrived. But it was tempting. The Vatican Project was hemorrhaging money. Though financed entirely by Teller, even

Anthony was concerned at the rate the cash was flowing with nothing to show for it. The Kansas proof-of-concept test had depleted their store of nanite-boosted bacteria, and Viktor still insisted on maintaining absolute control of their development. At Erkennen Labs, they were still growing the structure in beakers! At this rate, it would take him a century to produce enough nanites to seed the Earth's atmosphere.

H, her green eyes flashing, had dismissed the demonstration as a minor victory. "You've proven you can manage a fart in a phone booth, Anthony. We need to see meaningful progress. We're running out of time."

Tony only laughed at his father's predicament. Laughed! He'd never invented anything in his entire entitled existence, and here he was, laughing at the man who'd put him in charge of the greatest implementation of technology in human history. Anthony regretted giving the Mars project to his son. Like everything else in his life, the boy hadn't had to work for it. He just had it handed to him.

There was a stir across the restaurant just as Anthony's virtual warned him Ming Qinlao was arriving. The maître d'hôtel fussed over someone. Heads turned. People whispered.

Anthony smiled to himself. Dr. Qinlao certainly knew how to make an entrance. She made a gracious gesture at the Peninsula's head man and weaved her way through the dining room with a light step. Her sleeveless, ivory sheath dress caught the mood lighting, showing off her toned, shapely arms. A single strand of pearls graced her throat, and a stunning diamond bracelet hung on her left wrist. When she caught his eye, her gaze became animated, as if she'd just heard a great joke she couldn't wait to share.

Anthony stood to greet her. Ming thrust out her hand first.

"Mr. Taulke, I'm Ming Qinlao." Her grip was firm, dry.

"Call me Anthony, please." He held her chair out for her, unable to avoid comparing this young woman to Tony. Her eyes swept the table, then met his gaze without hesitation.

"I realize it's a bit early," she said. "But I've had a hell of a day and could use a drink. Would you join me for a Jameson's?"

Anthony ordered two whiskeys, ice on the side. They made small talk of travel and weather and safe corporate topics until the drinks arrived.

"We're just getting to know one another," Anthony said, "but do you mind if I ask about your day?"

Ming tilted her head with a you-asked-for-it smile. She took a long sip of her drink. "I'm surprised your people haven't pushed the press release to you yet." She shrugged, then leaned over: "I got married, then dumped my boyfriend." A frown contorted her face. "Well, not my boyfriend, really. An arranged match that I was going along with for political reasons. I imagine American companies have less family drama in the boardroom than the Chinese do."

Anthony laughed, a half-amused sound drowned in bitterness. "You imagine wrong."

He put two fingers in the air aimed at the waiter, then scanned the newsfeeds for the marriage notice. Kenneth Han. Fifteen years old? And he'd been self-conscious about marrying a much-younger Louisa! This young lady had what it took to succeed, that much was obvious. If her engineering expertise was as good as her political prowess, Taulke Industries would be lucky to have Qinlao Manufacturing as a partner.

"You're staring, Anthony. I'm a married woman, you know."

Anthony made apologies, his cheeks betraying his embarrassment. This was one thing he actually coveted in Tony. His case with women.

"What do you think of my son?" he asked on impulse.

Ming's face softened and she sat back in her chair.

"Tony and I ran in different circles at university. I was surprised by his call for this meeting, actually, but pleased at the same time. To your question—he always struck me as a bit of a playboy, honestly. He's in charge of your Mars project now? I've read everything about it, Anthony. It's brilliant." She put her tumbler down. "Maybe I should slow down. I'm gushing, and this is your meeting." She crossed her arms. "How can I help you?"

For the first time in weeks, Anthony felt a stirring of hope, a lightening of the load he'd been carrying. This woman was exactly the kind of partner he needed. Direct, honest, purposeful, everything he'd been at her age. A kindred spirit, and if her day so far was an example, willing to do whatever it took to get the job done.

Anthony decided to trust her. "I need a manufacturing partner for a very sensitive project. A game- ... make that world-changing project."

Ming leaned in. "You have my undivided attention, Anthony."

He dropped a silver privacy disk on the table and pressed the center button. It pulsed a soft blue. "Just a precaution." He scanned the room, his thoughts flashing to H and her ability to hack his schedule. "You never know who's listening."

Even with the privacy zone in place, Anthony chose his words carefully. "I have a need to mass produce nanites, a proprietary design." He pulsed her a stripped-down schematic. Ming studied it in her retinal display.

"Without exact details, I can't say for sure, but we've had experience with this kind of micro-manufacturing. We have a patent on a self-assembly process technique that ... yes, I think it would work." She turned her shrewd gaze back to Anthony. "But you already knew that or I wouldn't be here. Can I ask what it's for? I see there's a recombination link to bacteria."

"Sorry, but that's classified."

Ming raised her eyebrows and nodded slowly. "How much do you need?"

Anthony leaned back in his chair. He knew he was taking a chance using a Chinese firm to manufacture the prototype, but if it worked, surely the president would want other countries involved in the project when they took it global. And as Viktor had pointed out when Anthony recruited him, they'd need China onboard to be successful. Whatever influence Ming had with the Chinese government might even make the president's wooing of the United Nations that much easier. He threw out the biggest quantity he could fathom needing for full implementation.

Ming's eyes unfocused again as she studied the schematic more closely. "I can put my people on it immediately—as soon as you give me the detailed design."

"How long?"

"For the first batch? We'll have to spin up the Shanghai facility around the new self-assembly process... A week, maybe less. We can scale quickly, if you approve the samples."

"I can pay an expedite fee, if that helps." Was he being too needy? If this woman's company could manufacture samples of the Erkennen nanite design in a week, the Vatican Project would be back on schedule in no time.

"I'll take the fee, of course," Ming said with a wink. "But I want something else from you." Her eyes narrowed as she studied his face.

"Name it," Anthony said.

"I want you to take a place on the board of Qinlao Manufacturing. I need allies, Mr. Taulke. People I can trust."

He blinked, reaching for his whiskey. Whatever he'd thought she might want, it hadn't been that. She looked amused as he drank.

"I'd be honored, Miss Qinlao—I mean, Mrs. ... I'm sorry, I don't know what your married name is, Ming."

She gave him a wolfish smile. "Qinlao, forever and always." The steel in her voice reminded him just what a formidable young woman he was doing business with.

Anthony inclined his head. "Of course." He touched his glass to hers and they finished their drinks together.

As she talked about her time on the Moon, he studied her closely. She was the perfect first recruit for an idea he'd been toying with for the last few weeks: creating an informal alliance of business leaders to manage this revitalized planet they were creating. It was clear to him the political structures were not getting the job done. The population of Earth was not being served well by its leaders.

Maybe it was time for some new leadership. Business leadership that showed the kind of success he was used to. A kind of Council with a capital C, composed only of the most forward-thinking business leaders of the time. He was saving the world, after all; he needed a posse to do it with.

He'd ask Viktor Erkennen too, of course.

Ming set down her glass. "The sooner I get the detailed plans, the sooner I can—ah. Great minds."

He'd pulsed her the full schematics of the nanite design, less the detail about the carbon-consuming bacteria. "I'll have my people draw up a formal contract between our two companies," he said.

"You're a trusting soul, Anthony. I would've had you sign the contract before sharing proprietary information." Her eyes began scanning the detailed specifications.

"I trust you, Ming." He'd just met her. Hardly knew her. But it was true.

She refocused on Anthony. "I feel the same way. It's like this partnership was meant to happen. For both of us."

Anthony smiled gently. "I couldn't agree more. Let's have one more drink. I want to talk to you about another idea I have."

# 19

## REMY CADE • EARTH ORBIT

Remy spent most of his time on the Observation Deck of the Temple of Cassandra space station. The term *days* lost meaning when circling the earth, but he found odd comfort in the repetitive nature of the station's orbit.

While he moped, Elise was engaged and happy, obviously a devotee of the New Earth cause.

Remy, on the other hand, was a man without a job. On a space station filled with other weather cultists, there was nothing and no one to protect her from.

She worked on him every day. That's how Remy thought of Elise's attempts to get him to join the Neos. And yet, he couldn't—or wouldn't —join her.

In retrospect, a fight was inevitable.

"I got you back your WorldNet access, Remy. What more do you want?" A line of frustration furrowed the space between her dark, shaped eyebrows.

"We need to get out of here. Go home." Weeks of imprisonment—sorry, being *hosted*, Brother Donald insisted on calling it—aboard the station had put him on edge.

She looked at him with an emotion somewhere between disgust and pity. "Go home? To what? With the New Earth movement, with Cassandra, I am literally saving the Earth. What could be more important than that?"

"But your father—"

"My father is a fossil who thinks in terms of quarterly profits in his little corner of the world. I am talking bigger, much bigger—the whole planet bigger. Doesn't that mean anything to you?"

Remy was silent. He stared at Earth revolving below them. Saving the planet ... now there was a worthy cause. Maybe he could even prevent more catastrophes like Vicksburg from happening. And they *would* happen. He'd seen the YourVoice story just this morning: Graves had declared Miami uninhabitable months ago, and FEMA was still relocating its population inland. Except for the part about joining a cult, Elise made a good point. Someone had to do something.

She sidled up to him, placed her head on his shoulder. Together they gazed down on Earth. "It's okay, Remy. You can go. I'll be fine." She'd squeezed his hand and walked away, leaving him to his thoughts.

But he couldn't go. He told himself he was just doing his job, protecting her from these crazy Neos. He had been contracted by her family to protect Elise, and he was not one to break a contract. They'd brainwashed her, he told himself. She needed him.

But that wasn't it, either. He'd never seen a more orderly, respectful bunch, and they seemed to damned-near revere her. She was safe here at the Temple, of that he had no doubt.

The trouble with having too much time on his hands was thinking. Elise had been smart about restoring his WorldNet access. He'd gotten to see how her disappearance was playing out back home—and it wasn't good.

Remy Cade, former Army grunt discharged under the black cloud of the Vicksburg massacre, had wormed his way into the Kisaans' sphere, apparently intent on kidnapping their daughter. They blamed him!

Conspiracy theorists only fanned the flames. Investigative reporters wrote dark stories of how Remy Cade had become infatuated with Elise Kisaan. They even had vids, real footage of him and Elise together, appearing too familiar for his role as her bodyguard. Her apparent affection for Remy in the vids? Stockholm syndrome, of course. Hell, they even had *him* half-believing he'd kidnapped Elise.

The Kisaan family was publicly distraught and frequently in front of the cameras, blaming Remy Cade and the US government for Elise's disappearance. They offered a reward, they hired investigators, they promised revenge. Blackfish Security, his former employer, put out a statement denouncing Remy and issuing a public apology alongside a promise to bring him to justice.

Remy absorbed it all with growing panic. In theory, he could reach out, set the record straight. Give his version of what had happened in Alaska, though there were no vids to exonerate him. The only footage the media still possessed showed dead caribou, military men shooting, and the dead reporter in the clearing. Nothing of him carrying Elise to safety, of Rico's shooting him.

Who would believe him? The court of public opinion had already convicted him. No one was standing up and saying, "That's not the Remy Cade I know."

Elise was happy here, happier than he'd ever seen her. Remy was the first to admit that he didn't understand it, but it was real.

So he moped for days in the observation lounge, staring down at the planet. In the middle of one of his darker moods, he sensed General Roman Hattan approaching. They'd conversed once or twice over chow, the older officer never once asking him about Vicksburg. That alone rocketed him up Remy's likability scale. The man was crusty, a welcome relief from Brother Donald's placid demeanor.

"Saddle up, kid. Need your help." The general's voice made it clear he was drafting Remy, not asking for a volunteer.

Remy stood, tearing his eyes from the vista below. "Where to, sir?" The sign of respect was automatic. Hattan seemed not to notice and nodded toward the window.

"We're taking a field trip. You promise to behave?"

The eight-man corporate shuttle held only him, Hattan, and the pilot. It was corporate model, with leather trimmed seats and a bar in the back. Remy watched with interest as the shuttle undocked and they entered Earth orbit. In constant communication with someone planetside, the pilot used what sounded like commercial call signs.

Hiding in plain sight.

Remy twisted in his chair to get a look at the space station dropping away behind them. It looked like all the other large stations in orbit, just another corporate home-away-from-home in the Earth Orbital Network. But there was no company logo as far as he could see; certainly nothing identifying it as the Temple of Cassandra.

"If you pay your taxes, no one asks questions," Hattan said. Remy wasn't sure if the general thought that was a good thing or not.

"So Cassandra ... is a corporation?"

Hattan shrugged. "In a manner of speaking. There are shell companies, lawyers, all that sort of thing. Not my area of expertise."

"Financial camouflage," Remy said.

Hattan regarded him with an amused expression. "You're catching on, Cade."

"So, what *is* your area of expertise, General?"

Hattan stared at the approaching Earth. "I play offense." He turned to look out the window and said nothing more.

The shuttle entered a commercial orbital traffic pattern. They zipped by the Taulke space elevator, the station on the end of a tether looking like a weight on a string, then banked north. Remy could see the tiniest bit of polar ice, then the sweep of green and brown—Siberia?

They dropped out of orbit, leveling off in a high-altitude lane for a cooldown burn, then slowly ingressed into an airliner route over the Pacific Ocean. Remy thought he recognized Vancouver before they descended into clouds. When they emerged again, he could see a steep mountain range, and the sky around them was empty of other aircraft.

The pilot peeled off his headset, then dropped to an altitude below the highest peaks. They flitted in and out of sunshine as they weaved into the mountains.

After the distant vistas of space, Remy reveled in the visual texture of the rugged mountains. It only took being away from Earth for a little while to make you appreciate its beauty close up. Brown and rocky, only the very tallest peaks were touched with white, and most of those were shrouded in clouds. Repositioning the map in his mind around Vancouver, Remy figured they were deep in the Canadian Rockies, maybe Alberta.

The pilot slowed them down, aiming the shuttle straight at a mountain-side. Remy watched the sheer cliff grow large in the forward windshield. He glanced at Hattan, who appeared unconcerned. The shuttle came face to face with the rock face, then passed through sheer rock and into a huge cavern.

"Pretty realistic, huh?" Hattan grinned at him, obviously enjoying Remy's nerves. "Holographic camouflage."

The ship settled to the cave's rocky floor. "It's a larger version of holographic skinning technology," Hattan continued. "Like what the corporate types use to decorate their offices with waterfalls and mountain views."

Hattan unclipped his harness and swung to his feet. "Ready for the grand tour? We call this place Mount Doom, but the official name is Assault Base 7."

"Assault base?" Remy asked.

"Like I said before, I play offense. You'll see." As they exited the shuttle, the general returned a salute from a young man in a generic gray-green paramilitary battle-dress uniform. The only insignia was the Cassandra logo on his right shoulder. "We'll walk, Sergeant," he said to the young soldier.

Remy matched the general's brisk pace across the stone floor, their boots echoing in the open space.

"Most of this cavern was here when we found the place," Hattan said, his arm arcing over his head. "We carved out the rest. We use this level as a launch area. The hangars are below us." He stepped onto a vast, metal-plated, automated walkway, his footsteps ringing. As they descended to the hangar level, what Remy saw left him speechless. Dozens of troop carriers, fighters, heavy-lift airbuses, even tanks—all with the insignia of Cassandra painted on them.

He recognized the models. These were US military-grade weapons, current models. As the walkway ended, Hattan resumed his march. They passed through the hangar and into an armory. Rows and rows of assault weapons, missiles, ammunition.

"Where did all this come from?"

Hattan gave him a knowing glance. "Same place the military gets theirs. Remember those shell companies I mentioned? We have an arrangement with defense contractors."

An arrangement. Remy's mind reeled at the arrangement that could arm a fringe cult like the Neos. As they continued the tour, something struck him. Not all the craft were American manufactured. There were Chinese Chengdu J-42s, the latest in stealth fighter technology from the People's Republic. Russian BTR-129 troop carriers. Israeli Watcher observation drones that could spot the heat signature of a mouse from orbit.

Remy realized he'd stopped walking. He stood gawking instead.

"How'd you get this equipment across international borders without being spotted?"

Hattan turned around. "You recognize some of them as stealth craft, right?"

"Yeah."

"Answers your question, doesn't it?"

Remy reddened.

"If we couldn't fly it in, we brought it through smaller shipping yards, the ones without advanced scanning tech," Hattan said. "Label a container something unpleasant with a digital signature, and the human inspectors at the smaller facilities are less likely to randomly inspect it." He paused. "It's a lot to take in, I know, Cade. Come on, there's more."

Remy raced to catch up. "Where are all the personnel?" This was a whole lot of high-tech equipment for the dozen or so people he'd seen since they'd landed.

Hattan laughed. "In training, of course."

"Training? Where? You can't just fly a bunch of fighters around without attracting a lot of attention."

"Oh, they're getting the best training in the world," Hattan said, smiling. "All over the world. Canadian military, US military, private security. Mossad, Russian spetsnaz, you name it. We have people everywhere."

Hattan's expression became a mysterious grin. "Are you beginning to see the breadth of our movement now?"

He certainly was. This was no fringe cult with monks running around a single space station. This was a worldwide movement. A well-armed, worldwide *military* movement.

Remy had heard the conspiracy theories about a subculture of military men and women who'd taken a secret oath to a higher cause than their own country. He'd dismissed it as bunk, the modern equivalent of rural militias two centuries earlier. Myth fed by people's desperation to believe some greater power would reach down and save them from global catastrophe with the help of Robin Hood and his Merry Men. But with what he saw here...

"But, who will you fight?" Remy said. "I mean who's your enemy?"

Hattan shrugged. "To be determined. Whoever gets in our way. Look at it this way, son. The world order will not change on its own. It'll need to be overthrown, remade. 'People of the world unite; you have nothing to lose but your chains.'"

"Who said that?"

"Marx. *Communist Manifesto.*"

Remy almost laughed out loud. "So you're a communist?"

Hattan's eyes narrowed to slits. "The Neos are not about politics, Remy. We're realists. Humans have failed to take responsibility for the safekeeping of our home. I—*we*—are here to change that."

Remy glanced around. Enough firepower surrounded him to start a decent-sized war.

"Seven," Remy said. "You said this was Assault Base 7. How many bases like this are out there?"

"Twelve," Hattan said with pride. "Spread around the globe, armed and staffed with hundreds of thousands of loyal followers of Cassandra. Waiting for the call the arms."

The call to arms? The followers of Cassandra were disturbing enough when Remy had merely thought of them as a cult. Now...

Hattan stepped aside as an enlisted man approached. He nodded, then turned back to Remy. "Here's the deal, Remy. I can always use a good soldier and I've checked you out. You're the real deal. But I can't afford to have any loose operators in my outfit.

"It's time for you to make a decision. Elise thought bringing you here might help. It's against my better judgment, but if you want out, I'm under orders to provide you with enough food and gear to make it back to civilization. You can start a new life, somewhere where people don't ask a lot of questions, where you won't be recognized. That's our only requirement."

Remy's mind was spinning. His vision of an upstart cult had been shattered by what he'd seen in this stronghold full of the latest warfare tech. If it were up to him, Hattan's eyes seemed to say, Remy had a choice to join up or get a bullet in the back of the head.

"What about Elise?" he asked.

Hattan cleared his throat. "Elise Kisaan has made her choice, Remy. Now, you make yours. My shuttle leaves in an hour. If you're on board, I expect you to be a contributing member of my team." He spun on his heel and strode away with the enlisted man in tow.

Remy watched the two men walk back through the hangar, waited until their footsteps died away. They were offering to let him go, free and clear. Every nerve in his body screamed at him to get as far away from this crazy cult as possible.

And what about Elise? Could he leave her? What happened when she woke up from this insane dream and found out he'd abandoned her? Those were his choices: stay with Elise or leave her behind.

He placed his hand on the dark skin of a Chengdu J-42 fighter, all angles and sharp edges to confuse radar. The shield of Cassandra loomed over him on the cavern wall.

Whatever happened, he knew one thing. Elise needed him now more than ever.

Remy squared his shoulders and traced his steps back to Hattan's shuttle.

# 20

## ANTHONY TAULKE • NEW YORK, NEW YORK

Another sip of coffee, another grimace. Anthony set the cup aside. How was it possible to have a suite in one of the most exclusive hotels in New York and get served coffee this bad? Feeling stir crazy, he paced to the window.

H, sprawled on the couch with one foot on the coffee table, watched him. "Nervous much?" Her green eyes looked black through the glare of her data glasses.

"Are you sure he read my notes for the speech?" Anthony asked. The sun was shining down into the canyons formed by the arching architecture lining New York's city streets. The pedestrians below seemed to radiate life in the reflected light. It looked like a pleasant summer day from up here.

"He read your notes. Just relax. These are politicians, not scientists. The goal of today is to dazzle, get the public behind us so we can move to the next phase." She sounded bored with it all.

"I'm going for a walk."

"No, you're not."

His anger flared. "You can't tell me—"

H shifted her data screen to the wall of the suite. It showed President Teller mounting the steps to the speaker podium in front of the UN Security Council. He was ready for high-def. His dark skin glowed, and his hair was dusted with the perfect touch of distinguished gray at the temples. The heavy shoulder pads on his dark suit gave his upper body more heft and framed the red power tie. Teller acknowledged the applause with a stern nod of determination.

The first part of the speech was standard stuff: thank you's and general ass-kissing of the electorate, which in this case included the entire world community. Anthony realized he was tapping his foot and stilled his nervous action with a self-conscious glance at H. She couldn't suppress a mocking grin.

"Today, I am announcing a world-changing project." Teller's voice echoed across the UN General Assembly chamber. "We use that term loosely some days, but not today. For the past century, we have struggled with our planet's changing climate."

Anthony fretted when the president launched into a sidebar about climate change history and the bio-seeding results from Anthony's failed project two decades prior.

He blinked on his retinal display and tracked the president's flash-polling. An impressive upswing. That should make Teller happy.

"Here we go," H said.

Teller delivered a steely glare at the camera. "Today, I am introducing UN General Council Resolution 9875, a proposal to build a planetwide network of bio-seeding satellites. This effort, under the leadership of the United States, will solve our climate change problem once and for all." A smattering of halting applause swelled into a wave of enthusiasm. A few of the delegates even raised their voices in approval. The president smiled as he waved his hand modestly for silence.

Anthony switched back to his own retinal screen to watch Teller's numbers soar higher. He stared in disbelief. The president's flash-polling numbers weren't rising. They were falling.

"What the hell?" H was on her feet. "The Chinese just announced they won't support it. Neither will Russia. How could they react so quickly, without even knowing the details?" She advanced on Anthony. "Who did you tell?"

"No one." But he immediately thought of Viktor and Ming. Was it just coincidence that the home nations of his two partners were rejecting Teller's initiative? Could they have leaked the news? Doing so put everything at risk—as Teller's falling polling numbers clearly demonstrated.

H stormed back and forth across the room, her dark bob bouncing with each step.

"The Russians claim they need more time to study the results of our pilot test. How the fuck do they even know we did one?" Fuming, H's eyes flitted between Anthony, Teller's image on the wall, and the readout on her data glasses. "China says the move is irresponsible. Damn it! The Brits are out, too?" She ripped the glasses off her face, threw them across the room. "The boss is gonna be pissed, Anthony. This is killing his poll numbers. And the election is only a few months away!"

On the screen, Teller's speech had begun to falter. He'd been fed flash-polling results through his implant, Anthony guessed. That explained his backpedaling. "The United States will introduce this resolution in the very near future. My purpose here today was to make the world aware that we have a solution to our ever-growing climate crisis. Thank you."

The applause in the chamber was real, but the political sniping outside the UN had already escalated into a full-scale verbal assault. Teller's face as he exited the United Nations building was a grim, toothy mask of fury.

---

In person, President Teller made no attempt to smile away his anger. His dark eyes flashed as he entered the hotel suite. He dismissed his security team and ripped the red tie away from his neck. "How bad is it?"

H cleared her throat. "You dropped, sir." She shifted her feet, and Anthony realized this was the first time he'd seen this woman not in complete control of a situation. Her lack of attitude in this moment of crisis unnerved him.

"'You dropped, sir,'" Teller mimicked in a nasal, feminine voice. "How much?"

"Six points."

"Shit! That hurts. What are the trend lines saying?"

"Too soon to tell, sir," H said in a careful tone. Anthony suspected it wasn't too soon at all but that she'd thought it best to portion out the bad news.

Another curse. Teller wheeled on Anthony. "You need to get me out of this hole, Taulke. I have less than three months until the election, and this UN resolution was supposed to be the crowning event of my first term. Now, it's a shit sundae."

Anthony stared at him. The calm, visionary leader of the free world who'd recruited him in a cabin overlooking Los Alamos had been replaced by a craven politician willing to trade his planet for a reelection bid.

"Taulke! I'm talking to you!" Teller's skin took on an angry red undertone.

"Anthony," H intervened, "there's one sure way out of his mess for the president. We have to deploy your bio-seeding nanites. No one argues with success, right? All we need to do is—"

"Without a UN resolution?" Teller's voice was incredulous.

"Maybe we could do a limited deployment?" said H. Her voice was tremulous, and again Anthony felt a surge of prickling fear at her timidity. The more she talked, the less sure of anything he felt.

Anthony closed his eyes and held up a hand. Turning to face the president, he said, "Sir, I—we—need satellites to do the bio-seeding deployment properly."

"You didn't need satellites for your demonstration," the president said. In that moment, Anthony realized Teller hadn't read any of his briefing notes.

"We used a plane. But that was tens of square miles. There's not enough high-altitude aircraft in the world to make that happen."

"What about doing just the United States? What Helena suggested."

Anthony shook his head. "Sir, our biosphere doesn't stop at the border. With geoengineering at this level, we could cause catastrophic consequences. There's no modeling for—"

"Get your people here," the president shouted at him, flecks of spittle dusting Anthony's face. "Right now."

"Sir, I don't—"

H stepped between them. "Do it," she whispered. "There has to be another way, Anthony."

Ming and Viktor entered the president's suite together, as unlikely a pair as Anthony could have imagined. Ming wore an elegant crimson business suit, her hair swept back into a bun, while Viktor, as usual, looked as if he'd slept in his clothes.

Anthony was relieved to find the president had used their transit time to calm himself. Teller greeted Ming and Viktor with his usual polished grace and broad smile. He offered them coffee and poured himself a cup. Anthony declined.

"I'd like to thank all of you for your fine work so far," Teller said when they were seated around the coffee table. He offered a self-deprecating smile. "No doubt you've had a chance to hear how my UN proposal went this morning. Someone is trying to undermine me—us, I mean. I'll get to the bottom of that on my own, but we can't let this temporary setback slow our real progress." He paused to sample his coffee and made a face. Teller turned to H. "This coffee is atrocious, Helena. Get us something better immediately."

H nodded and sub-vocalized instructions to absent staff.

Teller leaned forward, elbows on knees. "We need a new strategy. It's not good enough to ask permission from the international community, I need to show them success so that they rally behind me—us, I mean. And I don't just mean lines on a graph. I need to show real results in the real world. But to do that we need to manufacture and deliver this bio-seed into our atmosphere on a planetary scale." He slapped his knees. "I need solutions."

It sounded like H had been talking to him, Anthony decided. Maybe Teller was willing to take the chance of global deployment, sans global endorsement, after all.

"Satellites are the best way to do it, sir," he said.

"I'm not looking for the best way, Taulke." The president's earlier anger shown through but was quickly replaced by contriteness. "Apologies, folks. It's been a long day."

Erkennen blew out a breath that was half a laugh. Ming remained impassive, but her expression was open.

"We need to move quickly," H said. "If we take too long to ramp this thing up, there are forces that will shut us down."

"Forces?" Ming said.

Teller nodded. "Ask Anthony. He's been through this before. There are profits to be made as long as the climate war rages. It's a sad truth, but it's a truth all the same. We saw a flash of that power today. Someone..." The president flashed a look at H, who shrugged. "Someone leaked the speech. Hell, maybe even the specs for the bio-seeding project. The Chinese and the Russians were announcing a no vote before I even announced what the project was."

"What are you suggesting, Mr. President?" Viktor Erkennen's tone had lost its easy humor. He drew up, and even in a dumpy suit, the Russian scientist looked ready to defend his honor.

"The president meant no disrespect, Doctor," H said, placing fingertips on the old man's knee. "Even the British chimed in."

"Right! Even the British!" Teller was becoming animated again. "And H is right. Dr. Erkennen, Miss Qinlao—pardon me, *Doctor* Qinlao. I meant no disrespect. But someone let the cat out of the bag!"

Silence reigned around the table. Anthony suspected they were each considering who might have betrayed the Vatican Project. Viktor's face was still flushed, but Ming looked pensive.

A knock at the door broke the tension. H received the service cart, then poured them all fresh cups of coffee without asking. Anthony took a tentative sip. Much better than the dreck he'd drunk earlier.

"I have an idea," Viktor said finally.

Teller smiled. "Well, let's hear it."

"Missiles," Viktor said. "We use missiles to disperse the bacteria."

"You mean surface-to-air missiles?" Teller asked.

"No." Viktor's jowls wobbled as he shook his head. "I mean intercontinental ballistic missiles."

H choked on her coffee. Viktor seemed not to notice.

"Take off the nuclear warheads," he continued, "and put on a bio-seeding warhead with shaped charges to aid dispersal."

"Mr. President," H said, coughing, "I don't think—"

"Is it possible?" Teller asked. His gaze swung around the room.

Anthony looked at Ming, who gave him a tiny, reluctant nod. "It's possible, sir, but could you really launch a bunch of missiles? I mean, wouldn't it cause some kind of international incident?"

"That's what the speech is for," Teller said, smiling broadly. He was in his element now.

"Speech, sir?" H's voice was barely a whisper.

"Yes, speech! I'll make sure the world knows what we're doing and why we're doing it. We'll leak stories between now and zero hour. The nuclear powers' intelligence services will pick them up. We'll have them primed for the fireworks show before we ever light them off."

"Those fireworks could destroy the planet, Mr. President," Anthony said. "Or cause an international incident at the very least."

Teller leaped to his feet and began pacing. "That's exactly what I want, Taulke. An international incident." He shot a gleeful look at H. "I like it. We turn swords into plowshares to save the planet. The ad copy practically writes itself." He projected his arms into the air as if holding a vidscreen between them. "Teller Tills the New Earth."

H didn't look convinced. She reached out and took the carafe of coffee. It tittered against the lip of her cup as she poured.

Her boss, on the other hand, was on a roll. "Taulke, we'll give you and your team access to one of our submarines—the latest and greatest. I want to be able to move this platform and hide it if I need to. Put the Army disaster colonel in charge—YourVoice's ratings go through the roof whenever his housewife-sexy stubble's in front of the camera. He'll be the face of this. What's his name again?"

H cleared her throat. "Graves, sir."

"Yeah, put Graves in charge."

Anthony grimaced. If only the man's name was anything other than Graves.

# 21

## WILLIAM GRAVES • BANGOR, WASHINGTON

Graves had been a soldier all his life. Duty, honor, country—the principles drilled into his head from his earliest days at West Point—had formed the foundation of his character. A marriage that hadn't panned out. No kids—that he knew of, as the old joke went. The only constant in his life had been the Army.

But somewhere along the way, the rules of the game changed. And no one bothered to tell him.

From his office perched above the massive covered drydock, Graves surveyed the five-hundred-foot, sleek shape of the ballistic missile submarine and wondered what in the holy hell had happened to his life. All thirty-six missile hatches, each as wide as a hot tub, were open. From this perspective, the massive war machine looked like a giant's toy.

*We will turn our swords of war into plowshares for peace.* That's what President Teller had said when he called Graves personally to offer him this job. It was a great political line, but was it even possible? Forget the risk of starting a nuclear war, were the logistics of what he'd been read in on even possible?

Another modified ICBM, suspended by a crane, hovered over the submarine, then slowly lowered into the launch tube. Workers—some in Navy uniforms, some in the red jumpsuits of Qinlao Manufacturing, and a few yellow-suited Taulke employees—swarmed the sub. It had been like this for the last six weeks, day and night. Around-the-clock crews brewing the bacteria, as he'd come to think of the process. Repurposing the missiles. Prepping the sub. Never a wasted moment.

Communicated by the ever-present, elfin-eared woman called H, President Teller's sense of urgency permeated the project. From the moment Graves had stepped aboard as the officer in charge, she had slashed red tape and torpedoed bureaucracy. The ICBMs had been stripped of their nuclear warheads and delivered to a Qinlao building adjacent to the drydock where the Chinese company mated them with pre-manufactured bio-seeding warheads—correction: dispersal units. Graves had been reprimanded more than once by H to ensure he used "science-sensitive language," when he spoke about the project, even if all communication was still private. The USS *Independence* was no longer a war machine, she said. It was a vessel of global salvation.

But Graves was a warrior, and old habits die hard. In his mind, a war on climate change was still a war—and one he was still willing to fight. As the project progressed, he'd come to believe in Taulke's crazy idea. At some point, Graves decided it might just work.

Maybe this was mankind's best shot. He'd seen enough Phoenixes. Enough Miamis. One too many Vicksburgs. Mother Nature was winning, and it was time to change the game.

That day in Kansas, seeing the results of Taulke's bio-seeding test, had planted the seed in Graves's mind. When he was honest with himself, a part of him needed this solution to work if only to avoid his going mad from the hopelessness of fighting a never-ending, losing war.

Those stakes were the very reason he felt rushed by political expediency. Graves turned to face H, who lounged in an office chair, eyes glued to her data glasses.

"We won't be ready," Graves said. "I need at least another ten days."

The data glasses came off, revealing dark circles under the woman's eyes. "We don't have ten days, Colonel. We have three days. And you will be finished in the next three days."

Graves shook his head. "We'll have all the modified missiles on board, but we won't have the targeting system finished and we don't have launch protocols worked out with Washington yet." He sat down behind his desk. His leg muscles ached, and he could use a quick nap to stay focused.

"You can take care of all those details at sea," she replied.

"We need more time. I'll call the president myself if I have to."

H hauled herself upright and put both hands on his desk. "Colonel, the wolves are at the door in Washington. Congress is starting investigations and talking about a bill to stop the project. Our only advantage is speed. If we can get the sub to sea, we can hide behind military operational security —the military is with us. Being on the front line, they want to see us do something about this problem, as you well know. We need to be ready to go in three days." She sat down again, clearly exhausted. "After that ... who knows?"

⸻⸻

### Ming Qinlao • Shanghai, China

Ming sat on the sofa in her home office, mesmerized by the newsfeeds, her knees pulled up under her chin. Every channel had a different take on the same headline: *US Submarine Puts to Sea Amid Worldwide Resistance, Protests, Hope*.

She turned off her YourVoice feed. The WorldNet was melting down with clashing cyber arguments about the End of the World.

Ming shivered in her thin nightdress. Whatever happened next, they'd done it: she, Anthony, and Viktor. The submarine *Independence*, armed with thirty-six bio-seeding warheads manufactured by Qinlao, was operational. Anthony had told her that once the *Independence* submerged in the open ocean, it would be almost impossible to find. If she could just get to sea...

Teller had been true to his word. He'd worked the back channels to all the nuclear-capable powers and had received assurances—after sharing results from the Kansas test—that the powers of the world would not see the United States' launching missiles from the *Independence* as provocative. Though loud protests were lodged through the UN, it seemed no one was willing to go to war over what many hoped to be the genuine solution to their shared, worldwide problem.

The waters around the ship were gun-metal gray and topped with whitecaps driven by a fitful wind. From a distance, the submarine was a small, dark shape in the water, hardly threatening at all. Most of the vessel lay hidden below the waterline. It churned a broad, white wake, stark against the dark sea and the darker hull.

Only when the Coast Guard cutters came into view could she get a better sense of perspective on the size of the massive vessel. There were three smaller boats around the sub now. Two on the near side, one partially hidden behind the submarine's sail that jutted out of the water like a metal cliff.

When the ships approached, she watched the tiny people on the flying bridge descend into the safety of the submarine's interior. It was safer that way, she figured. With all the hatches shut and the sub at speed, the Coast Guard seemed to hesitate, at a loss for what to do next. They couldn't board the *Independence*, and short of blocking the sub's path with another vessel the size of a cargo ship, there was nothing to slow her passage to sea.

Sying entered the room, her open robe showing a long, semi-transparent nightgown. Her fingers danced across the back of Ming's neck. "Come back to bed. It'll be hours before anything happens."

Ming's retinal display pulsed: Anthony. She pulled away from Sying's touch and slung the feed to the wall screen. Sying perched on the back of the couch.

"Anthony, I'm seeing the newsfeeds of the *Independence*. What's going on?"

Her business partner had a twisted smile on his face, half-exultant, half-fearful. His son, Tony, hovered in the background. His expression was less sanguine.

"We did it, Ming. The ship is headed out to sea. Once they make open water and submerge, we're home free. The president is going to make an announcement as soon as they leave the sound."

"What about the final trajectories and the dispersal testing?" Ming said. "Can we still test all that if they're underwater?"

"You go to war with the army you have, not the army you want," Anthony replied.

"I'll assume that's an American saying."

"It means—"

"I know what it means, Anthony." Her company's involvement with the American project had been a closely held secret. How would China's political class react? How would her board react? If the Vatican Project failed, Xi would have all the ammunition she needed to take Ming down. "We won't get a second chance at this."

Anthony cracked his neck. "Or a third, in my case."

Ming had to laugh a little at that. She was so nervous, it was either laugh or cry. Not too long ago, the entire endeavor had been a secret engineering project. Now, the whole world was watching. Success would vault Qinlao to the apex of global manufacturing companies: the one percent of the one percent. But failure would have devastating downsides. For everyone. Everywhere.

"We agreed that more testing—" she began.

"It's out of my hands, Ming. This is a political decision. It *will* work, I know it. And if not, then we get Viktor to trigger the kill switch."

Ming reached for Sying's hand. "Isn't that what they said about the *Titanic*?"

At that moment, Viktor joined the call. It looked as if Anthony had rousted the Russian out of bed. His appearance was even more disheveled than normal, his round face puffy with sleep.

"No *Titanic*!" he boomed. Then, stifling a yawn, "Enough with the negativity, Ming."

"Good morning, Viktor," Anthony sang out. "It's time to change the world, my friend." He filled in the Russian on the sudden change in plans. The older man's face came to life in a giddy smile.

"This is wonderful news," he said in his heavy accent. "I have good news to share as well. In the latest manufacturing process, I upgraded the nanite controls. Even if the dispersal is not perfect, we will have the ability to modify the bio-cloud in situ. Last minute change, but very useful to us now."

"You still have a kill-switch, right?" Ming asked. As an engineer, she hated last-minute changes. Humans made last-minute changes. Humans made errors.

Viktor nodded. "Absolutely. Unbreakable quantum crypto, the best in the world. There are only two keys in existence. This is one." He held up a slim silver suitcase.

"Where's the other one?" Anthony asked.

Viktor smiled slyly. "Someplace where no one will ever find it."

Cryptic answers like that one only encouraged Ming's nervousness. She made her goodbyes politely but quickly and ended the call.

Sying slid her arms around her. "You're cold," she whispered. "Come back to bed."

Ming allowed herself to fall back into the warmth of her lover's embrace, but the chill stayed with her.

The whole world was watching.

---

### Anthony Taulke • San Francisco, California

After the call, Anthony stretched his arms over his head. It was good to be home. Good to see the sun again after weeks of dreary Seattle and the smelly shipyard.

He peered over San Francisco Bay from his private office. Not a cloud in sight. Just the way he liked it. A positive portent of things to come, perhaps.

He drew another breath of pure, air-conditioned atmosphere. That Seattle shipyard had been like something from another age. Anthony expected modern war machines to be sleek, futuristic, laden with cutting-edge technology. The engineer in him looked forward to the chance to see the submarine up close. What he'd found were welded seams and painted metal, ancient technology better suited for the twenty-first century. And the smell! Everywhere, the dank scent of rotting seaweed and industrial grease with a steady undercurrent of sweaty workers. He'd destroyed the clothes he'd lived in there as soon as he returned home.

The captain had asked Anthony to "put to sea," as he called it, on the *Independence*. He seemed uneasy about Colonel Graves's grasp of the new technology. It was all Anthony could do not to laugh in his face. The closest he wanted to get to an ocean was to look at it from his eightieth-floor private office window.

He savored another sip of his personal coffee blend. That was perhaps the worst part of the whole experience. It was bad enough that the coffee inside the shipyard was terrible, but even if he brought coffee inside the drydock, the taste of the place permeated everything.

By this time the *Independence* would probably be somewhere underneath the waters of the Pacific Ocean, safely hidden while the president reassured the UN about the bio-seeding project. Anthony shivered. Hundreds of meters underneath the water in a steel coffin was not his idea of a life well-lived.

His virtual notified him of an incoming call. Anthony rejected it. No calls. Today was for contemplation and reflection. He'd done his part in saving the planet. Today was me-time.

*"Emergency override."*

Anthony grumbled but accepted the call.

President Teller's head and shoulders filled his retinal screen. He wore no makeup and his face looked tense, strained. "There you are. We have a problem."

Anthony blinked. "What happened? I thought they were at sea?"

Teller's face was worried. "They are. Well, trying to get there, anyway. *Independence* is in the Sound, but factions are trying to stop it."

"Factions?"

"Some congressmen have convinced the governor of Washington to hold the sub in port while they file an emergency injunction in court. Somehow they got the Coast Guard roped into this. I still command the military, but this is tricky. My poll numbers are all over the place. I can't get a read on public opinion."

Anthony did his best not to roll his eyes. "It's a modern submarine. Can't they force their way to sea?"

"Starting a shooting war with ourselves is not a way to improve my standing with the public."

"Okay," Anthony said. "Why are you calling me, Mr. President?"

"I want to launch now. From Puget Sound."

Anthony swallowed. Hard. "Now? We only have prelim targeting loaded. These are ICBMs. If another country thinks we've launched a nuclear weapon—"

"I'll make a public announcement. The other countries have already agreed in principle to the bio-seeding, and to launching the missiles from the *Independence*. If we have to go back to port, that sub will never get to sea again. It has to be now."

"Mr. President, that seems ... overly bold."

"That's exactly the point, Taulke. Bold. World-changing. I'm on the ropes here, politically speaking. I need a big win to get re-elected. What's bigger than this?"

"Sir, I don't think—"

"Do you believe in your technology or not, Taulke?" Teller demanded. "You assured me this is fail-safe. If we see any problems, we can shut it down, right?"

"Yes, sir, that's correct."

"Well?"

"I guess ... I support your decision, sir."

"You guess?" Teller's dark skin took on an angry red undertone. "Are you with me or not, Taulke? Yes or no?"

"Yes," Anthony replied in a firm voice. He was an engineer, and the numbers added up. Whatever else was true, that was the simple fact of the tech. "Vatican works, and we know how to control it."

"Good." The president composed himself. "Oh, and one more thing, Taulke. I'm changing the name of the project. I don't like Vatican."

"Okay..."

"I'm calling it Lazarus. The Lazarus Protocol. We're taking a dead world and bringing it back to life. The name polls well, too."

The call ended. Anthony spun his chair to look out over the serene Pacific.

The Lazarus Protocol... It did have a nice ring to it. Pseudo-biblical, but with a pop culture spin. And weren't they resurrecting his bio-seeding tech to work a miracle for the planet?

A smile of satisfaction bloomed. Closing his eyes, Anthony made note of every sensation, trying to lock this moment in his memory forever.

*This is the moment I saved the world.*

## 22

### REMY CADE • EARTH ORBIT

"I'm asking you to trust me, Remy."

Elise's voice was soft but determined. She was dressed in her UN uniform, the seal of the Office of Biodiversity stitched over her left breast. The high collar and her long hair hid the New Earth tattoo on her nape.

"Remy, please." She placed a hand on his arm. He wanted to stay mad at her, but her touch thrilled him, like always.

"This is a bad idea, Elise. Using your UN credentials to help these guys? That's a big step. Something you don't come back from." He took her hand and was rewarded with a warm squeeze of her fingers.

She shook her head. "Cassandra has ordered the attack and assigned me to lead it. I'm committed. What I need to know is whether you're committed to me."

Remy pulled away and paced the length of the station's observatory. The panoramic view of Earth rolled out under the windows. The Neos were convinced they were saving the planet, and behind it all was the ever-present Cassandra.

He'd give anything to meet this mystery cult leader in the flesh. She seemed to have unlimited access to everyone on the station, but in the days he'd been here, Remy hadn't seen or heard from her even once. She only talks to the faithful, was all they would say.

"I need you, Remy," Elise drew closer. The shadow line on the planet approached. "Especially now. This is going to be dangerous."

"Dangerous?" Remy knew she was playing on his fears for her safety. He knew it but it didn't matter, not really. His job was to protect Elise, and he took his work very seriously.

"Hattan is leading a raid—"

"A raid?" Remy turned to stare at her. "Now there's a raid?"

She placed a firm hand on his chest to stop the impending rant. Her palm was warm, her eyes a deep smoky hazel that made his breath catch in his throat.

"We're using the UN dropship to get past their security. I'm going and that's final. I want you with me. I need you there." Elise slid her hand down to his hip, and pulled him close. "Please. For me?"

Remy felt his resolve release with his breath. Her eyes, her voice, her touch. Nothing else mattered. "For you, then."

"For *us*." Elise kissed him, hard.

*Nothing else matters*, Remy thought, drunk on her taste, her scent.

The door to the lift opened and three men stepped out, dressed in UN military gear. Remy recognized Hattan, Brother Donald and Rico, the UN sergeant who'd shot him in Alaska. Rico nodded in recognition, a smirk ghosting his lips.

Remy set aside his temptation to kill him on the spot. The priority now was Elise. Time enough for Rico later.

Hattan ran the briefing using the holographic image projector in the ceiling. Remy studied the four-story circular structure with a red Greek letter epsilon emblazoned on the airlock door. Military-grade construction with built-in defensive gun emplacements.

The general spoke in clipped, precise terms. "What we have here is a Level 4 bioweapons facility surrounded by a state-of-the-art drone defensive perimeter. No way we're getting through that kind of hardware."

Remy glared at Elise who ignored him. This was just getting better and better.

"We're going in subtle. Under the guise of an unscheduled UN inspection visit, we'll use the commandeered UN vehicle and Secretary Kisaan's bona fides to get us safely to the dock." Hattan indicated a port on the top level. "We'll be wearing full face shields, except for the secretary, and transmitting false ID vitals to gain entrance to level 0. Remy and I will stay on the dock level to deal with security and safeguard the escape route. The rest of you will travel through the core elevator to secure the objective. We'll do nothing—I repeat, nothing—to create suspicion. If security suspects anything, they have the ability to lock down the entire station."

"No," Remy said. "I stay with Elise. Period."

Hattan shot a look at Elise, who nodded.

"Very well. Then Donald and I will stay topside and deal with security. Rico and Remy will accompany the secretary."

"What's this objective you keep talking about?" Remy asked. "Some kind of world-ending bioweapon?"

Another glance at Elise. Another nod. "A computer key."

"Not just any computer key," Rico said. "The biggest, baddest piece of code in history."

"Enough," Hattan snapped. "Need to know."

Remy pleaded with his eyes at Elise, who seemed not only relaxed but anxious to get started. He knew that look and she was going on this mission with him or without him. Best get his head in the game, then.

"This place is remote?" he said. "What if we need backup?"

Even Hattan cracked a smile. "No backup needed. Trust me, Remy. It's remote."

"Where?" Remy was getting tired of all the cloak-and-dagger bullshit. If he was in, he was all the way in.

"On the dark side of the Moon," Elise said.

---

The Moon grew in the shuttle's forward window. They'd taken a circuitous route, filing a false flight plan that traded authentication codes with several space stations as they passed.

In spite of himself, Remy was intrigued. The headline for years had been that LUNa City was mankind's next home. He'd never had the opportunity to visit it himself. Although, a clandestine raid on a Level 4 lunar facility hardly counted as a visit.

Remy was once again impressed with the Neos' attention to detail. The UN military uniforms were genuine, as were the standard-issue sidearms. He hoped their ability to fool the orbiting security drones was just as good.

"Don't get too used to the weapons," Hattan said. "Protocol says we'll have to leave them in the shuttle. No projectile weapons allowed in the facility."

"So we go in naked?" Remy asked.

"Nope, we go in old school," Rico replied. He opened a bag and pulled a blade out, then stuck it in his boot. He handed one to Remy.

"This knife will get past security?"

"Carbon smartglass," Hattan said. "As tough as a regular blade but scans bend around it. The latest in personal military stealth tech."

Remy accepted the blade. Perfectly balanced. He slid it into his boot sheath with no small feeling of trepidation. It had been a long time since he'd fought with a knife.

Elise touched his elbow and pointed out the window as they exited the lunar traffic lanes. "Look, Remy, an extractor."

Still tiny at this distance, the machine looked like a mechanical dinosaur with its broad, flat snout buried in the dirt. Through the surrounding dust cloud, Remy could make out a wide trail of lunar regolith entering the maw of the beast, and far behind it, a swath of rejected material. A yellow strobe winked at them as they passed over. He knew the machine was the size of a small town, but it was difficult to understand the scale of what he was seeing until a person stepped out of a tiny lunar vehicle. He gaped.

Hattan's expression was bleak as he studied the monstrous extractor. "We strip-mined Earth, now we're working on the Moon. They mine rare earth metals and Helium for fusion reactors up here. Anything to keep the great human experiment running."

The ship passed over one of the company towns that housed the lunar miners, a sad collection of surface buildings bermed with loose regolith. Most of the facilities were located underground to minimize the radiation, Remy remembered from a YourVoice documentary.

Elise took Remy's hand as LUNa City appeared on the horizon. Underneath the massive clear dome, a series of high-rise buildings were already growing up from the Moon's surface. The UN promoted the international lunar community as mankind's first step to the stars, but in Remy's opinion, they were losing the PR battle to Taulke's Mars Station.

The traffic thinned once they'd passed the beehive of LUNa City. After they crossed the sunline into the Moon's shadow, theirs was the only ship flying.

"Alright, people," said the pilot, "we're in range of the security drones. Sending our UN ID. Standby."

Remy thought he could see dark shapes outside the ship slipping by against the starlight. His pulse quickened. The familiar tingle of near-term action prickled his skin.

"We've been cleared. Passing the drone perimeter, approaching dock." The pilot's voice was far too relaxed for Remy's liking. He could see the multi-story facility approaching, the large Greek letter epsilon shining under the tracking lights of the shuttle as it slowed to line up with the docking port. There was a brief quivering of metal as the clamps locked on. "Docked. It's all yours, General."

Hattan stood, pulling his regulation face shield into place, leaving only his eyes exposed. "Alright, just like we briefed. Secretary Kisaan, lead the way, please." Remy moved to Elise's side, feeling naked with only the knife in his boot to protect her.

The light on the door blinked green. There was a hiss as the facility shared its air with the ship. The doors parted.

A thin man with dark, pockmarked skin stood on the other side. He was dressed in a heavy lab coat and flanked by a pair of security guards, armed only with Tasers and knives strapped on their hips.

"Secretary Kisaan, this is unexpected." The thin man spoke rapid-fire English with a thick accent Remy placed in Southeast Asia. "I was under the impression you were—"

"Don't believe everything you see on YourVoice, Dr. Okaga," Elise replied smoothly. She stepped past the doctor and his security guards. Remy followed, feeling clumsy in the low-gravity setting from constantly overpowering his movements. He was painfully aware that the guards moved with the easy grace of men who knew how to handle themselves in lunar gravity.

Elise seemed completely calm as she walked with the doctor. "The kidnapping was a cover story to get me off-planet. I'm here on a covert mission for the UN Committee for Global Reconstruction. Viktor sent me."

Okaga's surprise deepened. "Dr. Erkennen? I wasn't notified."

Elise eyed her companions. "You know what the term covert means, right?" She winked. "We're to go to level 4 and contact Viktor via secured communications. He should be calling in" —she made a show of pulling up the chronometer on her retinal display— "two minutes, thirty-seven seconds."

Despite his growing nervousness, Remy smiled to himself. Okaga picked up his pace. "Of course, Madam Secretary."

They passed a security area filled with screens and a drone workshop. Remy counted two more guards. When Okaga pushed the button for the elevator, Elise said, "Two of my team will stay here, Doctor. Two will accompany me."

Okaga frowned. "But have you not been briefed on the latest protocols? No more than four people on level 4 at any time—and I must be accompanied by security." He smiled nervously. "For obvious reasons."

Elise's pleasant expression never wavered. "Like I said, I've been under the radar. My mistake."

Remy felt Hattan tense behind him. There was a pause as the general exchanged a look with Elise.

"We'll remain here, ma'am," he said finally.

Dr. Okaga and Elise stepped aboard the waiting elevator, followed by Remy and the taller security guard.

The space was small, no larger than a modest closet, and smelled of ozone and recycled air. As they descended, Remy was acutely aware of his opposite number. The man was half a head taller and clearly accustomed to the reduced demands of the Moon's gravity. His penetrating, gray eyes stayed alert, and he fingered the Bowie knife on his hip. The handle was worn from use.

The elevator opened onto a small room. Flush storage panels like security deposit boxes lined the walls, and a computer console sat on a small desk in the far corner. Remy spotted a domed camera in the ceiling.

"Viktor will be calling in less than a minute. We need the second key to sync with a change he's made to the primary," Elise said. Okaga looked alarmed. "Viktor can explain everything. He needs this key synched to my DNA."

"He wants the quantum key synched to you?" Okaga's voice was tight. "That is most unusual, Madam Secretary."

"Viktor will explain," Elise said again. "All you need to do is get the key out, doctor. We are running out of time and we want to be ready for Viktor, right?"

"Okay, okay, just a second." Okaga, sweating now, shuffled to the wall beside the desk and touched his thumb, index, and little finger to the silver steel. A *phish* of air, and the compartment opened.

Okaga removed the case and set it on the desk. The computer screen sprang to life at his touch.

"It'll be just a moment to get the authorization program on line." His movements, like his speech, were quick and precise. He obviously wanted to be ready for his boss's call.

As the doctor bent over the terminal, Elise slipped a blade from her sleeve. She stepped behind Okaga and plunged the knife into the base of his neck.

Time froze for Remy, his mind refusing to process what he'd just seen. The doctor's body slumped over the terminal station, then crumpled to the floor in the slow motion created by the Moon's lesser gravity.

Elise turned, silver case in hand, a flush of exhilaration on her cheeks. A bloody knife in her fist.

This wasn't happening. Elise—his Elise—had just committed cold-blooded murder. She wasn't capable of...

The guard, only two steps to Remy's right, recovered first. He drew his Taser like a gunslinger. Even while his brain stayed frozen, Remy's training kicked in. He drove his shoulder into the larger man's chest, sending the Taser's electrodes into the dead scientist.

But in the low-g, Remy overpowered his attack. The bigger man shrugged off the hit and drew his blade. Remy bounced off the wall, landing on all fours.

The big Bowie knife looked like a sword compared to the slim blade in Remy's hand. The guard was light on his feet, at ease in the lunar gravity.

He sliced at the air in front of Remy, backing toward the elevator. The only sound was the hiss of his breath between his teeth.

Remy felt the glare of the ceiling camera overhead. If security locked this place down, he and Elise would be trapped. Hell, the guard had probably already pulsed for backup.

The guard paused, listening to his earpiece. He reversed course, charging into the room. Remy fell back against the steel wall, barely fending off the assault. The heavy Bowie knife sliced at his body armor, just missing the gap under Remy's armpit. He drove a knee into the guard's stomach to push the man back.

The guard feinted, Remy dodged, then sprawled backward, tripping over Okaga's prone body. He felt more than saw the coming attack as the guard loomed over him. Trapped between the dead body and the wall, Remy was out of space to maneuver. He lashed out with a boot and missed.

There was a flash of movement behind the guard, and the man dropped to floor like a puppet with its strings cut. Blood sprayed, and Remy realized Elise had hamstrung the guard.

With a shriek, Elise dove on top of the big man, her thin blade clenched in both hands. His legs might be useless, but his arms worked fine. He stabbed the Bowie knife downward. Elise dodged, and the blade slammed into her bionic leg.

The guard paused for a microsecond, expecting a response from what should have been a devastating wound. He grunted, tugging at the handle, but the knife was stuck.

Elise plunged her knife into the hollow of his throat.

The man gurgled once, blood welling over his lips. His death rattle splattered blood across the pristine white of her government uniform. Lifeless fingers released the Bowie knife, still stuck firmly in her mechanical limb.

"Jesus!" Remy said. "Jesus!"

"Pray later," Elise muttered, rolling off the guard's corpse. She worked to pry the big knife from her thigh. A brutal grin of satisfaction painted her face as the big knife came free.

Elise opened the case and took out a black ring, which she slipped over her wrist. She bent over the terminal and tapped at the keyboard. Remy could see Okaga's still-wet blood on the back of her hand.

She nodded to herself, then tucked the silver case under her arm. Pausing at the elevator door, Elise turned back to Remy. "We're on a bit of a schedule, lover. You coming?"

# 23

## WILLIAM GRAVES • BANGOR, WASHINGTON

The officer of the deck, a twenty-something young man with short red hair, gave an order and the massive submarine heeled in a slow turn. Water piled over the bow in white, creamy waves, creating a football field-sized churning wake behind them. Graves's stomach shifted. There was a reason he'd chosen the Army instead of the Navy.

On the flying bridge of the USS *Independence*, he studied the distant Seattle cityscape across the blue-gray waters of Puget Sound. Rain fell in a mist, collecting on his face like a second skin. After the closeness of the drydock, the open air and rain felt wonderful, like Mother Nature herself was washing him clean. That seemed somehow appropriate to Graves. If they were successful here, if Taulke's bio-seeding technology worked, Mother Nature and mankind would be getting along a lot better from now on.

Graves had been given command of the submarine's mission, but not operational control of the vessel itself. His partner in command was the CO of the *Independence*, a hard-eyed Navy vet named Richard Scobee, who didn't bother to hide his skepticism of Graves and their joint mission. Still, the captain was a professional and treated Graves with cold respect.

Dealing with H was another matter. The fast-talking, sardonic woman with the body morphs was the antithesis of the straight-laced naval officer, and the captain openly disdained her. For her part, H ignored him.

"Sir?" the OOD handed Graves a handset. "Captain wants to talk to you."

The colonel cleared the salt spray from his throat. "Graves."

"Colonel, I've just received a … request … from the Coast Guard for us to turn around."

"Turn around?" Graves caught H's eye. Lines appeared on her forehead. "The Coast Guard? Do they have jurisdiction over you?"

"Well, no, not technically. You'd better come down here, Colonel."

Graves passed the handset back to the OOD and turned to descend into the ship. H caught his arm, then tapped her glasses. "I just heard. Someone's making a play. Congress, maybe, I dunno. Whatever Scobee says down there, we are *not* turning around."

Pulling his arm away, Graves hurried down the ladder. The interior of the sub was a bewildering array of screens and switches and handles and pipes crammed into every available space like an old steampunk creation gone digital. And yet, every sailor seemed to know exactly where to find whatever they were looking for. After the bracing, fresh air of the bridge, the control room assaulted his nose with its humid funk of body odor, coffee, and seawater. Foreign, but not unpleasant to Graves. He stepped aside to let a sailor rush past—they were always rushing somewhere—and made his way down the swaying hallway to the wardroom.

Captain Scobee sat at the head of a red table. His XO, a heavyset woman with mouse-brown hair named Utsey, occupied the chair to his right. The two looked up when he entered. Scobee's face went flat as H stepped into the room.

Graves accepted a towel to wipe the sea from his face and a fresh cup of coffee from the steward. "What seems to be the problem, Captain?"

Instead of answering, the sub's CO put an audio call on the speakers. "USS *Independence*, USS *Independence*, this is Coast Guard Station Puget Sound. On the authority of the governor of the state of Washington, you are directed to reverse course and return to base. Repeat—"

Scobee killed the audio. "That's the problem."

"You said the Coast Guard had no authority over you, correct?" Graves asked.

"That's what I said."

"Then you keep going," H broke in.

"Young lady," Commander Utsey snapped, "you are not in our chain of command."

Graves held up his hand. "XO, please. We're all on the same team here." To Scobee: "How have you responded?"

"We haven't." The CO shrugged his broad shoulders. "Frankly it's an unprecedented situation. I'm not sure how to respond. I've been doing this for twenty years, and I've never let the Coast Guard tell me to do anything. I'm not planning to start now."

"Good—" Graves began.

"Bridge to Captain."

"Go ahead, OOD." Scobee threw the call from the officer of the deck onto the room's PA system. "This is the captain."

The young officer's voice sounded strained. "Captain, I've got three Coast Guard cutters approaching at high speed. It looks like they've got a boarding party on deck."

H started to talk, and the captain cut her off. "What are your orders, sir?" he said to Graves.

"Can we submerge?" Graves said.

Commander Utsey shook her head in a way that told Grave he should have known better. "Too shallow."

Scobee took a deep breath. "We could repel boarders. Clear the bridge, seal the ship. Short of an anti-ship missile, there's no way for them to get inside."

"Do it," Graves said. Utsey stood so fast her chair slammed back against the wall. She dashed from the room.

A moment later, a pulsing alarm sounded throughout the ship.

*"General quarters, general quarters, all hands standby to repel boarders!"*

Feet pounded in the hallway outside.

Graves swallowed his now-cold coffee in one gulp. He was out of his depth, and he knew it. But Scobee and Utsey seemed to know their shit.

Tearing off her data glasses, H sat up straight in her chair. "You need to launch the missiles. *Now*. I just got authorization from the president."

Scobee grimaced. "As my XO told you, you are not in the chain of command. And that's not how we do things in the Navy—"

"Get an outside newsfeed," H said. "The president is addressing the nation ... no, wait" —she looked at Graves, then Scobee— "the world."

The captain of the *Independence* threw a broadcast from YourVoice to the wall screen. The last time Graves had seen the president in public was at the UN address. He'd worn image-perfect makeup, the finest cut of suit. What he saw now was a man who'd just stepped out of a tough meeting. His sleeves were rolled up to the elbows, and his tie was missing. A gray sheen of stubble shadowed the dark skin of his jaw as he approached a podium with the seal of the President of the United States. His surroundings didn't look like the East Wing of the White House, where he traditionally spoke.

*More like a bunker somewhere*, Graves thought.

"My fellow Americans," Teller began. "For centuries, men and women in this office have addressed the people of this nation in just that way: my fellow Americans. Today, I break with that tradition. Today, I wish to address the entirety of humanity—that citizenship we all share, regardless of our national borders.

"My fellow world citizens, we have fought a losing battle against ourselves since long before any of us were even born. I am talking, of course, about the climate war. We've seen cities fall to drought and flooding. We've watched our coasts submerge, our people drowned and displaced. The refugee crisis grows worse each year. Every country on this Earth has been affected by evolving weather patterns. The scope of the problem is just so vast, so overwhelming, that the future without intervention seems only to lead, like a rushing river unchecked, to the fall of nations. And, in the end, to the death of mankind.

"But we can do something about that. We can redirect the course of the river before it drowns us all. Months ago at the United Nations, I proposed a worldwide bio-seeding program to dramatically reduce the amount of carbon-based compounds in our atmosphere. We can reverse the warming of our planet and the volatile, destructive weather patterns." Teller leveled his steely gaze at the screen. "But political interests fought against this measure."

"His ratings are off-the-chart high," H whispered, her eyes snapping back and forth behind her glasses. "This is bitching!"

Scobee passed her a sour look.

"What you do not know," Teller continued, "is that the United States continued developing this program in secret. We've outfitted the USS *Independence*, our latest ballistic missile submarine, with bio-seeding dispersal units in place of nuclear warheads. We have turned a weapon of war into a vessel of peaceful science that can heal our planet."

Teller's words took on a mesmerizing cadence. "Today, even as the *Independence* puts to sea, a group of rogue operatives are planning an attack. My fellow world citizens, we can wait no longer. We cannot miss this chance at salvation. Like Lazarus in the Bible, we will raise our planet from the grave to live another day. Therefore, by the powers vested in me by the War Powers Act, I am ordering a launch of the bio-seeding missiles aboard *Independence*."

Teller paused for a breath. "To the leaders of the world, I want to reiterate: launching these ballistic missiles is not—I repeat, *not*—a hostile action. It's are our gift to the planet. Good night, my fellow citizens of Earth ... and may God, in whatever form you worship, bless you all."

The screen went dark.

"Holy shit," Scobee said.

Graves released a breath he hadn't known he'd been holding.

H leaned over the wardroom table. "Captain, you need to launch those missiles."

The CO slammed his fist on the table so hard, Graves's coffee cup jumped. "How many times do I have to say it? I don't take orders from you!" He shifted his glare to Graves, who felt his mouth go dry.

Graves groped in his breast pocket for his data glasses and put them on. There was a red light indicating an incoming transmission. He blinked an acceptance.

"There you are, Colonel." Teller's voice was tired, his eyes weary. "I assume you saw my address? I'm ordering you to—"

The display fritzed, then went blank.

"We're being jammed!" H said, her voice ratcheting up. "You got the order, right? Teller said launch, right, Colonel?" Her green eyes drilled into Graves.

Technically, Graves knew, the answer was *no*. But they were here now, at the brink of history. All he'd experienced on the ground came back to him: the refugees, the constant, forced retreats from an unbeatable adversary in a losing war ... the mother and her daughters in that minivan, who'd died with hope in their hearts but no air in their lungs.

The decision was his now.

Graves stood and pulled the launch key from under his t-shirt. The metal was warm in his hand. "Captain," he said, "I order you to launch all missiles." His voice was in its lowest register, weighed down by the words he spoke.

Scobee stood, pulling his own launch key from under his shirt front. The two men stared at one another for half a moment too long.

"Launch all missiles, aye, sir," Scobee said.

## 24

## ANTHONY TAULKE • SAN FRANCISCO, CALIFORNIA

Coffee wasn't doing it for him, so Anthony popped two stim tabs in the form of chewing gum. The rhythm of his jaws helped him to think. After YourVoice crowned him as the mastermind behind the global launch of thirty-six bio-seeding missiles, there was not much need for secrecy anymore. He'd moved from his private office in the penthouse down to the boardroom, filling the walls with virtual screens showing media feeds and data streams from all over the world. His handpicked technicians manned workstations to ensure he had the best possible information at hand.

On one of the screens, Anthony kept the missile launch from the USS *Independence* showing on a loop. The news drone had a perfect angle on the shot, a quarter mile or so in front of the sub. Far enough away to get the entire ship framed with Seattle lurking in the misty background, but close enough to see the arcing trails of the missiles as they carried their payload skyward.

Thirty-six intercontinental ballistic missiles in ripple fire, an impressive sight. The hatches were popping open like champagne corks, gouts of smoke and fire blasting into the air. Then each missile emerged, white like a candlestick with the bright-red Qinlao warhead up top carrying the carbon-eating, nanite-enhanced bacteria.

*The power of the private sector*, Anthony thought. *Coming together for the benefit of mankind*. He'd done that, *he'd* made it happen. He'd go down in the history books as the man who saved the planet.

The newsfeed cycled to a shot from the Taulke space elevator showing the white missile contrails blossoming away from the Washington coastline to their designated dispersal points across the globe. Each warhead —*dispersal unit*, he reminded himself—carried a dozen smaller units, called multiple reentry vehicles, and each of those were independently targeted. Each MERV broke away from the main missile trajectory, then culminated in a white circle as they deployed the nanites, creating a starburst effect onscreen. The nanite payload showed as an ever-expanding ring of soft-glowing green that softened as it was absorbed by the atmosphere.

He'd seen this same vid over fifty times now in the past few hours, but it still gave him chills. Anthony wanted to shout and pump his fist in the air every time. It had worked! Every single one of those goddamned, beautiful missiles had worked flawlessly. The governments of the world had believed Teller. None of them had seen the launch as an act of aggression. The whole world watched and waited for a scientific miracle.

Waited for the good news to come rolling in.

Anthony tore his attention away from the looping vid to focus on a map of Central America. Green circles floated over the topographical features. Carbon readings from local monitors. Spotty data, but the best they had available.

"You're sure these are right?" he asked one of the scientists, a young woman with an unruly mass of bright blue hair.

She shrugged. "It's what we have," she said in a clipped voice. She seemed annoyed by not having a better answer. Her dark eyes flitted across the screen. "I'm not sure about the quality of the data. We're making up how to interpret it as we go along."

Anthony couldn't help but take her words as a none-too-subtle rebuke. They'd fast-tracked the deployment of a world-altering technology without the means to accurately measure what it was actually doing. Generating meaningful performance measures was Phase II of the plan. Unfortunately, they'd barely completed Phase I before Teller had ordered a launch.

He pushed down his frustration at her tone. He was imagining things.

He'd been up for more than twenty-four hours now. Take a deep breath; don't react.

"If the data are correct, what does that mean in real terms?"

"Well, we're seeing a gradient in C-based concentrations between Mexico and Guatemala." She slashed a line across the Gulf of Mexico on the screen. "In theory, that means uneven heating, which means we can expect instability in the weather. Wind storms? Flash hurricane? Impossible to tell. We've taken the normally well-mixed carbon factors and changed them, literally, overnight."

"Will it stabilize? It should have stabilized by now, right?"

She shrugged again, not bothering to face him. "It should, I guess, but it's not. Honestly, this is all new science. There are so many variables to consider in a test on this scale."

*Test?*

Anthony popped another piece of stim gum to occupy his hands. Feeling suddenly nervous, he sought out Viktor.

The big man was slouched in an extra-wide chair he'd brought with him from Russia, shoes off, looking drowsy. It fit his ass perfectly, Viktor claimed, and by God, if he was going to save the world, he was going to do so comfortably. Anthony flopped into an open chair next to him.

His old friend grunted a greeting. "The gradients are still there?"

Anthony nodded. "Getting worse, I think."

"What do the models say?"

Anthony threw a dirty look at the blue-haired meteorologist. "No one knows. Or they're afraid to say." He closed his eyes. "I'm worried, Viktor."

"Don't worry." Viktor patted the silver case wedged between his butt cheek and the arm of the chair. "If it gets too bad, we kill them. Start over."

"Somehow, I don't think we're getting a second chance on this one, buddy." *Or a third*, he thought, recalling his conversation with Ming the day before. "If this fails, our benefactor might not be around much longer."

"You mean the president?" asked a new voice. Anthony's spirit dipped before he even opened his eyes. H stood there, the tips of her pointy ears sharp in the light, a hand resting on a cocked hip. She seemed to have rediscovered her mojo for smugness.

Anthony's tired muscles protested as he lifted himself to his feet. "I didn't know you were back, H."

She bent the corners of her lips, but Anthony could see the tension in the lines around her eyes. H hadn't been sleeping much either lately. "My boss is worried that your save-the-world plan is not working. That would be bad, Anthony. He sent me to get a real update, not that don't-worry, be-happy crap you've been putting out through your media department."

"We've got a storm forming in the Gulf," Blue Hair called out. "A big one."

Anthony bolted across the room, H and Viktor in tow. Blue Hair was hunched over the screen studying a tight circle of clouds that looked to Anthony like a wand of white cotton candy. "It's incredible," she said. "It formed in minutes, out of nowhere. The carbon gradients are causing sharp temperature differentials. Storms are spinning up. It's almost like they have a life of their own." The superstitious lilt in her voice swam up Anthony's spine like an eel.

The YourVoice newsfeed opened a segment with a reporter in Beijing, his location stamped by the crawler at the bottom of the feed. The reporter was a scant meter from the camera. In the background was a swirling mist of reddish-brown particulate matter, with vague shapes moving in and out of focus.

The commentator spoke in rapid-fire Mandarin. Anthony pulsed his virtual to activate its translator and the soft interpreter's voice whispered in his ear.

"The capital of China is engulfed in a massive dust storm that has overwhelmed the city's normal weather defenses. The Chinese government has declared a state of emergency for a fifty-kilometer radius around the city. Experts say the storm, which developed quickly and without warning, has destroyed the desert reclamation project around Beijing..."

Anthony closed his eyes. This was *not* his fault. Beijing had dust storms all the time. Hurricanes in the Gulf were normal.

"Is the bio-seeding causing the storm in the Gulf?" Viktor demanded. He walked to the screen where Blue Hair had the Chinese map annotated with weather data. "What about in China?" The Russian was fully awake now.

Blue Hair threw up her hands. "I can't say for sure. There's a strong suggestion, but causation does not equal—"

"Stop talking," Anthony said. "Assume the two are linked. Will the atmosphere reach a new equilibrium?"

"Mr. Taulke." Her voice took on the clipped tone again. "I told you before, models aren't refined enough yet—"

Anthony spun, herding Viktor and H away from the team of scientists. "Viktor," he said in an urgent voice, "you said you could control the nanites. Can you use that control to affect local events?" He looked at H. Her face was tight, bereft of its usual dominant sneer.

Viktor pulled the silver case out from under his arm. "Of course." His grizzled smile was oily, confident.

He settled his bulk at the conference room table and opened the case. While Anthony gave him access to the global data feeds they had running in the room, Viktor donned a pair of wide data glasses and slid a black ring over his wrist. "Establishing satellite uplink."

Viktor worked his protocols. Anthony's heart hammered in his chest. There was a part of him—a very big part—that wanted to let the experiment proceed. Admitting defeat for a second time... Hell, he'd have to make Mars viable just to find a place where he could live unhounded by the constant reminders of another failure.

He sneaked a look at the screen showing the dust storm in Beijing. It was spreading.

"Hurry, Viktor."

The Russian scientist's eyes darted behind the shimmering lenses. "Acquiring the data for the Gulf ... sending a command to reduce the carbon consumption." His pudgy hand carved the air, then he closed his fist. "Done."

Anthony called to Blue Hair. "We've adjusted the seeding levels in your area. What do you see?"

The young woman peered at her screen. A full minute ticked by.

"Well?" Anthony said.

"I'm not seeing any change." The clipped tone again.

"Nothing?" Anthony replied. "Look again."

She returned to her monitors. "No change, sir. Might even be slightly worse now."

Minutes ticked by. Anthony felt a sheen of sweat grease his forehead. Blue Hair shook her head when he queried her again.

*Be patient*, he told himself. *We're looking at hundreds of square miles of ocean. It takes time.* But fear gnawed at him. Something was wrong. He could feel it.

Anthony bent to whisper in Viktor's ear. "Try to adjust the levels around Beijing." He caught the sharp scent of armpit sweat from his Russian friend.

Viktor's gloved hand grabbed at the air, the screen on the tiny computer in front of him continuing to spool data. "Done."

Another thirty minutes passed, agonizing in their slowness. Blue Hair reported no apparent difference in the Gulf, and the live shot from Beijing was still a dust cloud of brown debris. If he believed YourVoice, the city was being buried alive.

H's hand gripped Anthony's elbow. "You and me, outside. Now."

He followed her into the hallway and shut the door behind them. "What is going on, Anthony?"

He tried to meet her eyes and failed. "The control feature on the nanites has never been tested at this scale. You need to give us more time."

"There is no more time! People are dying out there! Tell me, right now. You can still shut this down, right?"

Anthony glared at her. "Of course, we can."

H's eyes flicked behind her glasses. "Yes, of course, Mr. President. I'm tying him in now, sir."

A pulse overrode Anthony's virtual, denying him the option to refuse the call. Teller's face appeared. "Taulke, what the fuck is happening out there?"

Anthony fumbled for words. "The bio-seeding is causing large carbon gradients, sir, which drives weather instability. That's the cause of the storms, we think."

"You think? Did you see this coming?"

"No, sir. We've never tested the bio-seeding nanites on this scale before.

It's a side effect ... over time, we should see mixing that evens out the effects."

The president's face went slack. "Side effect? People are dying and you want more time? The UN is talking about designating me a war criminal for unlawfully violating the atmosphere over other sovereign nations. My polls are in the tank—the fucking tank, do you hear me? How much time do you need to make this problem go away?"

Anthony shook his head. "I—we—don't know, sir."

H intervened: "Sir, I recommend we shut it down. Kill the project. If we have more storms, your unfavorables will just continue to rise."

Teller's haggard features gathered into a scowl. "What about you, Taulke? What do you recommend?"

Anthony closed his stinging eyes for a moment. What he wanted to do was take a nap—just a short one to gather his wits and his strength. Then he could make an informed decision.

"I'm waiting, Taulke."

Anthony opened his eyes. "I agree with H, sir. We should activate the kill switch."

Teller cursed, smashing both fists down on his desk. "Damn it, damn it, damn it!" The man's whole body quivered with emotion. "Do it. Kill the fucking little monsters. Let's hope to God we get something positive out of this mess. You have screwed me, Taulke, and I won't forget it. If I go down for this, you can bet your ass you're going down too!"

The feed died.

H nudged him toward the door. "Let's go," she said, her voice shaking. Whether with rage or fear, Anthony couldn't tell.

As he leaned in to open the door, another message pulsed his display. Encrypted text, designed to erase itself as soon as he'd seen it.

*"Pop, I have a car waiting for you. Coordinates loaded."*

The message disappeared. Anthony bit back a surge of anger at his own son's selfishness. He was here to save the world, not run away.

He stepped to the center of the room and raised his hands for silence. "Everyone, I've just spoken to President Teller. We've decided to throw the kill switch." A rush of suppressed groans swept through the room. "There are too many side effects, too many unintended consequences that are hurting too many people. Don't worry. We'll be back to save the world another day."

H grunted. "Not fucking likely," she said under her breath.

Ignoring her, Anthony put his hand on Viktor's shoulder, feeling the heat of sweaty, soft flesh under his palm. "Shut it down, Viktor."

The Russian nodded. His hand slashed across the screen. He paused, his eyes flicking across the data screen on his glasses. He gestured again.

And again.

"There seems to be a problem," he muttered in accented English.

Anthony's stomach clenched. His balls drew up. He felt the air around him, the space occupied by H, crackle with tension.

"Explain," he said in as calm a voice as he could muster.

"My quantum key is being overridden," Viktor whispered.

"What does that mean?" H's voice was taut. "You've been hacked?"

Her voice carried to every corner of the room. Chairs moved as scientists reacted to what she'd said. Blue Hair half rose from her seat. To Anthony, his tech team looked ready to make a run for it.

Viktor licked his lips. "Not possible. There are two keys. One is primary, one is secondary. The order is set by whichever logs in first. The secondary takes over if the first key logs off." Viktor spoke slowly as if explaining the details to a small child. "It's a failsafe! To ensure someone is always in control and can kill the nanites."

"Someone?" H asked, her anger growing.

"The other key is in a secure location," Viktor said.

"Let me get this straight," H said. "The only way one of these keys won't work is if the other is currently logged in?"

"Yes, that is correct," confirmed the scientist.

"And yours doesn't work."

"Yes ... but—"

"Someone else logged in with the other key," Anthony said, the full impact of what he was saying weighing him down. "Someone else is controlling the nanites."

"That's not possible," Viktor said. When he got excited, his accent got thicker. To Anthony's ear, he was all but incomprehensible now. "The other key is in a secure location!"

"*Was* in a secure location," whispered H.

"Where, Viktor?"

"It's safe, Anthony. I'm sure of it."

"Where?" H demanded.

"The Moon."

Save for the newsfeeds reporting the expanding chaos around the globe, the room fell silent.

H exhaled slowly, as if afraid to give up the air.

"Look, we can still salvage this," Anthony said. "We can get the second key—"

"You idiot!" H yelled. "Don't you get it? Someone's already stolen it!"

The doors to the boardroom opened. Two men in uniform entered, taking up station on either side of the doors.

Anthony's thoughts flashed to Tony and his message.

Then H locked down his virtual.

## 25

## MING QINLAO • SHANGHAI, CHINA

"Ming."

Although Ito spoke in a whisper and didn't touch her, the sound of her own name snapped her awake. There was urgency in his voice—and more than that: fear.

She slipped from under the comforter, careful not to wake Sying. Ito retreated to the hallway as she pulled on one of Sying's silk robes. He was still wearing his gray uniform, and the dusky patches under his eyes told her he hadn't yet slept tonight. Her retinal display indicated it was half past three in the morning.

"What is it?" The situation seemed to call for hushed voices.

"Your aunt," Ito said in the tone he usually reserved for describing lawyers. "She's called a meeting of the board for later this morning. It's a vote of no confidence, Ming."

Ming tugged the robe tighter around her shoulders. The cold, marble floor chilled the soles of her feet. Auntie Xi ... Somehow, someway, she'd found out the Shanghai plant had been used to produce Anthony's nanite-dispersing warheads. And Ming had been so careful in hiding the paperwork. There hadn't been a single mark associating them with Qinlao Manufacturing. Only a patriotic impulse to paint the warheads People's Republic red.

And yet, Xi must have discovered Ming's part in causing the chaos that had somehow made the world's weather worse. She supposed she could always argue that Qinlao had simply manufactured the replacement warheads to specifications provided to her by Anthony, like it would for any other paying client. But that sounded lame even to her ears. The board would think her actions incompetent at best. Traitorous on a world scale at worst.

"Come, Little Tiger. All is not lost."

Ito led her to her father's office—she still thought of this working apartment that way, even after all these months and filling the house with her mother, her lover, and her new husband.

"The central government has relocated from Beijing to Xian for now," he said, throwing the news to the wallscreen. "A dust storm buried the city." Ito pinged someone on his retinal display, then threw the second image beside the newsfeed.

Marcus Sun's face appeared immediately. He was awake, his eyes alive. His robe and disheveled hair were the only signs of the morning's early hours.

"Ming, thank goodness," he said.

"Marcus! I think Xi—"

Sun held up a hand.

"I have my spies, too, Ming. Your aunt is meeting with the Minister of Manufacturing first thing in the morning. She will use your connection to Taulke to discredit you. With the minister's support, she can force a vote of no-confidence with your board of directors. She will take the company from you if that happens."

Ming opened her mouth to speak, then closed it again. Boards and ministers and under-the-table tricks. Frustrated, she killed the newsfeed—she needed no reminders of the trouble she was in—and reskinned the wall as a hearth with a huge, crackling fire. Ming gripped the back of the couch, her fingernails digging into the leather. Would that bitter old woman never give up her quest for power? Did family mean nothing to her?

She squeezed her eyes shut. She was a queen, a powerful woman.

"Don't despair," Marcus said. "There's a way we can thwart her. Perhaps."

Ming looked up.

"There's a bylaw that covers this eventuality. Something your father included when he founded the company. The physical presence of the CEO is required for a no-confidence vote. Not virtual presence—the CEO must be in the boardroom when facing a no-confidence vote."

"The accused facing his accuser," Ito said.

"Precisely," Marcus said. "Jie Qinlao was nothing if not traditional."

"I ... I don't understand," Ming said. "We don't have the votes. How does this help us?"

"The only exception," Marcus continued as if he hadn't heard her question, "is death, proven by an official death notice. If you're not legally dead and you're not present, they can't take a vote of no-confidence. At most, they can appoint an interim CEO to run the company in your absence."

"Alright," she said. "But I still don't—"

"Ming," Ito said, the urgency back in his voice. "You need to go into hiding."

"No!" Ming slapped the leather so hard her hand stung. "We fight her."

"No, you don't." Sying's red-silk robe hung open, her breasts poking at the sheer material of her nightgown. Ito looked away, and Sying drew her robe closed.

"No," she said again as she crossed the room. "You are a lone queen on the board. Xi has all the pieces. If you stay and fight, you're trapped. The best course of action is retreat." She took Ming's hand, squeezing it. "For now."

"Sying is correct," Marcus said. "Your father was wise, Ming. The rules of this game are on your side. Use them."

A look to Ito, who nodded. The three people she trusted most were all in agreement. She had to flee.

Ming gripped her lover's hand. "You come with me."

Sying smiled faintly. "No, I'll stay here. Your aunt dares not touch a daughter of the House of Zhu. I'm safe. And we need someone on the board who can speak on your behalf."

Ming nodded. The relief on Ito's face was a rare show of inner feeling. "Fine. I'll go to—"

Sying placed a gentle palm just above where the silk of Ming's robe formed a V on her chest. Her fingertips were hot against Ming's skin. "I don't want to know. I can't reveal information I don't possess."

"I need to see my mother," Ming said, choking with emotion as she realized the price of her chosen course. "And Ken. To say goodbye."

As she turned, Marcus said, "Go with your father's grace, Ming. He'd be very proud of you."

Ming regarded the old lawyer's lined face, the calm expression of support she saw there.

*Would he?* she wondered. Beijing smothered in the dust of her ambition. Maybe Xi was right to want her out.

"Hurry, Ming," Ito said. "I'll meet you at the dock."

---

Wenqian, barely awake, rested at an angle in her maglev chair.

"Ito said you were leaving," she said without preamble as Ming entered.

"Yes." Guilt roiled Ming's gut. How often had she cursed her father for leaving her mother? "I'm sorry, Mama. Marcus can tell you the details. It's necessary—"

"Don't explain. If Marcus says you need to go, then go, before it's too late." Wenqian tried to lift an arm and failed. Ming took her hand. It was withered and cold in her grip. She squeezed the lifeless flesh anyway.

"I'm sorry about—"

Her mother's hand came to life and grasped her daughter's fingers. "No apologies. You are your father's daughter. He would be proud of you."

Ming felt her face grow hot. "That's what Marcus said. I'm not so sure."

The withered claw found its strength again. "You blaze your own path. Take risks. Reward will come for those who fight with honor."

"But I'm running," Ming said bitterly.

"You fight on your terms." Her mother's breath grew labored. "Only the foolish fight a battle they know they will lose."

Ming swiped at her cheeks, aware of time slipping away. "I love you, Mama."

Wenqian's eyes closed. Ming felt the pulse of a data packet arriving in her retinal display. "What's this?" she asked.

"Something for when the time is right, Daughter. Be safe." Wenqian fell back into sleep, exhausted from the mere effort of holding their brief conversation.

Ming kissed her mother's ice-cold forehead.

She had no time for puzzles now. She stored the data packet in a folder labeled *Later*.

Ming slipped through the door to Ken's room and turned on a dim light. Her husband lay sprawled across the bed, his mouth open in the sleep of the unencumbered mind. It had been a long time since she'd enjoyed that kind of bliss.

The light didn't wake him. She sat on the edge of the bed and poked him.

"Ken, wake up."

He surfaced from sleep slowly, his eyes blinking, stretching his arms as teenagers will when they've rediscovered the waking world. Ming felt strangely sorry for him, but also detached, as she had on their wedding day. Would his family be able to keep him safe? Would she even care if anything happened to him?

She was not surprised when her heart answered no. He'd become a pawn in this game of power against Xi. Her pawn, but a pawn all the same.

"I'm going away," she said.

"Okay." He sat up, rubbing sleep from his eyes with his pudgy fingers. "Can I come with you?"

Ming shook her head. "I might be gone a long time." She hesitated, then reached out to stroke his cheek. "It's best if you went to stay with your family. Tonight. Ito will arrange it."

"Tonight?" He was fully awake now, and something in her tone made him straighten up. "What's wrong?"

"Maybe nothing. I'm not sure. But we're being safe." She leaned forward and kissed him on the forehead. His skin was warm, alive, pulsing with life. "Go home."

"But—" he said, as he tried to grab her hand.

Ming evaded him and slid off the bed. "I need to go. I'm sorry."

Ken pouted. "We're married. We're supposed to stick together."

The whine in his voice urged Ming toward the door. "Take care of yourself, Ken."

Sying was not in their bedroom. Ming darted into her closet and pulled on the least-conspicuous outfit she had, a simple button-down shirt, heavy trousers, sensible shoes, and a smart-jacket she could alter to make waterproof or heavier, to fend off the cold. She grabbed a small canvas go-bag from the top shelf. Ito had long ago schooled her in the principles of survival. The bag contained cash, a change of clothes, access to an anonymous ByteCoin account, and a few toiletries.

All that Ming would need to seed the start of a life elsewhere until she could reclaim her own.

---

Ito waited for her on the dock. Five aircars and four drivers were standing by. Her oldest friend, the sensei of her childhood, appeared even older in the dockside's dim light. The skin of his face sagged, and a sheen of peppered stubble shadowed his chin.

"Four pawns to guard our queen." Ito gestured to the drivers as they turned to enter their vehicles.

He held a pair of cheap data glasses in one hand, offering her a tired smile as she approached. In his other was a steel hoop.

"We need to deactivate your implanted data device. It's not going to be pleasant, but we can't risk Xi being able to track you. Your code and tetradecimal number are a part of the corporate database."

Ming gave a tight nod of acceptance. Ito helped her fit the hoop around her head at eye level.

"Stare straight ahead—"

"Wait!" Ming said. She thought about the data packet her mother had pulsed to her. She wouldn't be able to access it once she was disconnected.

"No time, Ming," Ito said in a strained voice. "Stare straight ahead ... in three ... two—" Before he finished the countdown, a bright flash pierced her eyes, frying the retinal implant and its internal transponder connected to QM's security. Only her implant's memory board, now inaccessible, survived the surge.

"Fuck!" She tore off the hoop and threw it to the ground. Groaning, Ming tried to push the pain out of her head with her hands.

"Apologies, Little Tiger. The pain will fade quickly." Through flashing afterimages, she thought she saw a look of contrition on Ito's face. "Can you see?" he asked.

Ming nodded. Almost.

"Good. You need to get going, now. Both of you."

Both? She turned and there was Sying, walking toward her. Oddly, still wearing her thin, silk robe.

"Wait..."

Ruben walked beside his mother, dressed in rough trousers and a smart-jacket over a blue-checked shirt. He carried a small canvas bag like hers.

*He thinks he's coming with me.*

Ming shook her head. "No, no, no—"

Sying stepped forward and seized her by the shoulders. "You promised me, Ming. You promised you would teach my son."

"But I meant—"

"No!" Sying's judgment cut like cold steel. "If he stays here, he's a weakness to me. If he goes with you, I will be more effective ... If you love me, you will do this for me."

Ming felt her eyes well with tears again. He was a boy, a kid. What did she know about kids? Ruben's face was pale with apprehension. His chest rose and fell rapidly.

But there was something in the way he stood up straight that compelled Ming to hold out her hand to him. The boy's palm was clammy, but his grip was strong.

She kissed Sying. Quickly, a mere touch of her lips. Far too little to last her God knew how long. "I'll bring him back safely. I promise."

Sying's eyes were shining. It was the first time Ming had ever seen her cry.

Ito stood next to the third aircar. He slipped passport bracelets around first Ming's wrist, then Ruben's. "Clean passports. The transponders on all the cars are deactivated. We'll launch all of them at the same time." He regarded her a moment as if to impress her face on his memory, then crushed Ming to his broad chest. His heart hammered against hers.

"Stay safe, Little Tiger," he whispered in her ear. "Remember all that I've taught you. Come back to me."

Ming tightened her arms around the old man, wondering if she'd ever see him—any of them—again. This was wrong. She should stay and fight. Her mother, Ito, Sying, even Ken, they were all staying while she ran off like a scared animal with Ruben. How long? Would she see any of them ever again?

Ito let her go, and the chill of the early dawn air wrapped itself around her. "I'll be here when you return," he said.

She boarded the vehicle and snapped into the three-point harness, tugging the webbing tight across her chest. After making sure Ruben was strapped in tight, she gave his hand a squeeze. Through the virtual dash curving around her upper body, Ming could see the bright lights of Shanghai at night. Her city no more.

She ignored her loved ones standing on the dock. Ignored Ruben's tears as he waved goodbye to his mother. Ignored Ito's rigid, gray uniform so close to the car that if she lowered the window, she could touch him one last time.

It was time to look ahead ... to the future.

"Hang on, kid," she said.

Ming released the docking clamp, and the car fell into the night.

## 26

### ANTHONY TAULKE • SAN FRANCISCO, CALIFORNIA

Even the Pacific Ocean had lost its ability to quiet Anthony's troubled mind. For the thousandth time he asked himself: what had gone wrong? The randomness of the weather events, their severity, the massive loss of life— none of the models could account for what had happened.

Apparently, H wasn't buying it. Pizza boxes and Chinese fast food containers littered the table of the boardroom, though Blue Hair and the rest of the Taulke Industries scientists had been moved out. Taken for questioning, H said.

He and Victor Erkennen stayed, their compliance ensured by the troops stationed at the door. Government agents brought them clothes and food, but they'd been told very little. Viktor manned his oversized chair, napping. How could the man sleep at a time like this?

After deactivating Anthony's virtual, H had erected a dampening field around the room. She allowed them a single wall screen and access to commercial newsfeeds to entertain themselves. Anthony suspected having the 24/7 newsfeeds playing was also her way of reinforcing to him the scope of his screw-up.

It'd been years since he'd watched an uncurated newsfeed. How did people watch this stuff and really know anything? It was nearly impossible to distinguish between actual news, opined propaganda, and commercials by the same sponsors who bought and paid for said propaganda. After a few hours, it all merged into a meaningless chorus of drivel.

*This is how they used to torture prisoners*, Anthony thought. *Sat them down and pried their eyes open and overloaded them with artificial stimuli to make them pliable.* He half-wondered if that's what H was doing now.

The newsfeeds constantly replayed some of the most extreme moments of the last few days. For the hundredth time, he watched the massive dust storm grow out of the Gobi Desert and consume Beijing. Viewed from space, it showed up as an enormous brown blob, lightning arcing across its ruddy interior, burying China's capital. The few drone pictures from inside the storm were even worse. Chaotic winds seemed to battle one another as they whipped dust and dirt and sand and flogged them against Beijing like a cat-o'nine-tails.

Anthony worried about Ming. Thanks to H, he'd heard nothing from her since before the launch. They'd been careful about keeping her part in Lazarus secret, but Anthony knew that anyone with the technical know how could mine the project data and find out. H wouldn't even let him call Tony or Louisa to check on them.

*Lazarus.* Anthony cringed at the name now. Frankenstein's Monster would have been a better name for the creation he'd unleashed on the world.

The screen flashed up the aftermath from the micro-hurricane in the Gulf that had swept across Mexico like a lawnmower. News drones showed unbelievable pictures of denuded countryside and bare foundations where homes had once stood.

In London, a bomb cyclone had dropped temperatures to minus forty Celsius in only a few hours. Water mains froze and burst. The homeless were frozen where they lay outdoors, most simply slumped in sleep but some in positions of agony, making them seem like icy descendants of the victims of Pompeii. Trees stood like crystal statues sheathed in ice. A brave newswoman, bundled like an Eskimo, had ventured out to touch her glove to a bough of flash-frozen leaves, and the whole world watched as they shattered like the wings of a butterfly.

And on the East Coast of the United States, the weather was a beautiful spring day—in autumn.

"She's gone."

Anthony turned to find H entering the room. The guards secured the door behind her.

"You can't keep us here," Anthony said, ignoring her entree. "I'm an American citizen."

H regarded him with a pitying look. "I wouldn't say that so loud outside this country. They're liable to lynch you in the street."

Viktor woke up and slumped forward to rest his elbows on his knees. "I need to contact my government," he said. "I will request political asylum in the Russian embassy until—"

"Until this blows over?" H finished for him before checking something on her data glasses. She pointed at the screen which was showing the devastation in Mexico again. "That ship has sailed, doctor."

"Funny," Anthony said. "Who's gone?"

H dismissed the guards. They exited and secured the door from the hallway.

When they were alone, H sagged against the conference table. She looked suddenly worn down. It was clear to Anthony that her previous bravado, so recognizable and expected, had merely been an act for the soldiers. When she met his gaze again, Anthony saw something else there —fear. A worm of unease slid into his belly.

"What's going on?" he asked. "Who's gone?"

H muted the newsfeeds. The sudden quiet let Anthony hear the rush of blood in his own ears.

"Ming Qinlao has disappeared," H said. Her voice was dry.

"Disappeared? You mean her government took her?"

H shrugged. "She's just gone. Fled Shanghai. Police tried to take her into custody and she ran."

"But she's alright?" Anthony asked.

Another shrug. "She's off the grid, that's all we know. We don't know if she was involved or not."

"Involved in what?" Viktor asked.

"We've confirmed that your second key was stolen, Viktor," H said. "The secret, unbreachable Erkennen facility on the dark side of the Moon was attacked. Everyone's dead. All the security vids were wiped, and the key is gone."

Anthony felt the worm burrowing deeper in his guts. "Stolen by whom?"

H pursed her lips, her eyes dark pits of rage. "It looks like an inside job."

Was that possible? Viktor had certainly dragged his feet in developing the nanites, whatever his professed reason. But a sidelong glance at his friend showed only a graying scientist with poor laundry habits aghast at the news H had just delivered.

H watched Anthony process the news. "I can tell you what it looks like," she said. "China's been hit with a massive dust storm, London with the deep freeze ... and the old U-S-of-A?" She turned back to stare at the two men standing in the middle of the room. "From sea to shining sea: perfect weather."

Anthony blinked. "You think Teller's behind this?" he whispered.

H met his eyes, her own accusing. "He says *you* are."

---

## Ming Qinlao • Shanghai, China

After clearing the dock superstructure of Qinlao headquarters, Ming angled upward away from Shanghai. Flying without transponders meant no collision avoidance system to protect her from wayward flyers, so her four escorts fell into loose formation, two on either side. She set a steep climb to the transcontinental traffic lanes.

A pair of police cars, red and blue lights flashing, swept up from the city below on a course to intercept the climbing formation. The police slaved the comms of Ming's aircar, demanding all five vehicles return to the ground.

Two of the Qinlao cars peeled off. They made a beeline for the cops, veering at the last minute to sideswipe the police vehicles.

Ming worked hard to keep her own car stable. She'd never been great at hands-on, unassisted flying. Ruben gave her a frightened look, his hands clutching his seat, knuckles white.

The cars flown by the Qinlao operatives and their police targets lost altitude rapidly, then leveled out as the cops gave chase to their attackers. The two remaining aircars tightened up on Ming and Ruben. She punched the throttle and heard a grunt from her brother as their bodies pushed back into the seat cushions. Ming gritted her teeth. Speed was all they had now.

Her navigational sensors showed another car heading into the sky ahead, also on a trajectory to intercept. Cursing, she tightened her arc of ascent to cruise at a lower altitude. She wanted to go southeast but dared not be so obvious with someone on her tail.

Ming whipped the steering wheel hard, setting a course due east. Her air guardians followed smoothly. A thin line of pale pink shown on the far horizon.

The pursuing car fell in behind them. Sensors identified it as a jet-black Fiero model with blacked-out windows, illegal in China. Fieros were favored by freelance drivers, especially Japan's Yakuza mobsters. Ming watched how the car handled. Its lazy arc and slow turns meant it was armored—and likely armed.

*First the cops, now the mob?* she thought, punching the throttle again.

The Fiero's forward hatches opened. Ming's sensors screamed an alert at her.

Two missiles launched, their contrails angling upward, moving far faster than Ming's aircar.

Auto defenses sprang into her dashboard's virtual display. She quick-scanned to find the countermeasures, but her wingmen were faster. Both of them cut speed and fell behind, swinging across the flight paths of the missiles to draw them off. Two explosions lit the night sky behind her. At the last minute, she saw ejection notices from both vehicles and breathed a sigh of relief.

*Two pawns,* Ming thought grimly, protecting their queen.

But now she was alone in the open sky with her pursuer. Ming fretted as the minutes ticked by. The Fiero seemed to have spent its long-range arsenal, and the driver appeared content to follow, forcing her to maintain her eastward course.

Perhaps she hadn't been the target of the missiles after all. Maybe the goal had been simply to rid her of her escorts.

Ming climbed to the highest possible altitude. The Fiero might be slow on turns, but it would eventually catch her in a straight-out race. The car was visible now without sensors. Soon, it would be in machine-gun range, and Ming had no countermeasures for bullets. She glanced down at Ruben, whose taut face reflected the strain on her own.

"Are we going to die?" he asked quietly.

"No, Ruben," she said, wanting for his sake to mean it. "We're not going to die."

This was a problem to be solved like any problem. Ito had prepared her for this kind of battle. When she was young, everyone she fought was bigger and stronger than her. But she learned how to beat them. "Use your skills, Little Tiger," Ito would say to her.

Her skills. Her engineering skills.

The inkling of a plan flashed into her mind.

"Is your seatbelt on tight?" she asked Ruben. The boy nodded.

The Fiero was only a few hundred meters behind. Ming allowed her speed to decay slightly as they drove toward the new dawn.

She struck when the sun peeked over the horizon. As blinding sunlight flooded her windshield, Ming threw the throttle into reverse for a second, then powered into an aerial loop. Ruben screamed at the sudden, nauseating shift in gravity. The driver of the Fiero, lulled into the monotony of pursuit and temporarily blinded by the sun, shot by beneath her.

Ming slammed the throttle forward and dove down on to her pursuer. Her undercarriage crashed onto the blackened windshield of the Fiero with a sickening crunch of metal on metal. Ming jerked up on the steering wheel, then slammed down again, and again. With each impact, Ruben's cries grew more terrified, his grip on his seat more desperate.

Now Ming was the pursuer. The Fiero tried to dive, but Ming was faster. She caught him again and smashed down on the heavier car. The Fiero dove again.

"I've got you now," Ming said through clenched teeth. She put the aircar into a steep dive, aiming again for the Fiero.

But the other driver banked into a sharp turn, forcing Ming's aircar to glance off his fuselage. In that split second, she lost her advantage. The Fiero appeared behind them.

Alarms blared from the dashboard. Ming heard the *chunk-chunk-chunk* of bullets hitting the frame of their aircar. The steering wheel trembled in her hands. She spun them into a turn, but the Fiero had his range down now.

*Think...*

Below, the open Pacific Ocean loomed in the early morning light. Even as her brain measured the steepest possible angle of descent, Ming pushed the steering wheel all the way to the stops. The Fiero, guns blazing, pursued.

The flat gray of the Pacific took on texture as they hurtled toward it. She ignored the sound of bullets hitting her car. When she could make out the details of individual waves, she pulled up on the steering wheel.

"Hold on, Ruben!"

The double engines of her aircar strained, vibrating the cabin from the base of the superstructure up through their shaking seats. Ming flattened her body into the cushioned chair, pushing the soles of her feet against the car's floor, as if trying to ward off the hard ocean surface with her feet. The water kept rising to meet them.

Just as her screams joined Ruben's, their aircar leveled out.

The heavier, armored Fiero had followed closely. Too closely. Ming craned her neck as they ascended again. A white geyser erupted from the indigo sea behind them. The Fiero's ping on the dashboard winked out.

She throttled back the screeching engines, and the sympathetic humming of the aircar's stressed frame diminished. Ming even remembered how to breathe.

Her little brother looked at her, wide eyes floating over tear-streaked cheeks.

The readouts of the aircar's integrity showed nominal. A relief. The Fiero's fire hadn't hit anything vital. Ming turned them due south.

As they settled in for the long trip across the Philippine Sea, she put the car on autopilot and sat back in her seat. Ming made her hands into fists to stop their shaking.

She was in a fight for her life—and Ruben's. If she'd had any doubt before, it was gone now.

Was her aunt so desperate to see her dead, and Jie's only son too?

Ming's hole card, she realized—Jie's bylaw that protected her from being ousted—was also Xi's motivation for murder.

Two birds, one stone. If Xi succeeded in taking them both out in a "traffic accident," no one could stand in her way. A little recovered DNA from an accidental crash into the ocean would be all the evidence Xi needed to take over Qinlao Manufacturing.

But, Ming realized, this wasn't just about her anymore.

"You okay?" she said to Ruben after the silence had grown too long. Too loud.

Ruben nodded, but said nothing. In the light of the rising sun, he looked very young.

## 27

## REMY CADE • EARTH ORBIT

From the observation window of the Temple of Cassandra Station, Remy tried to find comfort once again in the predictability of Earth's rotation. Behind him, in the small briefing room where they'd planned the raid on the Erkennen facility, Hattan, Elise, and Rico had been meeting for over an hour. Apparently, Cassandra herself was joining them for the debrief, and despite his actions on the Moon, Remy wasn't yet a fully trusted member of the team. He wasn't even allowed to see her image, in-person or projected.

Only the faithful, he reminded himself.

But being excluded was the least of his worries. After their return, they'd cut off his WorldNet access again. Without the always-on distraction and outside stimulation, his brain percolated with his own thoughts. Right now, that wasn't a good thing.

Earth turned below. Cloud cover was forming over the blue Pacific in large, finger-like bands.

Why was he still here? *To be with Elise*, he told himself. *To protect Elise.* But that was a joke now. On the Moon, she'd been the protector, and she'd done it with ruthless efficiency and an unhesitating focus on the mission.

*The mission*, he thought. *The mission was all that mattered to her.*

The Elise Kisaan he knew today was worlds away from the shy, highly educated invalid he'd met five years ago on a searing New Delhi afternoon in her father's garden. That Elise could barely meet his gaze. That Elise, despite being the envy of New Delhi society, never left her father's compound. That Elise had never had a real friend—or a lover.

In hindsight, their relationship seemed fated. He'd been cashiered out of the army, pursued nightly by the horrors of Vicksburg, and relegated to the role of personal bodyguard to a woman who never went anywhere. A young woman terrified by the life-altering surgeries about to come.

They both needed comfort, so they found it in each other.

Remy's role gradually transformed from bodyguard to personal aide. Eventually, Elise would allow no one else to help her do anything. Only Remy was allowed to walk with her. Only Remy was allowed to transfer her from her chair to her bed. It was during those moments of forced intimacy that he came to realize Elise Kisaan was more than a spoiled little rich girl.

When her surgeries came, Remy was by her side every horrifying step of the way. Removing her dead legs and enduring the phantom pain of their loss, laying the bio-circuits and sensors that would mesh with her own DNA to become nerves, bone-welding the support anchors in her hips, and finally the permanent attachment of her bionic limbs. From this crucible of pain, the pampered girl was transformed into a formidable young woman like a sword blade forged by a blacksmith's fire and hammer.

Still demure when decorum called for it, Elise was more likely now to curse like a sailor in private when angry. She'd borne her bio-transformation with a dignity well beyond her years and a fierce determination to direct her life rather than accept what was offered. By the time she took her first steps on her new bionic legs, she was smiling through each tiny victory with him. Remy had become her best friend.

They slept together for the first time on the night after the first day she walked on her own. Their lovemaking was a passionate celebration of life, fed by the knowledge that it was also forbidden. It wouldn't do in Indian society, so entrenched in its caste system of propriety and expectation, for the aristocrat's daughter from Madhya Pradesh to be involved with the disgraced son of Kansas insect farmers.

Remy became Elise's way of discovering excitement for life again. And she became his drug of choice in laying to rest the Vicksburg nightmares.

With her maglev chair a thing of the past, her father launched an intensive grooming campaign to entrench his daughter into the upper echelons of the global elite. A posting as an intern at the United Nations led to the Deputy Assistant Secretary of Biodiversity position. A series of mysterious illnesses among the ranks of the BioD department got Elise promoted to Assistant Secretary of BioD. A scant six months later, the secretary was caught up in by a pay-for-play scandal involving the First Nations of Canada, and she was named permanently to the post.

Her political rise seemed charmed, Remy thought at the time. Now, as he watched a circular cloud formation swirl over Beijing, he knew the Neos were behind it all. They had pushed her to the top of her profession with the same ruthlessness she'd shown herself in killing two men in cold blood on the dark side of the Moon.

The briefing room door opened, calling Remy back from contemplation. Rico exited first without looking his way, followed by Hattan who offered Remy a nod before he disappeared. Elise came last, her lips swept upward, happy. There was no sign of Cassandra.

Elise joined him at the window. "It's done, Remy. It's done!"

"What's done?" he asked, wondering if she'd actually tell him.

Sure enough, her face clouded, then brightened. Apropos of nothing, she said, "They weren't sure about you, Remy. The way you hesitated down there—"

"Hesitated? What are you talking about?"

Elise raised her hands. "It's all good. I explained it. Your inexperience with the Moon's gravity, the fact that the plan was changed. It should've been Rico down there with me. It was too soon—"

"What are you talking about?" His anger vomited out of him, a sign of his desperation to have order restored—to be sure, again, who Elise Kisaan, his lover and best friend, truly was. Remy closed his eyes a moment, saying, "I'm sorry."

"It's alright. There was some concern that you're not fully committed to us." At his expression, her hands came up again. "Despite everything that went on down there. Because of it, really. The team felt you might've frozen out of a lack of commitment."

"The team. You mean Rico."

Elise's silence confirmed his theory. "Hattan defended you. So did I."

"And what did Cassandra think?"

The question seemed to catch her off-guard. "Cassandra?"

"She was in there, right? That's why I was kept out of the meeting."

Elise seemed to think her answer through. "She deferred to General Hattan on the matter."

"And Rico?"

"Fuck Rico!"

He released a breath. There, at least, was the Elise he'd known and fallen in love with. Cursing like a sailor. "How's your leg?"

She brushed her fingers over the still-visible slit where the Bowie knife had entered. "Functional, obviously. No major biocircuitry damage, thank Cassandra. My next stop is the infirmary. They'll patch me up and regrow the pseudo-skin in no time."

Remy chewed his lip and leaned against the railing of the observation window. "These people—the Neos—are not what I expected." His eyes tracked to the tattoo under her ponytail. "Somehow, I don't think this is what your father had in mind for your career."

Elise laughed bitterly. "My father. No, I don't think Aarav Kisaan would approve. But it's his own fault. He's as much to blame as anyone for what's happened. I'm here to make the best of his mess."

"Look, I don't think he appreciates the impact of his agricultural business on the planet—" He broke off when he saw a mocking smile trace Elise's lips. "What?"

"You think I'm upset with father because he's made his farms too big? Oh come on, Remy. I never took you for a back-to-the-land type, even if you are a farm boy."

He cocked his head. "I'm confused."

"My problem with my father and his generation is that they're not thinking big enough. We have a global catastrophe unfolding, one that's been centuries in the making. We need a solution that's just as big and bold as the problem. The New Earth movement is that solution."

Remy felt the beginnings of a headache. "I still don't understand."

Elise held out her hand. "You're cleared now. Let me show you."

She held his hand as they walked to the lift and descended through the heart of the station, past the crew quarters, deeper than Remy had ever gone before. The lift's lit panel button read *Control*.

The doors opened onto a dim room surrounded by arena-style seating. Below an observation railing, a massive holographic representation of the Earth dominated the center of the room. When Remy looked closer, he saw clusters of tiny red dots covering the globe. Technicians worked at various stations around the projected image.

"Nearly one in ten people on Earth are followers of Cassandra, the second largest faith on the planet," Elise explained. Remy's eyebrows went up. He knew their membership was large, but he'd never suspected *that* large. Elise continued, "We don't advertise that fact, of course. It would undermine our effectiveness."

"Effectiveness at doing what?" Remy asked in a whisper.

"Just watch."

A man paced on the other side of the Earth hologram, hands clasped behind his back, studying an overlay of a massive cyclone in the Java Sea.

"Bring up Jakarta," he ordered. As they got closer, Remy recognized the voice as Hattan's.

An enlarged image of Indonesia filled the air in front of the general. He squinted at the image, then touched three of the dots. "Reassign these assets to close-in observation."

Elise touched his arm. "You know how for a natural disaster, there's always a few Neos that show up and seem to sacrifice themselves to the situation?"

Remy nodded.

"We assign them from here. Each of those dots represents a team of Cassandra's disciples, observing—witnessing—an extreme weather event." Her hand touched her nape as if to demonstrate what that meant. "We're all connected back to the Temple, sending our environmental data back to Cassandra to be mapped and refined and modeled. Those three assets he just assigned to the cyclone are giving their lives in the name of science."

During her time at the UN, Elise had worked with a speech coach to Americanize her speech patterns, but when she spoke from the heart, her native Indian accent reappeared. Usually it reminded Remy of a simpler time when it had just been the two of them. Now, it scared the hell out of him.

"You can communicate with individual followers from here?" Remy looked around the room then back at the Earth hologram. This center connected a few billion people? Impossible. "Using their tattoos? But why? What does Cassandra do with all that data?"

Elise's lips turned up at the edges. Not the kind of smile that lit up her face, but an expression of secrecy. "To the chosen come the answers," she said, repeating one of Cassandra's famous one-liners.

He was still trying to reconcile his first impression of the New Earth Order as a fringe group of crackpots with the highly professional, highly organized, well-funded operation that had just conducted a military raid on a secure lunar facility. And had twelve operational bases scattered around the world, stocked full of the latest in military tech.

A chill ran through him. No one knew about the threat they posed to the existing world order. No one.

Elise drew him to the back of the room. "You have questions," she said.

Remy's head was still swimming, but he needed answers. Anchors that could tether him to the reality around him. "The device we stole from the Erkennen facility. How does that fit into all this?"

"I can't talk about that, Remy." Her voice was gently chiding.

"You expect me to trust you. You said I was cleared. I need some answers, Elise."

Her face tightened. "All right, then. You want to know about truth?" She held up her wrist showing him the black ring from Erkennen's lab. "This is what we've been waiting for."

"Rico said it was computer code. A key or something."

"Yes. And it's working perfectly." Elise nodded the three-dimensional hologram of Earth. Data screens floating in the air over specific geographic locations pulsed with information. Hattan watched the readouts closely. "Erkennen's a genius!"

"What does it control?" Remy asked.

"It controls *everything*, Remy. All of it" —she pointed to Europe on the map where Remy saw a blue circle over southern England— "a bomb cyclone over London, a massive dust storm covering Beijing, an uber-powerful hurricane marching across Mexico. And wonderful weather along the US eastern seaboard." She laughed, winking at him. "Let's see what the UN makes of that!"

Remy followed her world tour of natural catastrophes with growing alarm. "Wait ... you're telling me that the code you stole from Erkennen ... you're causing these disasters?"

Elise laughed again. "Cassandra's a prophet, Remy. She can predict the future. She foresaw Anthony Taulke's ego, Teller's greed, Viktor Erkennen's belief in his own brilliance. She saw all of that and used it to get what she needed."

Elise held out the black bracelet. "With this, Cassandra doesn't just predict the future. She controls the future of Earth."

Remy stared at the blue circle over London. There were how many millions of people in just that city alone, all being subjected to a deep freeze—for what? Cassandra's whim? "But what about the people? Won't this kill a lot of people, Elise?"

Lit by the greenish glow from the hologram, her face beautiful in profile, Elise's eyes shone with an inner light. But there was a hardness to her now, an alien coldness that chilled him to his core.

"People? For fuck's sake, Remy," she said, her voice boiling in its native accent, "the people are the problem."

# 28

## WILLIAM GRAVES • COAST OF MAINE

The waiting was the worst part, Graves decided. Whatever had gone wrong, knowing would be infinitely easier than the ignorance of waiting.

He stared upward into the darkness along the circular stairway of the Maine lighthouse. It had been in the Graves family for generations, purchased for pennies on the dollar when the Coast Guard abandoned it more than a hundred years ago. When he was a child, it was his secret place, his treehouse-without-a-tree, where he fantasized his future as a real-life G.I. Joe. He marveled how his young body had carried him up these rusting steps to the very top without stopping then. Now he paused, waiting on his old man's knees, wobbly and threatening to roll out from under him before he was halfway up.

Hurry up and wait was the military way, but this limbo he was in had no hurry-up component, nothing to occupy mind or body. There was just the waiting with his fears, in the absence of real knowledge, foreshadowing the details to come.

He'd stopped watching the newsfeeds. The whiplash of good news/bad news did nothing but tease his conscience with what punishment he deserved for his actions. One moment President Teller was the savior of the human species, the next he was an international terrorist bent on destroying the same. Graves was no politician, but he had the good sense to realize that his own fate was tied to Teller's.

He'd followed a legal order from the President of the United States to launch the missiles. Yet, the United Nations openly talked of charging Teller as a war criminal. Did that make Graves equally culpable? Like the Nazi officers in World War Two, was his public defense to be, "I was only following orders"?

Graves resumed his ascent. How had he gone from saving people to killing them? His heart ached with the weight of responsibility. Once he reached the top of the lighthouse, maybe he should just throw himself and his troubled mind into the white-capped waters below.

He relived the moment of the launch again and again, but still the question nagged at the back of his mind. Teller had never actually completed the order to launch before their connection had been jammed. It was clear what the president wanted, though. Graves knew with moral certainty he'd followed the president's expressed intent.

The United Nations was a cacophony of angry voices from all over the globe, blasting the United States for further destabilizing an already unpredictable climate. The irresponsible actions of a rogue nation under a cowboy president had made the situation much more volatile, the headlines proclaimed along with their blame. On the side of public opinion, YourVoice and the rest of the media had screamed without pause for Teller's head.

Finally reaching the top, Graves popped the hatch that led onto the light deck. The dirty Fresnel lenses glared at him like the vacant eye of some long-dead sea monster.

A crisp wind snapped across his face, stinging his eyes with tears. He edged out onto the deck, where he could feel the building sway with the winds coming off the Atlantic. Graves squinted straight out at the fading blue horizon, avoiding the vertigo-inducing view of the creamy surf smashing into the base of the rocky cliffs below. As a boy, he'd been afraid to venture onto the light deck, only going so far as to poke his head out the trapdoor for a peek at the horizon.

His sister had been the daredevil in the family. Jane would skip up the ladder and rush to the railing, leaning over to scream at the fury of the ocean, her long, brown hair trailing in the wind like a pennant. There was always wind up here, fresh and new.

Fighting down his boyhood fear, Graves gripped the railing and smiled grimly at this tiny victory over his childhood phobia. Jane would have been proud. But she was gone, killed in an earthquake in Mexico while working for the Red Cross disaster services. That was his sister, always running toward danger, always helping those less fortunate. Saving the world one person at a time.

He guessed it was her death that propelled him to request a transfer to the newly formed Army Disaster Mitigation Corps. He'd picked up saving the world where Jane had left off. Graves wondered what she would think of him now, after the catastrophe of the launch.

He'd given that launch order with the best of intentions. Those missiles were meant to save the world. Graves believed that. Still believed it, even now.

But his heart sank as the disturbing early results filtered in. Only hours after the bio-seeding dispersal, after the world had avoided a nuclear response, a phenomenon the scientists dubbed a *micro-hurricane* developed in the Gulf of Mexico. It slashed, quick and deadly, across the narrowest section of the Mexican mainland, battering the city of Veracruz. The death toll was in the thousands. The hurricane had spun up so quickly, no evacuation had been possible. They hadn't even named the damned thing until there were already bodies in its wake. A dust storm the size of Kansas buried Beijing.

These disasters and many more were caused by the missiles he had launched. Graves believed that, too.

Yet, in other regions, like the East Coast of the US, where he was, the weather was wonderful, spring-like even, despite the calendar showing September. He shook his head. It made no sense.

A speck appeared on the horizon. He squinted at it, wishing he'd brought binoculars with him. Its speed brought its detail quickly, and he recognized the design of the military aircar long before it swung past the lighthouse in a long arc on approach for a landing.

Graves hurried to the trapdoor, taking the steps carefully to favor his middle-aged legs. Around and around the steps wound down until he was dizzy. He caught his breath at the base of the stairs before opening the door. Whatever they wanted, at least the waiting was over.

Two soldiers stood outside: a lean man with dark skin and a short Korean woman with the shoulders of a bodybuilder. They were dressed in Army working fatigues.

"Colonel Graves?" said the woman.

He nodded, letting the lighthouse door close behind him. Hearing its creaking hinges, perhaps for the last time, evoked a sinking sadness in Graves.

"You need to come with us, sir."

So, this was it then. "I'm under arrest?"

The pair exchanged a look, then the man spoke. "We've been sent to escort you to the Pentagon, sir. We're activating Operation Haven."

# 29

## MING QINLAO • DARWIN, AUSTRALIA

From a distance, Taulke's space elevator looked like a strand of silver spider silk reaching from the Earth to Heaven. Ruben's eyes widened in wonder as Ming explained how she'd ridden it several times on the way to her job on the Moon. Its tiny transit pods terminated at an intermediate station called the Low-Earth Terminal, she told him, and from the LET, passengers could book passage to Mars, if they worked for Taulke, or the Moon if they were bound for LUNa City. There was even talk of one day establishing hydrocarbon extraction stations on Titan. Ruben listened with rapt attention.

Ming headed for a blue-collar section of town. It was packed with hotels to accommodate Darwin's large, transient population awaiting their ride to a life beyond Earth. Parking lots doubled as automated sales lots for workers never intending to come back, and Ming sold their aircar for a deposit of ByteCoin she used to purchase work licenses for her and Ruben. Though he was only fourteen, two years below the minimum age for off-planet work, the fake ID Ito provided secured him his slot. No one looked too closely at workers willing to work in space. She also bought them third-class tickets on the space-vator's morning lift.

They had the rest of the day and a night to pass before embarking, and Ming was glad to have the downtime. She lay on the bed in their hotel room, eyes shut against a mind that wouldn't stop trying to outthink her aunt. Without her implant, Ming found the quiet disturbing. It encouraged her to think too much.

Ruben stared out the fourth-floor window to the half-empty parking lot below. Unlike Shanghai, this was not a vertical city, and the boy seemed fascinated by that fact. Stretching as far as the eye could see, Darwin teemed with human life.

"Would you like to take a walk?" she asked. A walk would do them both good.

He turned to her and nodded, a brave half-smile on his face, and soon they were strolling along a Darwin street looking like tourists in floppy hats and dark glasses she'd purchased at the hotel gift shop. Ming pinned one-time-use face blurring devices on their lapels to fool any cameras that might catch them. After the chase with the Fiero, she wouldn't feel safe until they were in space.

As they walked, Ming began to relax. She could feel her brother relaxing too, through Ruben's hand. Holding it made her feel like a mother must feel, a role she'd never imagined for herself. A cool, ocean breeze swept out the sweaty scent of the city, leaving only the fresh smell of salt water, soothing the hot afternoon sun. A beautiful day—almost beautiful enough to make them forget they were running for their lives.

Auntie Xi was playing for keeps this time. Ming shivered, recalling how close they'd both come to oblivion in the cold waters of the Pacific.

Ruben squeezed her hand. "Are you okay?"

Ming nodded.

"Thank you," he said. "I ... I'm glad I'm with you."

Ming offered her little brother a faint smile. "Same here, kid. Come on. Let's enjoy this sunshine and fresh air while we still can."

They walked another block in silence.

"Can we go to the beach?"

Ming smiled, for real this time. "Sure."

Once they reached the oceanfront, they took their shoes off before leaving the grass, then walked barefoot into the hot, shifting sand. Ruben giggled as the grains squeezed between his toes. He'd never been to a beach before.

"Let's sit," Ming said.

Ruben looked down. "But we'll get sand in our ... in our clothes."

She shrugged. "Who cares?"

Smiling wide, Ruben plopped down. Ming joined him, and they laughed together at the feel of the wet beach beneath them.

The surf pounded, the sea wind roared. Ming said nothing for a long time. Ruben seemed content to stare into the distance at where the dark blue of the ocean met the light blue sky.

*This is what you'll miss*, she wanted to tell him. The vast openness of life on-planet, the breeze that doesn't come from a machine, the ability to focus on anything more than a few meters away.

When she'd been called back to Earth, she'd only returned out of a sense of family duty. Now she found herself missing the planet already. She'd come to think of it as home again.

How things change.

"Will we ever come back, Ming?"

She barely heard Ruben's voice over the constant *shush* of the surf.

Ming slid her arm around his shoulder and pulled him tight against her side. Together, they watched the water come ashore, then retreat again.

"We'll be back," she said. "I promise."

Ruben looked up at her, seeming to gather his courage. "Will I see my mother again?"

Ming said nothing.

---

It was just as she remembered it. The same smell of dust and rebreathed air, the same muffled clang of her boots on the stairs, the same pillars of reflected sunlight in the common spaces.

Ming moved with urgency, her footsteps quick and light on the stone floor. Ruben lagged. He was tired, she knew. Tired from the intensity and frequency of new sensations, tired of avoiding the probing stares of others, tired of holding his sister's hand.

"We're almost there," she said. "Keep up."

He stumbled, and Ming caught his arm. She was tempted to yell at him, to tell Ruben how life from now on wouldn't be the easy lifestyle of corporate royalty he'd known. Instead, she slowed her pace, reminding herself that he was just a boy and this was all new to him. You had to practice holding back the muscles overdeveloped in Earth's greater gravity. Eventually, they got lazy as they acclimated to the new norm.

"We're almost there," she said again. Her chest tightened as she made the final turn into the long hallway, half-dragging Ruben now, who was beginning to whine.

Ming counted the doors as they walked. One, two, three, four...

She pulled up short, uncertainty creeping in at the last moment.

"Is this it?" Ruben's tone begged for a positive answer.

Ming nodded, her mouth dry. Before she could stop him, Ruben reached past her and rang the doorbell. A buzzer sounded from inside.

Sounds of movement. The door slid open, and Ruben smiled at the pretty woman who'd opened it.

Ming took in the pale skin of her face, the band of freckles on her nose, the blonde hair drawn into a loose braid. The wetness of her lips, open in surprise.

"Ming?"

Ming tried to keep her voice steady, but failed.

"Lily."

## CASSANDRA'S WAR
### Book 2 of The SynCorp Saga

The Lazarus Protocol, the corporate plan to reengineer the Earth's atmosphere, has failed. The mysterious Cassandra and her Neo zealots have weaponized the weather, Anthony Taulke is in jail, Ming Qinlao is on the run, and Colonel Graves is left to clean up the mess.

Meanwhile, we the people pay the price—in blood and treasure.

But the machinery of the corporation is not yet dead yet. As Anthony hatches a new scheme to undo the damage caused by the Lazarus Protocol, he makes new alliances and stabs old friends in the back. Flushed out of hiding, Ming Qinlao risks everything to reclaim her family name. And a war-weary William Graves is forced to choose between his duty and his conscience.

Edge-of-your-seat space battles. Cloak-and-dagger corporate intrigue. Heartbreaking stories of love and betrayal. *Cassandra's War* is the second exciting chapter in *The SynCorp Saga*, the dark sci-fi series brought to you by the bestselling writing team of Bruns & Pourteau.

### Get your copy today at
### severnriverbooks.com/series/the-syncorp-saga

## ACKNOWLEDGMENTS

*The Lazarus Protocol* was a labor of love that had a few other hands involved in its birth.

Besides the unflagging support of our wives, Alison and Christine, a number of individuals were generous with their time and insightful with their comments as beta-readers. Jennifer Schumacher, David's sister, was the first person to read the completed novel and gave us great feedback. Jason Anspach, Rhett C. Bruno, Jennifer Ellis, Jon Frater, and Terry R. Hill —thank you for helping us make this a better book. E.E. Giorgi and Bill Patterson answered some technical questions we had, and David's daughter, Cate Bruns, conducted a close, final read-through when our own eyes were crossing—any remaining errors are entirely our own.

Severn River Publishing has picked up this original trilogy for republication as a second edition. Thanks to Andrew, Amber, and Cate for believing in the series and giving it a second shot at Sci-Fi life.

We also want to take a moment to thank you for your time spent reading *The Lazarus Protocol*. It's the first novel in what we hope will be an exciting, fruitful collaboration. We hope you enjoyed it.

David Bruns & Chris Pourteau

# ABOUT THE AUTHORS

**David Bruns** is a former officer on a nuclear-powered submarine turned high-tech executive turned speculative-fiction writer. He mostly writes sci-fi/fantasy and military thrillers.

**Chris Pourteau** is a technical writer and editor by day, a writer of original fiction and editor of short story collections by night (or whenever else he can find the time).

Sign up for Bruns and Pourteau's newsletter at severnriverbooks.com/series/the-syncorp-saga

Printed in the United States
by Baker & Taylor Publisher Services